COLE

Standish Bay, Book One

CHRISTINE DONOVAN

This book is dedicated to my husband Michael.
I love you!

I want to thank my husband, my four sons, Shawn, Matt, Danny and Joey for all your support over the years and my three-year-old granddaughter, Olivia, for brightening up my days. My mother, Alberta Murray and my sister, Karen Gomer, for always being there for me. Also, thank you to Sammie Grace for being the first to read BlackJack and giving me valuable information.

Prologue

GROPING THE WALL BLINDLY, HOPING TO STEADY HIS rubbery legs, Cole Jackson swore as he realized he was totally wasted. The hotel hallway seemed to sway violently like a ship caught in a serious gale—the kind small boats don't survive intact.

"Shit," he yelled as he collapsed to one knee then slowly raised himself up and continued shuffling toward the room he shared with his wife, Lindsey.

From a distant haze, voices pummeled through the buzz surrounding his brain. Faces blurred and flashed in and out and around the black spots plaguing his eyesight.

One person asked, "How'd the show go tonight, Mr. Jackson?"

"Great, just great," Cole thought he replied. The words formed in his brain—he just wasn't sure they managed to escape his mouth.

Another man remarked, "Do you need any assistance?"

"Hell no," Cole muttered aloud this time as he tripped along mumbling to himself. Why did everyone assume he needed assistance just because he had a damn good buzz on? It was his life, wasn't it? And if he chose to blur it with alcohol it was his business and nobody else's.

Cole slid the stupid plastic key card in the door for the third time. "Damn, damn, damn." He pounded the door with his fist. "I need sleep. All I want to do is crawl into bed. Come on, fourth time's the charm."

As he turned the knob, he prayed Lindsey slept *alone.* He'd stayed away as long as he could without passing out in the hotel bar. *Not like he'd never done that before.*

"What the hell," he swore as he shoved the door open, banging it into something. Once inside with the door shut, he looked down, blinked several times, forcing his eyes to focus, and saw Lindsey lying on the floor. A deep red stain encompassed her chest and a potent metallic smell suddenly floored his senses. Cole swayed and tried to steady himself as blackness descended, swallowing him up. The last thing he remembered as he collapsed next to Lindsey was his hand landing in something warm, wet and sticky.

Chapter One

Fifteen years later

COLE JACKSON SAT IN THE SUITE HIS BAND BLACKJACK reserved at the Four Seasons in Boston. Every muscle in his body was tense, making it difficult to pick away on his acoustic guitar. He hated to admit it to himself, or anyone else but nerves plagued him like hell. Not nerves exactly, more precisely he was scared shitless. Tonight BlackJack opened their tour in Boston, and Cole's thoughts were filled with insecurities about how he'd be received. He swallowed, hoping to stop the waves sloshing inside his stomach, causing him to gag. It would be miraculous if he kept any food down today.

He worried about what people *saw* when they looked at him. Did they see a killer? Or did they see a man who had some bad luck? It shouldn't matter one way or another to him, but it did. If only he could adopt that, *who gives a shit what anyone thinks,* attitude. Fifteen years in prison for second-degree murder had destroyed his self-esteem and self-respect. There was nothing like going to jail for something you didn't do.

All his friends, the close few he allowed near, kept telling him to talk about his ordeal, get it out in the open, and things would improve. His soul would heal. Like hell it would. People would just know what he went through. He had no intentions of letting the entire world experience prison life through his eyes. So, he buried the memories in the recesses of his mind, never to be dug up.

Tonight, a new chapter of his life would begin. He was back playing his music, his life's dream. During his days in jail he had hoped and prayed to play again someday, but he'd never thought it would happen. And truth be told, there were days during his prison confinement he surprised himself by seeing another sunrise. So here he sat, his favorite guitar cradled in his arms, his fingers gripping the pick like a vise, and the music he usually played so effortlessly sounding like crap.

"Hey, Cole." AJ Macleod, BlackJack's bass guitarist, back-up vocalist and also Cole's best friend, charged into the band's suite. "You won't believe who's signing books at the Prudential Center today."

Cole glanced up, not the least bit interested. His mind heavily centered on tonight's concert and trying to keep his body from jumping out of its skin. He finally asked, knowing AJ wouldn't leave until he had his say. "Who?"

"Guess? And ah'll give ye a hint—ye read all her books."

"Shit, AJ. I don't have time for your games. Just give me the damn name of the bloody writer."

His friend grinned from ear to ear. "Shannon Gallagher."

Cole caught his guitar moments before it hit the floor.

"Thought that might get ye." AJ chuckled. "Man, ye

should see yer face. Stunned doesn't even begin to describe it. Ah'm heading over tae the bookstore, wanna tag along?"

Cole thought about it for all of one second. He had kept a low profile since his release from prison, and he and AJ together might cause people to recognize them. He couldn't face all the questions and looks that would be directed toward him. Someday he would have to face it, but not today. He just couldn't do it. All his energy and emotional charge needed to be focused on tonight. Getting through this concert was crucial. If he survived it, his first public appearance since going to prison, he could survive the rest of the concert tour and possibly the rest of his life.

He had to admit though, the name kick-started his pulse and made him curious to what she—he shook his head. "I appreciate the invite, AJ, but I'm staying put...ah, lying low." He settled in with his guitar once again. "Just going to strum my Betty here and try to relax."

AJ shrugged. "Suit yourself, man. But ah hear she's quite a looker."

As Cole watched AJ leave, loneliness slammed into him. "Stupid idiot," he muttered to himself. He should have gone. It would have done him good to get his mind off tonight.

Shannon Gallagher had driven Route 3 from her home in Standish Bay, heading north to Hingham to pick up her sixteen-year-old son, Cameron at her ex-husband's house. Tonight she was surprising him with tickets to a BlackJack concert at the Garden so it made sense for him to tag along on a book signing she had at the Prudential. He could shop around and kill time, something teenagers were good at.

She could hardly wait to see her son's expression when she waved the tickets in front of his eyes, not to mention they were spending the night in Boston. A city they both loved.

She had been signing books for one full hour and was riddled with guilt for the people still waiting in line. It humbled and amazed her when people came to see her and buy her books. She would never take it for granted. One day success existed and the next puff, it vanished right along with health and happiness. Fortunately for her, she'd been blessed with all three so she never understood the unsettledness and yearning that nagged her at times. She daydreamed and reached out constantly for something that eluded her. She had a notion what it was and wondered if it would ever be close enough to grasp.

Someone cleared his throat, interrupting her thoughts. She looked up into the eyes—well she would have looked at his eyes, if he wasn't wearing dark sunglasses—of a tall man with shoulder-length brown hair and a mustache. He wore jeans and a black leather jacket. She quickly apologized for not paying attention. "I'm sorry. My mind wandered."

He smiled and handed Shannon her newest book. "Quite all right, luv. Ye've been busy." He glanced at his watch. "Ah think ah've been queued up in line for forty-five minutes." He paused and took in the crowd. "Nice turnout."

"Thank you. And I'm sorry you had to wait so long."

"Not a problem, ah've nothing pressing."

Shannon flipped the book open to the title page and glanced back to the gentleman with the foreign accent. "Are you from England?"

"Not originally, no, but ah used tae live there. ah'm from Scotland."

"Ah. I've been once. It's beautiful."

"Aye. That it is."

"Is this book for you?" she asked, pen in hand.

He shook his head. "No, luv, it's for a good friend. His name is Cole, spelled C.O.L.E. He's a big fan of yers. He's back at the hotel. Ah couldn't convince him tae come."

She signed the book with her curvy, Parochial school penmanship. *Cole, you need to get out more. But if you're going to stay in, you've picked a great book to keep you company. Enjoy, Shannon Gallagher.*

The Scottish man laughed as he read what she wrote. "He'll like that. Thank ye."

She smiled. "Thank you and I hope your friend enjoys the book."

He took off his glasses and winked at her. "He'll enjoy it, luv. He reads all yer books. Good day."

"Good day," she replied with a touch of Scottish accent in her voice as it was contagious not to do so.

Shannon's eyes followed the man out of the store. There was something vaguely familiar about him. But, oh well, she didn't have time to ponder it now, she still had a line of people waiting to meet her, and she didn't want to keep anyone waiting longer than necessary.

At two-fifteen, Cameron returned from meandering through the shops inside the Prudential Center just as Shannon completed signing the last book. As they left the bookstore, she spotted the Scottish gentleman approaching. Once again she had a nagging feeling he looked familiar.

He again removed his glasses and glanced from her to Cameron and back. "Excuse me, ah dinnae mean tae intrude, but ah hoped maybe ye, if ye dinnae have any plans for this evening—"

"I'm sorry," Shannon interrupted him. This would spoil her surprise. But, oh well, she had to tell him some-time. "I'm taking my son to the BlackJack concert."

Cameron yelled and picked her up for a crushing hug. "Mom, how *did* you? The concert's been sold out *forever!*"

"I can't breathe, and I have my sources," she choked out.

He let her go quickly. "Sorry."

Shannon turned to the man. "I'm sorry. If you'll excuse us, we must be going." She offered him her hand.

He surprised her by holding it tightly cradled between both of his. "So ye like BlackJack?"

Smiling, she studied him, trying to read his expression. He seemed amused at something. "Yes, I do. My son, Cameron, as well. We're huge fans."

"Ah'm AJ Macleod. Ye signed the book ah bought today for Cole Jackson."

Shannon's pulse jumped. She removed her hand from AJ's and placed it on her speeding heart. Cole Jackson read her books, *the* Cole Jackson. Oh my, she locked her knees before they buckled and she collapsed to the floor.

Cameron looked at her. "Mom, are you okay? Did you *hear* what he said? You signed a book for Cole Jackson and he is...oh shit man...you're AJ, bass guitarist. I thought you looked like him...but...you're *really* him?"

AJ laughed. "Aye, that's me. Listen, Cole doesn't get out much, and he'd be thrilled if ye came by the hotel tae meet him. We're staying at the Four Seasons."

"So are we," she breathed, hardly believing this conversation.

"We are?" Cameron asked, sounding even more shocked than before.

"Perfect. We're in suite 526, come on up and visit before the concert. We usually have a jam session tae loosen up and relax, then a light dinner." He turned to leave, paused, pivoted back and looked right into her eyes, his green ones hypnotic. "Please say ye'll come, luv."

How could she not? If not for her, but for Cameron who would positively hate her if she refused. "I...um...yes, I suppose we will," she answered, her voice sounding distant and nervous to her own ears.

———

As they drove to the hotel, Cameron never shut up. She didn't remember the last time she heard him talk so much or be so excited about something.

"Do you think they'll mind if I bring my guitar?"

"I suppose not," she replied, hoping it was true.

Shannon pulled up in front of the hotel, handed the keys over to the valet parking attendant and waited as their bags were unloaded. After checking in, they went up to their room so Shannon could change. She removed her pantsuit and slid into her favorite jeans, sweater and black leather boots. After she brushed her long brown hair, her teeth, and touched up her makeup her hand flew to her stomach as her insides churned. Her body trembled in fear and excitement knowing that minutes from now she would meet Cole Jackson in person. Her dream come true since she was sixteen and BlackJack first hit the music scene. She took a drink of water and prayed she didn't embarrass herself and throw up during her introduction to him.

Now she stood with Cameron, outside the door to suite 526, and on the other side stood her idol. Okay, so she was a little old to have an idol, but he was something. The sound of someone singing and playing guitar drifted through the door. *Cole.* She reached out with an unsteady hand to knock on the door, only to pull back and groan.

"Cameron, I don't know if I can. I've always wanted to meet him. What if I make a fool of myself?"

Cameron shot her a teenager's exasperated look, complete with an eye roll. "Mom, get real. You're like the coolest Mom ever."

Before she had a chance to flee, Cameron knocked on the door. It flung open, and her stomach took a silent tumble. AJ greeted them with a warm smile and stepped aside, sweeping his arm out. "Welcome."

Shannon scanned the room anxiously until she found Cole sitting on the arm of a couch, strumming an acoustic guitar. Her lungs constricted and she couldn't breathe, nor could she tear her eyes off him. He was mesmerizing. She drank in every detail she could make out from this vantage point. His dark blond hair was pulled off his face, and he sported the in-fashion five o'clock shadow. She also noticed some hard lines on his face he didn't have in his twenties. He didn't look like a pretty boy anymore. Oh, no—he looked better—much better. Older, more handsome, and she detected a vulnerability most people might not see, but she had a trained eye for detail. He wore old jeans with holes at the knees, a plain black T-shirt that hugged his ripped body and black leather boots all scuffed and well broken in. She knew from his pictures he was tall, but she never imagined the muscles rippling in his arms as he played his guitar.

"Mom, you're staring," Cameron whispered.

"Huh, what?" she said, emerging from her daze. "Oh God, I was. I was staring."

AJ chuckled. "Cole has that affect on women. Come, let me introduce ye."

Shannon stepped back and shook her head. "No, I can't."

AJ's easy going expression turned to confusion. "Why not, 'tis not because...?"

Shannon placed her hands on her scalding cheeks. "Oh God, no, it's just, well, like he's been my fantasy man since I was sixteen. I wouldn't know what to say. Just listen to me now. I sound like a moron." *Where was the person who wrote so eloquently?* Cole *had* been her fantasy man. Having married her ex-husband John McKenzie at seventeen because she was pregnant with Cameron had her growing up fast. Times were tough. She coped by either submersing herself fully into being Cameron's mother, putting her stories to paper or engrossing in BlackJack music and dreaming about Cole.

AJ curled his large, warm hand around her elbow and tugged her along with him. "Aye, he's every woman's fantasy. But let me tell ye." He lowered his voice several octaves. "Cole's extremely shy. He'll be as nervous as ye." He wiggled his brows at her and his eyes sparkled with mischief. "If ye tell him ah said that luv, I'll deny it."

They waited off to the side until Cole finished his song. So tuned into his music, Shannon figured he probably didn't even know anyone else breathed in the room with him. Watching him now brought back memories of his trial and how she never believed he was guilty. Her eyes had been glued to the television set, since it was broadcast live, and nothing anyone said could persuade her Cole could kill his wife. Something had seemed wrong. The jury had blinders on because the quiet, grieving young man on trial screamed innocence out of every pore in his dejected body.

Cole spotted the beautiful, tall brunette the minute she stepped into the suite, causing his pulse to kick up several notches. He had a way of playing his music and being aware of every minute detail that went on around him with no one knowing it. There was something vaguely familiar about her, but he couldn't quite put his finger on it. It would come to him in due time. He had a great memory, and he never forgot a face. At least he didn't think he'd forget one as gorgeous as hers.

She arrived with a tall, gangly teenager carrying a guitar. As AJ led them over, he pretended to be engrossed in his music and fought to control the rampart beat of his heart. AJ would never interrupt him in the middle of a song, which was good. It enabled him to study the woman more closely. She seemed fairly young—maybe late twenties or early thirties—and her son or younger brother accompanied her, as the resemblance was uncanny.

His body sizzled as he drank in her appearance. A tight black sweater molded perfectly shaped breasts, faded jeans enhanced her mile-long legs causing him to groan and think about them wrapped around his waist. *Where did that thought come from?* Black boots poked out from the frayed bottoms of her jeans. He snorted. They dressed alike, he and this beautiful stranger.

When he strummed his last chord, he looked straight at her and was bombarded with the most incredible blue eyes. She smiled at him and blushed, warming his insides. He couldn't help but smile back.

"Cole." AJ came forward. "Ah'd like ye to meet Shannon Gallagher and her son, Cameron."

Chapter Two

COLE'S BRAIN INSTANTLY SCREAMED OUT, *BACK UP, BACK UP, back up.* Did he just say Shannon Gallagher? That's why she looked so familiar. Her picture appeared on the back of all her books. A picture he spent countless hours staring at and imagining many what ifs? A one-dimensional picture showed her attractiveness, but nothing prepared him for meeting her in person. He became hyper-aware of her. His body stirred and burned for her in a way he'd never known before. And shit, introductions were not even completed yet. Something he'd rectify at once.

He casually—at least he hoped he pulled off casual— unfolded his lean frame from the arm of the sofa. He held out his hand to her, willing it not to quiver, giving away his nervousness. "Nice to meet you, Shannon," he said. When their hands connected, it was electric. The megawatt current transferred from her warm delicate hand into his and shot straight throughout his entire body. He let go quickly, least he get fried. He turned to Cameron and shook his hand. "Nice to meet you, Cameron."

Cameron didn't let go right away. He babbled. "Nice to

meet you...Cole...I mean...Mr. Jackson...nice to meet you, sir."

Cole pulled his hand away, smiled and pointed to Cameron's guitar case. "I take it you play?"

"Huh?"

"The guitar, you play?"

"Oh, yeah," Cameron replied.

"Let's sit. We can play something together," he said, gesturing to the sofa.

Cameron hesitated. "It's okay, Mr. Jackson. You don't have to."

"Come on, it's why you brought it. And call me Cole. Everybody does."

Shannon stood mesmerized, watching Cole with her son. She could not drag her eyes off his long graceful fingers as they strummed his guitar. The thought of those fingers had her body tingling in all the right places. They played a song or two she recognized from one of BlackJack's older albums. Cole's voice sounded different from what she remembered. It sounded deeper, raspier, but still beautiful to her ears.

The song he played now brought back startling memories of her life with John. He'd always tried to convince her he loved her and married her for that reason, not because of their son they'd created in the backseat of his father's Buick. But she never quite believed him. Oh, she knew he loved her as she loved him, but it wasn't head-over-heels in love. The song, *Will You Ever Love Me*, reminded her so much of that time in her life.

Then to her surprise, Cameron played and sang one of his own songs. Shannon's favorite, and it never ceased to bring tears to her eyes. It was a love ballad with just enough of a beat to keep your foot tapping. Cole caught on quickly and joined in with his guitar.

A hand settled on her arm, startling her for a second until she realized it belonged to AJ. He leaned close to her ear and whispered, "Cameron's extremely talented. Did he write that?"

Shannon smiled at her son, and her heart soared with pride. "Yes, he did."

"He is good, aye, very good," AJ said with strong conviction.

AJ and Shannon applauded after they finished. Cole and Cameron exchanged silent looks, then stood together and bowed dramatically, which caused Shannon to laugh. Then they continued to play, and AJ led Shannon over to a small serving table and invited her to fix a plate.

"Where are the rest of the band members?" Shannon inquired as she put a small amount of fruit and pasta on her plate. She had no idea if she could consume any of it. Since she had found out she was meeting Cole Jackson, her insides had hurt from the nervous shutters vibrating there.

"With their wives," he replied as he fixed a plate. "They should be here shortly. We've another hour tae go before we leave for the Garden. Aye, speaking of which, here they are."

Two men and two women walked in. Shannon recognized Ted Pierce, the band's drummer and Brad Nolan, keyboard and guitar player immediately. Brad was average height with a slight build, his dark hair buzzed short and he wore wire-rimmed glasses and large diamond studs in both ears that sparkled against the light. Shannon didn't think of him as classically handsome but not bad-looking either. Linked to his arm stood a petite, voluptuous blonde, clearly his wife. At least Shannon thought so.

Ted was tall, largely built, but not heavy. To his side stood a woman of average height even in spiked heels, Shannon thought she was attractive in a dark, exotic way.

AJ made introductions. The men had British accents, which didn't surprise her, their wives were American. They seemed nice and receptive to her, which helped calm her down some, but not much.

After the introductions, her attention was drawn back to Cole and Cameron who played Cameron's song once again. She watched Cole with complete and utter fascination. He seemed like a genuinely nice person and he treated Cameron like a peer. Complimenting him on his music and giving him suggestions without hurting his feelings or offending him. Occasionally, he would glance up and smile at her, turning her insides to mush. A terribly intriguing spider web tattoo flanked nearly his entire left arm. Before she knew it, her legs ate up the distance between them giving her a better peek at the tattoo and her breath vanished. Tangled in the spider web were many interesting things. The one thing, however, that caught her eye instantly was a nearly naked, beautiful woman. The details astounded her. Her tattoo experience was limited to small three-leaf clovers, roses, sharks or Celtic crosses. But Cole's tattoo amazed her. It was a true work of art. He glanced up, locked eyes with hers, tilted his head and stared intently for what seemed like an eternity to Shannon. All the while she couldn't manage a single breath. Then he finally broke contact, put his guitar down, said something to Cameron and stood up to approach her.

Oh God. Shannon's hand fumbled for the back of the nearest chair as the room tilted. Cole came and stood right beside her, and she breathed in his potent male scent sending her reeling even more. Their shoulders brushed, causing a tingling sensation to travel from her shoulder and beyond. *Way beyond*. They stood almost the same height, thanks to the one-inch heels on her boots. Why had she always hated being five-ten?

"Your son's talented," he said with a British accent that melted her bones. "What would you say if I invited him on stage tonight to perform his song?"

It took a moment for her to comprehend what he said and for her brain to compute an answer. Few people threw her off guard. This man beside her did and big time. She was blown away from the physical attraction that slammed into her at first sight to his genuine interest in Cameron. As she continued to watch her son play his guitar, she pretended Cole's closeness did not set her body ablaze and her mind spinning.

"I would say that's kind of you. It's fine by me if Cameron agrees."

"Would you like to ask him, or should I?" he said, raising his eyebrows and his eyes sparkling with excitement.

Shannon unconsciously touched her hand to his arm and pulled it back immediately because of the jolt she received. And it was one hell of a jolt. Exactly like the one she'd felt when they shook hands earlier. Startled by the bodily contact once again, she struggled for words, then finally replied, "I think it would mean a lot coming from you."

She watched her son's face as Cole spoke to him. His expression one of shock, then it turned to ecstasy. He jumped up, did a little dance then came running toward her. He exuded such exuberance his face lit up like a Christmas tree strung with a million tiny twinkling lights. "Did you hear? Cole invited me." He pointed to himself. "Me, on stage to sing my song. Oh, man." He clutched his stomach. "I think I'm gonna puke."

"Where's he going?" Cole queried as he watched Cameron sprint from the room.

Shannon shook her head. "He's going to be sick. I think he's a little nervous."

Cole snorted. "Yeah, well, I know the feeling."

With his comment, Shannon studied Cole closer, more intently than before, and to her amazement she found he appeared nervous. Could what AJ had said be true? That he was shy?

"Would you and Cameron like to ride to the Garden with us in the limo?"

"I don't want to impose," she replied.

He looked disappointed. "You won't. Say you'll come."

How could she refuse? Cameron would never forgive her if he found out, which he probably would. Also, she wouldn't mind spending more time with this sexy, interesting man standing beside her, causing her body to take on a life of its own. "Okay."

"If you'll excuse me, I'm going to my room. Have AJ walk you down to the lobby in fifteen minutes. And oh," he paused and glanced at the sofa where two guitars rested. "Don't let Cameron forget his guitar."

"I won't," she replied, knowing she had an, *I can't believe this is happening*, expression etched on her face.

There was no way she could not watch him as he stopped and spoke briefly with each band member, then left through an adjoining door. She breathed deeply, and freely, finally able to take her first true breath in over an hour. Cameron came back in, looking white as a sheet. He placed his guitar in the case, and before he closed it, Shannon went up to him and placed a comforting hand on his arm.

"Cameron, are you okay? If you're not ready for this, I'm sure Cole will understand."

He rolled his eyes. "Yeah, right Mom. I'm fine. Just a little panic attack, but hey, Cole says he gets them all the time too. Can you believe it? Cole Jackson scared shit-less before a concert?"

Shannon sighed and shook her head. Reminding Cameron about his language these days wasted good air. There was something about teenagers and swearing. She knew it was normal. She'd been the same way—well, maybe not her, but John had, if her memory served her correctly.

"Just because he's famous doesn't mean he's not human," she said.

Cameron's color slowly returned. "You're right. He's really cool inviting me to play with him on stage. Who would have thought?"

"Yeah, who would have thought?" Shannon agreed. Cole was a smart man. He knew raw talent when he saw it, or in Cameron's case, when he heard it.

AJ approached. "The limo awaits."

Cameron's eyes lit up. "No shit, are we riding with the band?"

Shannon rolled her eyes. "Sorry about his language." She smacked Cameron's arm in jest.

"No problem luv, part of being a teenager and an adult too." He winked at Cameron. "Ah've gotta serious trash mouth."

Chapter Three

Parked under the main hotel entrance canopy gleamed not one limousine, but two. Shannon, Cameron, AJ and Cole climbed in one and the other band members and their wives in the other. Shannon, all too aware of Cole's presence sitting opposite her, found herself once again flustered by him. She did not like this new experience whatsoever. She didn't know where to look or what to do with her hands as Cole looked at her. It excited her and petrified her at the same time. He suddenly seemed more relaxed. He folded his arms across his chest and his bedroom brown eyes penetrated to her soul. AJ and Cameron carried on a boisterous conversation. For the life of her she did not understand what they were talking about. She finally resigned herself to looking out the window and clasping her hands together on her lap, holding her favorite purse in a death grip.

She watched the stop-and-go traffic as they drove to the Garden, almost in a daze. She loved busy Saturdays in Boston and she imagined all the concert attendees were scrambling for the various parking garages in the area. The limo pulled down a narrow street to a side door. Shannon's eyes widened, and her heart sped up when she saw the mob of fans. Fortunately, concert security held them at bay long enough for everyone to get inside the door safely.

Cole led Shannon and Cameron to a large room heavy with the aroma of Italian food. He introduced them to several people. Shannon would never remember their names, but their faces she would remember. She considered herself a visual person. Most of the people present were the equipment and road crew, scrambling in and out, juggling food and work. She also met the members of the opening band. She'd never heard of them, but Cameron had, and he was off engrossed in an animated conversation with their lead singer.

Cole turned to Shannon, looking serious. "Would you be fine for a bit? I'm going to my dressing room."

"I will, but thanks for asking," she said, touched by his concern. Although she'd much rather he stayed with her, she could perfectly mingle alone. And God, as her eyes drank him in again, he was nothing like she expected and everything she thought he would be. He was incredibly handsome, dynamic and sexy. Not at all aware of the effect he had on people, especially her. Or was he? He appeared shy and unsure of himself, and she wondered if he had always been that way, or had it been caused by his years in prison?

After he left, she shivered, and it had nothing to do with the air-conditioning blasting in the room. She missed the heat radiating from his body. Shrugging it off, she made a beeline to the drinks, opened a bottle of lemon-flavored water, and sat on a loveseat tucked in a corner. While sitting there sipping her drink, she watched as her son, in all his glory, talked about music. This was his life's dream. And seeing him here, he fit. Music came naturally to him. She and John joked all the time about where he got his musical ability and singing voice from. It hadn't come from either of them. Maybe the creative writing of lyrics came from her, but his musical talent did not. She couldn't sing on key to save her life or play an instrument. Neither could John. Buried somewhere deep in their family tree was a musically talented genius, and she silently thanked whoever hung on that particular branch for passing such incredible genes onto Cameron.

Her eyes followed the members of the opening band as they left for their time on stage. Cameron grabbed a root beer and joined her, looking ecstatic. "Mom, this is so awesome. Did you know, Adam, he's the singer for Road Trip. Did you know he's only twenty-one? And God," Cameron paused from his rambling, and his eyes took on a look of awe. "How lucky is he to be traveling with Black-Jack?" He took a gulp of soda. "Can you imagine what that would be like? Anyway, I can't believe we're here."

"It is amazing." Shannon laughed nervously. "I can't believe we're here either, and I can't wait to hear you play tonight."

He choked on his root beer and Shannon's hand flew to his back.

"I'm sorry. Don't be nervous. You'll be great." She continued rubbing his back, regretting her comment. She tilted her head toward the door and smiled. "Look. Here comes the band now."

They had changed clothes. Everyone wore jeans, boots or sneakers and T-shirts. Cole's long hair was no longer confined but hung loose. He wore the same clothes, only he'd added a black leather vest. Her body began to quiver. It started in her toes and shot to every outer extremity imaginable. She hugged herself, trying to stop it and while she did, she noticed how pale he looked. Concern for him slammed into her and she wondered if he'd eaten anything during the day. She never saw him eat. As she watched, he grabbed a bottle of water and sat down on a loveseat. He closed his eyes and appeared to meditate. God, he truly fascinated her. He had all these different facets to his personality.

The press had exploited him before and after his wife's death. The stories written about Cole, at the time of Lindsey's death, seemed like articles written about a totally different person. He had been only twenty-three. Did a person really change that much? She remembered reading back then he never granted interviews, making her wonder where they got their information from? And since his release from prison, she could understand his desire to keep his personal life private and still not grant interviews. There had been a media frenzy at his release. A popular public figure had wanted him deported to England, believing him to be a British citizen. The truth was Cole had been born in the United States to an American father and a British mother. He spent most of his life in England, but he was an American citizen and could not get deported.

Shannon didn't think Cole had anything against reporters. Instead, she had the feeling, even though he lived in the public eye, he tried his hardest to live a private life. And let's face it, some, not all, but some reporters would twist his words just to juice up the story so they could sell more copies. And Shannon hated to admit it, but she was one of those people who bought anything remotely connected to Cole Jackson, but not anymore. Now that she met him, she didn't need to rely on the half-truths written about him. She could get to know the *real* Cole Jackson all by herself. The question was, did she have the guts to?

Cole was, without a doubt, in a full-blown panic attack. He had puked up what little food he'd had in his stomach, and now he felt like shit again. He knew once he took the stage everything would click into place. The musician, performer and actor would take over. Fortunately, he could bury his self-doubt, his panic from being in a crowd, and his, *I am not worthy of this life*, in the back of his mind as his alter ego took over on stage. However, there posed one monstrous problem? He had to fight, claw and drag his way to the stage first.

Cole tried to meditate, something he'd learned to do in prison. It had gotten him through some tough times. But with Shannon Gallagher in the room, the only thing he could think of was her, which caused his heart to skip a beat. While in prison he had read everything he could get his hands on. AJ sent him many books including hers. At first Cole never understood why her books? She wrote romantic suspense, and he had never made a habit of reading romances. He had to admit though, her books were well written and entertaining. She knew police procedure and the law, and her sex scenes gave him something to fantasize about during the long, lonely nights. Cole might not have known he enjoyed her style of writing, but somehow AJ had.

He spent hours obsessively looking at her picture. There had been something about her eyes that had drawn him in. But nothing, absolutely nothing, could have prepared him for the emotional jolt he'd felt when he looked into her majestic blue eyes in person for the first time. The thought of diving into them and losing himself in them forever occurred to him at once.

He'd felt an instant connection. She had as well. He

knew she had felt the jolt when they shook hands the first time, as it was hard not to see the shock and confusion on her face. It had taken both of them by surprise. Even with his eyes closed now, he knew she watched him. He could feel the warmth from her eyes like tiny, heated pinpricks. Not painful or uncomfortable, just intense enough to make him all too aware of her presence in the room.

Her son, shit, he had what people would refer to as pure, raw talent. He had what it took, talent-wise, to go far in this business. Cole just hoped he had a good head on his shoulders because the music industry was a tough gig. The job was physically demanding during concert tours and emotionally draining at other times. Everyone wanted a piece of you, and if you let them, they would take, take, take, until they left nothing. Nothing, but the outer shell of a man with an empty soul.

It was a business for the thick-skinned and strong. Cole shook his head. Didn't he know it? Neither had existed in him in the early days. He had relied on drugs and alcohol to help him be tough and look where it had gotten him. It had taken him to a place unfit for any decent human being, but not anymore. No chemicals would ever touch his lips or body again. He would become thick-skinned on his own. This time he planned on surviving the emotional roller coaster ride. He would be in complete control and in charge of his own destiny from here on in. It was easier said than done.

Cracking his eyes open just a smidgen, he studied the lovely Shannon Gallagher. What fates brought her to him today? She surprised him with her shyness, although why should it? Most writers were introverts, whether they wrote books or songs. He tried to remember what her bio stated on her jacket cover. He didn't think she was married. No wedding ring. She couldn't have been out of her teenage years when she had Cameron. He wondered what her life was like. Did the glitz and glamour touch her at all? Did she have any heartbreak or dark skeletons in her closet? *Damn if he didn't want to know all.*

Someone approached him and cleared his throat. Cole knew AJ stood in front of him without having to look since all his senses were on high alert. Their manager, Todd Cavanaugh, stayed in the wings so to speak, and AJ pretty much ran the show. The band members preferred it that way.

"Cole, we need tae go. Ah'll have Shannon and Cameron wait at the bottom of the stairs tae the left of the stage."

Cole opened his eyes and stared into the face of his closest friend, the friend who had also loved his wife. AJ didn't know he knew, but he did. He may have been drunk all those years ago, but not stupid, not by a long shot. He also knew others received her favors besides AJ. The prick, Mr. Ex-New York Senator himself was included among the long list. Cole would never forgive him for his cruel words spoken right after Lindsey's death when he'd needed his close friends support as much as he'd needed air to breathe. If the senator had publically acknowledged that he believed in his innocence, things might have gone differently at his trial. He sighed. *Ancient history, man, ancient history.*

"Cole, ye okay, man?"

Taking a deep breath, he pushed those memories of Lindsey back into the recesses of his mind. He didn't need to be thinking about all the things that had gone wrong in their marriage, in their life. Now would be a bad time for the rage that sometimes consumed him when he thought about her unfaithfulness. Never mind the melancholy because she no longer walked the earth.

"Yeah, go on. I'll be right there."

"Aye, don't be long. Our fans have waited fifteen long years for this."

Once alone, Cole grabbed crackers and a Coke and headed down the hall to the stairs leading up to the stage. The stage hustled with road crew members putting the finishing touches to the set. Hard to believe behind Black-Jack's enormous banner sat thousands of fans in darkness waiting for them to appear. He could hear the enthusiastic hum of the crowd and see the flames from lighters and the glow from cell phones. Not an empty seat in the house, with approximately eighteen thousand fans. Oh shit, he mused as his stomach protested again. He shouldn't have eaten those crackers.

He barely made it to the barrel in time before he lost the contents of his stomach once again. As he straightened, mortification slammed into him at finding Shannon and Cameron standing close by, having witnessed it. His stomach took another roll. His hand fished in his front jeans pocket and came out with a small tin of mints. He popped one into his mouth to kill the awful taste.

"Hey, Cameron, you ready?" *Was that really his voice?*

Cameron shook his head in return. "Hell no."

"After the third song you're up." He tossed him the mints and turned his back. His hand gripped the railing as he pulled himself up one metal stair at a time, silently praying he could pull this off.

Shannon held her breath and counted the beats of her pounding heart as Cole walked onto the dark stage. Several seconds later the lights exploded, momentarily blinding her as they opened with one of their biggest hits, "Misty

Mornings." She inched closer up the stairs, careful to stay out of the spotlights, and stood captivated by Cole's stage presence. One would never know by watching him now that he'd thrown up before taking the stage. And boy, did he know how to play to a crowd, and they welcomed him with open arms. Shannon's eyes stung with unshed tears. She knew this must be hard on him. Fortunately the fans from Boston welcomed him enthusiastically.

He traded in his acoustic guitar after the opening song for an electric one and everyone and everything going on around her melted into oblivion, except Cole. Her undivided attention centered on him. He stood at a microphone stand, strummed his guitar and belted out a heavy metal tune that left her ears ringing and her body humming with energy. His hair flung in the air as he played his guitar over his head, behind his back and not at all. Then he swung it around in the air as though it weighed nothing.

Her hands flew to her heart as it swelled for him. This was his element, his life's blood. And my God, nobody did it better. She couldn't help but think of all those years wasted in prison when he should have been doing this.

The next song took on the melody of a love ballad. Cole ditched the guitar, pulled the microphone from its stand, and walked the stage singing and slapping hands with the audience. His tight jeans hugged his butt as he bent over, causing Shannon to groan. His arm muscles bulged as he cradled the microphone in his hands. God, Shannon mused, it appeared he serenaded and made love to every woman in the audience. *She wanted it to be her.*

When Cole introduced Cameron, Shannon flew out of her trance, and her heart swelled for her son. Cole introduced him as a local teenager from the Boston area with incredible talent. Cameron didn't disappoint the fans either. He played and sang like a pro. Cole stood right there alongside him, silently supporting him, playing and singing backup.

Tears streamed down Shannon's face and she had trouble breathing. She had always known Cameron had talent, but it hit her, at precisely this moment, how much. From tonight on, his life would never be the same. She only hoped he was ready for it. Mature enough to handle it. And, oh my God, what would John say?

Cameron stayed, playing his guitar on stage with the band until they took a short break. "Mom, that was so awesome!" He bound down the stairs breathless from all the excursion and excitement, not to mention hot, sweaty and grinning from ear to ear.

Cole came up beside Shannon also sweaty and looking hot. Somehow the combination of the smell of sweat and watching it drip down his face turned her on. She stared as he chugged a bottle of water. Watched his Adam's apple bob up and down when he swallowed, and she nearly groaned out loud. After tossing the empty into a barrel, he handed a full one to Cameron, then smiled at Shannon. The smile lit up his molten brown eyes.

"Your boy did great. He picked up on every one of our songs like a pro. If you don't mind, I asked him to sit in on the next set."

Shannon didn't know what to say. No matter what Cole said, she didn't want Cameron being a burden. "I don't know. You've done so much already."

"Mom, please," her son pleaded, focusing his sad puppy dog eyes on her. When a teenager wanted something bad enough, somehow they knew how to beg for it just the right way. Shannon figured this was inbred in them at birth.

"You can't imagine what it's like out there. It's always

been my dream to be standing on stage with thousands of fans cheering and singing along with me. I know they're here for BlackJack, but I can *feel* the connection with them and with the music. Please don't ruin this for me." He clasped his hands together and dropped to his knees. "P*lease, please, please,*" he begged.

"Cole, can I talk to you for a sec," Shannon said, tilting her head, showing the need for privacy.

They stepped away from Cameron and her mind reeled, trying to figure out how to approach what bothered her. She decided there was no way except to take a deep breath, swallow and forge forward. "Cole, there are girls, women actually, flashing their, ah, um...naked, um...breasts at you guys on stage. I don't want Cameron up there."

"Shannon," Cole said enjoying himself. "We can hardly see anything from the stage because of the lights. Besides, if you were in the audience you might find your-selves sitting next to one of these women."

She was somewhat relieved by his explanation, albeit embarrassed by the content of the conversation. "Oh, I never thought of that."

"But did you see." He put his hands out in front of his chest to indicate large breasts. "The woman in the front row with the—"

"Cole!" she yelled.

His arm snaked around her back and he whispered close to her ear, causing her heart to palpitate. "I'm kidding. Let him come on stage, who knows when he'll get another chance."

This was not a man she could easily resist. "Fine, but I'm counting on him not seeing any more naked breasts."

Cole laughed as he let his arm drop. "You think it's his first time?"

Shannon looked at him, shocked by his comment. "Yeah, I do."

Cole cocked a brow.

"Okay, well maybe not, I can only hope. He's only sixteen."

"And what were you doing at sixteen?"

"None of your damn business," she choked out.

Cole burst out laughing and dropped a quick kiss on Shannon's cheek. Then he pulled Cameron on stage with him. The kid's eyes were bugging out of his head from having witnessed the kiss.

As the concert went on, the audience demanded more. Cole and the other members did not disappoint. They delivered big time, especially Cole, who had the most to prove and the most to lose.

When the concert ended, the band members vanished into their dressing rooms, she presumed to shower and change. Shannon and a hot, sweaty and stinky Cameron waited for them in the backstage room. The room swelled to capacity with people, some Shannon recognized from earlier and many new faces she'd never seen before.

AJ, the first band member to join them said, "Hey Cameron, do ye want tae shower and clean up?"

Cameron raised his arm slightly and sniffed. "Why? Do I smell ripe?"

AJ laughed and made a face. "Aye man, ye do. Go tae the second door on the right. Shower and grab a clean T-shirt out of my bag."

Shannon smiled at AJ in relief as she watched her son stroll away. It amazed her his feet touched the ground after what he'd just experienced. The opportunity of a lifetime most people could only dream about. "Thanks, he reeked. It would have been a long ride back to the hotel."

"Aye, luv. It would have. Listen, we have tae hang out

here for a bit tae speak with some radio people and those fans lucky enough tae have nabbed backstage passes. And ah'm told one local television station has come hoping for an interview with Cole. Boy, won't they be disappointed when he's a no show. Also, some guy from a Boston radio station wants tae interview Cameron. Would that be fine?"

Shannon frowned. "I don't know... did you just say Cole won't be here?"

AJ's brows drew together and his lips tightened. "Cole's not ready tae face any interviews just yet. He kens the subject of his wife's death will come up and he doesn't want tae talk about it. We'll meet him back at the hotel. Now, about the interview with Cameron, can he do it?"

Had her imagination run wild or had she witnessed sadness flash in his eyes as he spoke about Lindsey? It must have been horrible for all the band members to lose her. And why, with there being so much more to Cole than a dead wife, couldn't reporters come up with something else to talk to him about?

Glancing around the room at the crowd, she hoped her son knew what he was doing. "Only if I supervise," she finally replied to AJ's question.

"Without a doubt, wouldnae have it any other way. Ah and here's Cameron now."

AJ, Brad and Ted spoke to the local radio D.J. and the one local television entertainment reporter. She recognized the woman as the reporter who'd written a story on her a while back. AJ then introduced Cameron. He appeared nervous, but handled himself well. Answering all their questions truthfully and expressing his thanks to all four members of the band for letting him jam with them. Shannon's heart swelled with pride. Sometimes he seemed way beyond his years.

When they returned to the hotel, Shannon and

Cameron went to the band's suite and found Cole sitting on the sofa eating a sandwich. He smiled at her with a mouth full of food and waved her over.

She stood frozen to the floor, her legs refusing to move and her palms damp with sweat. She'd just met this man, and he had such power over her body physically, and her mind...well he had power over that too. Because, no matter what she tried to tell herself, her mind betrayed her thoughts and her thoughts drifted to Cole. What would it be like to have someone like him love her? He was such an intense man, she imagined he did everything that way. He'd be a fabulous lover, passionate and totally focused on the carnal pleasures he gave and received. Oh my God! Here she was standing in front of him, fantasizing about him, and by his expression it was as though he could read her thoughts. How mortifying to think he knew her brain centered on sex. And not just sex, sex with him!

Since her divorce she'd barely dated anyone long enough to feel anything but a slight attraction, which had suited her. So why now, after all these long years, did her whole being sit up and take notice of this man?

Cameron headed to the food table and somehow she managed to walk over to the sofa and casually sit down next to him, although she actually collapsed because her knees finally gave way. She hoped he didn't notice the shaking of her hands. And she swore if he listened carefully enough he'd hear her heart beating a loud staccato inside her chest. To help her calm down, as if she could calm down sitting next to Cole's strong, lean, hot body, smelling of sandalwood, she focused on the other people in the room. It didn't work. It might have if his muscular jean-clad thigh wasn't burning an out-of-control inferno against her thigh.

"Thank you for letting Cameron play with us tonight."

Cole raked his long fingers through his still-damp hair. Shannon's eyes followed every sensual stroke, imagining him doing that to her. "Whether or not you know it, he has the gift.

Shannon hesitated looking Cole in the eye. She knew it was rude to speak to someone while avoiding their gaze, but she didn't want him to see how nervous he made her. *Jeez, she couldn't win.*

"Shannon."

She'd always been and still was a huge Cole Jackson and BlackJack fan. She had every CD, including their latest, and Cole had bled his heart out in the songs he had written for that one. One particular heartbreaking song made her tear up every time she heard it. During that song he opened the door and let the world into his heart and soul. It made her feel nineteen and in love with him all over again.

"Oh, I'm sorry. My mind—well, it has a mind of its own sometimes. About tonight, thank you. It meant an awful lot to Cameron." She blinked back tears, suddenly wanting to make an appearance. "And to me."

He gave Shannon a lopsided grin. "Yeah well, me too. He's a great kid. You did all right by him."

Surprised by his compliment and thrown off by his sexy smile, she finally replied, "I can't take all the credit. My ex-husband and I share custody."

"Has it been hard for you?"

Confused and unsure about what he referred to she hesitated. Obviously he picked up on her confusion because he clarified himself.

"The divorce, was it hard for you?"

What did she share and not share with the man sitting next to her? She wondered if she needed to pinch herself or not because of how could Cole Jackson be interested in her life? One Shannon had never been comfortable talking about. But, for some strange reason, she wanted to tell Cole about herself and she wanted to know all about him. The only way she figured she would learn about him was to talk about herself.

"John and I married young, before we truly knew ourselves, never mind each other. Unfortunately, several years after we married, we realized how much we loved one another as friends but not..." The heat from the blush crept up her face. "Not as husband and wife, not as lovers." Pausing, she wet her suddenly parched lips with her tongue. "We divorced when Cameron was five. John has since remarried and I found out today he and his wife, Cheryl, are expecting baby number four."

Cole remained quiet. He couldn't help but wonder about her and the ex-husband and why they didn't fit as lovers. "That's nice about the baby." Standing, he slowly unfolded his tall frame and mumbled, "I'll be right back." He strolled across the room to speak to Cameron, who still stuffed his face with food. Everyone else had left for the night. Cole smiled to himself as he watched Cameron, and he felt a pull to his heart. This was one special kid.

"Hey, Cameron," Cole said.

The boy nodded his head as his mouth swelled with food.

"I have a question to ask and I want you to answer truthfully," Cole said in a serious tone, which got Cameron's undivided attention.

Cole stole a look at Shannon, who had sat back on the couch and watched him with keen interest. His pulse raced. Frowning, he wondered suddenly what he was doing. What would someone like Shannon Gallagher possibly see in someone like him? He, Cole Jackson, an aging rocker who'd spent his best years behind bars and had nothing to offer her at this most crazy time in his life. *Confidence man. Have some confidence in your ability to read women. Oh, that's right, silly him, he hadn't been around that many women.* But he could see the interested signs radiating from her, and he planned on finding out just how interested she was.

"Would you mind if I asked your mom out on a date?"

Cameron choked on his mouthful of food. "My mom," he said with his eyes bugging out of his head. "Why?"

"Because she's smart, talented, warm and kind, and hell, I've only known her for a few hours—can you imagine how many more fascinating traits she has?" His eyes collided with hers. The heat sparkling from her eyes and shooting across the room at him had his blood pumping south at an alarming rate.

"I guess it would be okay. Better than okay, it would be way cool," Cameron replied, still appearing a little stunned.

Cole still hadn't broken eye contact with Shannon. "Great Cameron, it's late. Go to bed."

"Huh." Cameron glanced from Cole to his mother and took the hint. After saying goodnight to him, he went over to his mom and Cole heard him say. "Night Mom, I'm exhausted. I think I'll turn in. Stay here with Cole."

Shannon's whole body sizzled from Cole's intense stare as he causally strolled toward the couch and turned the television on to *Saturday Night Live*. Sitting down beside her, he surprised her by wrapping his arms around her waist and pulling her close so their heads rested against each other. It seemed natural for her to be here like this with him. They sat for a time, neither one speaking.

Every nerve ending in her body rose up and took notice of him. From his manly smell of sandalwood with a hint of leather to his breath tickling her cheek. Add the warmth coming from his strong arms and the heat from his thighs brushing up against hers; it was a wonder she didn't self-combust.

God knew she had written enough about love at first sight and strong physical attractions over the years. But had she honestly believed it existed? Whether she did before, she was a believer now. Somehow she felt connected to this man. A piercing bond that ran deep within the marrow of her bones, and she did not understand why. And now was not the time she wanted to question it.

She wanted to enjoy it.

Revel in it.

Exist with it.

Shannon snapped out of her reverie at the sound of Cole's deep voice saying things that surprised her.

"My marriage to Lindsey was not your typical marriage. I had loved her since I was seventeen." His voice held no emotion. "After we formed the band and started traveling she…" He paused and Shannon felt and heard him take a deep breath and let it out. "Well, she definitely stopped loving me. Let's just say she loved everyone but me. I think that's why I drank so much and snorted cocaine. I was embarrassed and ashamed by Lindsey's careless treatment of my heart. I never let on I knew about her affairs, and she had no plans to change our relationship." He squeezed his arms around Shannon tighter and buried his head in her hair, inhaling deeply. "During the last two years of our marriage, I never touched her. I touched nobody. I could have had dozens of women, but as unconventional as our marriage was, I would not break our wedding vows."

Shannon's chest and throat constricted painfully in response to what he said. Lindsey had hurt him badly, and she said the only thing she could. "I'm sorry."

He snorted. "Yes well, I'm sorry about a lot of things. I'm sorry Lindsey died. I'm sorry I never found out who really killed her. I'm sorry I spent fifteen years rotting in jail for a murder I didn't commit." His voice suddenly softened. "And I'm sorry we didn't meet years ago."

Tears pooled in her eyes and his name came out as a whisper. "Cole."

He sniffed. "You're not afraid of me, Shannon, are you? Please tell me you're not afraid."

Stunned by his pleading, Shannon took a moment to think. No. She was not afraid of him. Although he probably believed most women were afraid of a man who'd been convicted of killing his wife, whether or not they believed it. She did not believe it. At least she didn't think so, and she would prove it.

His body trembled against hers as he waited for her answer. She had something much better in mind than words. Pivoting into him, she cradled his devastatingly handsome, somber face with her unsteady hands, giving him her most endearing smile as she tugged his mouth to hers.

He hesitated, and she believed he was afraid to let himself go. She continued tasting him, running her tongue along his soft lips until she felt him sigh and open his warm, wet mouth to let her in. A deep guttural moan came from deep inside his throat and vibrated into hers. He pulled her so close their bodies molded together as one, and he took over the kiss and deepened it still. He tasted her, devoured her air and explored every speck of her. There wasn't any part of her mouth, tongue, face, neck or lips he hadn't tasted, and it rocked her world.

Shannon's whole body burned with desire for him. However, she heard little warning bells go off inside her head. It's too soon and too fast. Sanity broke through her hormones, reached her mind and she pulled back and tried to catch her breath. It was then she realized her hands were still on his face. Giving him an uncertain smile, she dropped her hands to her lap. "I never believed you harmed Lindsey, and I am most definitely not afraid of you." Her voice held a strong conviction and sounded in complete control, contrary to how she really felt inside. Her insides burned with longing for Cole. She trembled with the need to have his hands and mouth all over every inch of her body.

Cole closed his eyes and held her tightly as his heart rate lowered to a more normal speed. Breathing in her unique scent, he realized he never wanted to let her go. Did she have any idea how much those words meant to him? How much they soothed his broken, needy heart? She couldn't know, or could she? Her eyes shone with such intelligence. There probably wasn't much that went on around her she didn't notice. Could she possibly know how he felt about her? She probably did, just as he suspected her feelings for him ran along the same parallel lines. But the million-dollar question was could they could join those lines?

"I better walk you to your room," he breathed out. He had to, before something neither one of them was prepared for happened. And if he held her much longer, there was no doubt in his mind *it* would happen.

"Hmm, yes you better."

They walked hand in hand down two floors to Shannon's room. Once outside her room they heard the mumble of the television coming from inside. Cole ran his hands through her silky hair. Had anyone's hair ever felt better? "When we have some time, I'd like to hear about your writing and how it all came about. Meanwhile," he whispered, "what are your plans for tomorrow?" Shannon's eyes were closed and her lips slightly parted as he continued caressing her hair.

"Hmm, I have a book signing at Copley Place from twelve to three."

He leaned in close and placed soft, silky kisses along her neck and up to her ear, causing her to moan. "Would you mind if I stopped by?"

"Hmm ... oh, no, I mean yes, please do."

He grinned at her as his hands cupped her face, and he kissed her gently. "Goodnight, Shannon Gallagher," he murmured.

As he walked away, he heard her soft reply, "Goodnight, Cole Jackson."

When she stepped inside her hotel room, she saw Cameron asleep and sighed with relief. She didn't want him seeing her all ... all what? Acting like a lovesick teenager and floating on top of cloud nine as though she'd been kissed for the first time? Smiling, she touched her fingers to her lips and twirled around. Cole Jackson was quite a man. She would never have thought in her wildest dreams, well yes, in her dreams, but not in real life, that she would ever meet Cole Jackson, never mind kiss him. Never mind losing her heart to him in a matter of hours. Damn, her stomach had butterflies swarming inside it. Her whole body tingled with...something indescribable: nerves, excitement, terror, and longing, both emotionally and physically.

Shannon didn't believe Cole killed his wife. Being a romantic at heart, she couldn't help but bleed for the man convicted of his wife's murder. At the time every picture depicted of him told a heartbreaking tale. His eyes were so incredibly sad. You could tell he had truly loved his wife and grieved deeply for losing her.

Nothing Shannon had heard all those years ago would make her believe one of her biggest rock idols committed murder. She remembered exactly where she was when she'd heard the guilty verdict. Sitting at her kitchen table eating lunch with her son, she cried as she listened as each juror voiced the words guilty. Cried as they handcuffed and leg shackled a stunned Cole Jackson who had tears streaming down his handsome face. And here she was, so many years later fancying herself in love with him.

It had been so long, actually never, since she felt this way, and it unsettled her, considering who her feelings were for. Not because he had been to prison but because of the man himself. She headed into the bathroom and took an extra-long hot shower. Dressed in shorts and a T-shirt, she climbed into the nice soft bed, burrowed deep into the covers and fell asleep dreaming about Cole. She'd dreamed about him before, but it was the first time her dreams were based on reality, and reality far surpassed the imagination.

Cole lay awake in bed arguing with himself about this thing with Shannon—whatever it was. Hoping he wasn't making a mistake starting something with her when his life was in shambles. Not to mention, he hadn't befriended nor slept with a woman in almost fifteen years, and in his book it put him out of practice. Well, not exactly true. Two days after his release from prison, he had hired a high-priced call girl from an escort service in New York. He'd hired her for the entire night, wanting to feel a warm body sleeping beside him. His twelve hours with her set him back a pretty penny, but it had done wonders in bringing back his manhood and some of his self-esteem. Other than the call girl, and this would come as a shock to most people, especially considering what his lifestyle had been like, Lindsey was the only other woman he'd ever been with. They had lost their virginity together.

There had been plenty of opportunities for other women. Women came backstage all the time offering to give all the band members blow jobs. Since no one else in the band was married at the time, they took the sex offered. Cole would sit and watch the orgies going on around him through a drug-induced haze because it never stopped at oral sex.

Before Lindsey began sleeping around, they would join in, but only with each other. After the affairs began, Cole wouldn't—couldn't make love to Lindsey. He was dead, emotionally and physically where she was concerned. As he'd told Shannon earlier in the evening, he could not, would not, break his wedding vows. Stupid, considering Lindsey didn't give a damn about them.

Now, he felt more than a little frightened at the prospect of having a relationship with Shannon. He hoped they had one because he didn't think his heart would ever be the same after meeting her. This brought his mind back to the real reason for the uncertainty: Did Shannon truly believe in his innocence? Why? No one else did.

He would never forget the day the verdict came in. It

had seemed like a lifetime waiting for the jurors to deliberate when, in fact, only two days had gone by. Cole remembered standing in the courtroom dressed uncomfortably in a suit, which only added to the bizarreness of the day. His head hung down and tears streamed down his face as they read the verdict. He barely stifled a sob as he heard the word "guilty" and then the pain of a knife eviscerating his heart, over and over. A jury of his peers had found him guilty of second-degree murder for killing his wife.

He pictured his beautiful Lindsey in his mind. They had known one another their whole lives and had been in love for most of it. Married at twenty, she was dead at twenty-three. And God help him—he didn't do it. Even if he didn't remember much about the night, he knew one thing for certain—he could *never* have harmed her. But, it didn't matter what he knew, it only mattered what everyone else believed and what they believed to be the truth condemned him.

They saw a young, budding rock star in his twenties who spent his days and nights drinking, drugging and partying. The prosecutor's closing argument easily swayed them. He depicted him as a self-absorbed twenty-three-year-old-spoiled brat who would do anything to get his way, and he somehow convinced the jury his wife had gotten in his way.

Cole's defense attorney was Arthur Monroe. Some considered him the best in the country, but sometimes the best wasn't good enough. The evidence against him was circumstantial at best, and the murder weapon was never found. Mr. Monroe argued every case point and objected to every defamation of Cole's character. He called to the stand a long list of character witnesses attesting to Cole's upstanding and peaceful personality. None of it mattered.

The jury heard only what they wanted to hear, that Cole had been high on cocaine, drunk on beer and in the heat of the moment had stabbed Lindsey Jackson once in the heart. He never went for help, it wouldn't have mattered anyway—she'd died instantly. He had disposed of the murder weapon, passed out on the floor next to her body and woke up the next morning covered in his dead wife's blood. How could he not be guilty?

Cole remembered feeling his lawyer's hand pressed against the middle of his back. Small comfort to a man whose life just crashed down around him? His lungs burned, making it impossible to breathe as the knife lodged deeper into his chest. His body began to tremble painfully, and Cole thought he would be sick as the reality of the situation slammed into him. He was to be transferred to a maximum security prison in upstate New York for a stay of twenty years. He was eligible for parole after fifteen.

They denied the appeal filed by his lawyer.

Some say they railroaded him. Others say he got his just due.

Only Cole and Lindsey Jackson's true killer knew justice had not prevailed that dark day in the New York City Courtroom.

John McKenzie stared at his cell phone in his hand, tossed it on the sofa and then picked it up again. He had every right to question Shannon's motives when it involved their son. She may think, with his job, the never-ending suck the life out of him house, his kids by his second wife, and another one on the way, that he was in over his head. Which he was, hell he didn't even have time to take a crap. Well, he did, although interruptions always happened, making him understand why he guzzled bottles of pink medicine. Anyway, he was not too busy he would let this thing with Cole Jackson slide. He heard his son's voice last night when he called him and it sounded to him like he idolized the man. Now there were many other musicians he wouldn't mind his son worshiping, but Cole Jackson? Come on. He punched in the numbers for Shannon's cell phone. He placed the phone to his ear. His knuckles turned white from his relentless grip, and he began counting the rings.

Chapter Four

SHANNON, STARTLED AWAKE IN THE MORNING BY THE MUSIC of her cell phone, groaned as she slid the little arrow across. "Hello."

"Shannon, what the hell were you thinking letting our son socialize with a murderer?"

She groaned again and lay back down in bed, holding the phone away from her ear to let John rant and rave. She'd known this was coming. Knew there would be a price to pay for last night. John enjoyed controlling the people in his life, and her name still graced his list.

"And you, when I talked to Cameron last night, he told me Cole Jackson asked you out on a date." His voice climbed high on the Richter scale. "Are you out of your fucking mind? He killed his wife. I can't let you date him! I won't let you date him!"

How dare he tell her what she could and couldn't do? He gave up that right after they divorced, not that he ever had it to begin with. Although she had the feeling, he would have a different opinion on that subject.

"My mind is fine, thank you very much. I have every

right to decide for Cameron and myself. And I take offense to you thinking otherwise." Her body shook in tandem with her voice, testifying to her anger and frustration. Many times, they had loud, emotionally-filled conversations, and nothing ever got resolved, so she took a deep breath and spoke calmly. At least one of them would act sane and reasonable this morning. "Calm down, John, and while you listen to me, why don't you grab a bar of soap and wash out your foul mouth?" She heard him curse again. "First, Cameron had the time of his life last night. You should've seen him. He was awesome. This is his life's dream and being exposed to the business now is a good thing. Besides, I was with him the whole time and let me tell you, every single member of BlackJack is a role model. And there were no drugs or booze anywhere."

"Yeah, because they're all recovering drug addicts and alcoholics."

"Only Cole is, smart ass, which does not make him a bad person in my book or anyone else's. Second, Cole didn't kill his wife. And third," she continued no longer capable of keeping the anger out of her voice. "Where do you get off telling me what I can and cannot do?"

"Oh, Shannon, please!" John said, exasperated.

"I truly believe he didn't do it. If you met him, you would feel the same way." She heard him yell at the dog, something in the tune of, go wipe your muddy paws.

"Shannon, be reasonable, don't date this man. Please."

"Whether or not I date him, it's none of your business. And just so I make myself perfectly clear and there is no confusion, I *do* want to go out with him."

"Fine. If that's your decision, however, I don't want Cameron anywhere near him."

She growled into the phone. He was determined to

make her lose it. "Don't do this. If you'd seen them togeth-er." She flinched when she heard him bang something.

"Shit! I think I broke my hand. I'm coming to the hotel to pick him up in an hour. Wake him."

"Cole leaves town tomorrow, what's the big deal?"

He exhaled. "I love you Shan. I don't want anything to happen to you."

"Nothing will."

"That remains to be seen. I'll see you in an hour, be in the lobby."

Before she could respond, he'd hung up. She dragged her suddenly weary body out of bed and took a long, scalding hot shower. Why was John being so unreasonable? Sometimes he drove her crazy. She didn't know how Cheryl put up with him. He could be so pigheaded. She just thanked her lucky stars he wasn't her husband anymore. As much as she loved him, he drove her nuts. After drying her hair and getting dressed, she woke Cameron up by lightly shaking him and pulling off his covers.

"Meet me downstairs in thirty minutes all packed. Your father's picking you up." She hoped her voice didn't betray her anger with John.

He gave an unintelligible groan and rolled over. Wouldn't that tick John off more if Cameron showed up late? Shannon smiled as she left the room. It would serve John right if Cameron kept him waiting.

She entered the dining room, paid for Sunday morning brunch even though all she could stomach was coffee and a muffin. She took a table next to a window facing the street. The sun shined brightly, guaranteeing another beautiful day. Too bad, after her conversation with John, she would have trouble enjoying it. Then her eyes found *him* as he entered the restaurant, causing her heart to soar. He wore jeans and a blue chambray shirt with the sleeves rolled up to his elbows. His eyes scanned the room and when they locked on hers, he smiled and nodded in greeting. Immediately her body quivered with anticipation. She watched him pile food on his plate and stroll over to her. My God, even the way he walked screamed out sex.

"Good morning Shannon, you're up early," he said as he slid into the chair opposite hers.

"Morning Cole, so are you."

———

His radar spiked. Something had changed since last night. He took a sip of his steaming coffee and studied her. Yup, something was definitely wrong and his stomach took a dive. Was it him? Did she regret kissing him? Only one way to find out.

"Mind telling me what the matter is?"

She forced a smile. "What makes you think something's the matter?"

He sat back, cradling his coffee mug in his hands, his brows drawn together. "I may have only met you yesterday, but I'm a perceptive person and something's screaming at me something's wrong."

She played with her muffin, breaking off pieces and letting them crumble onto her plate. "John called."

"Ahh, John, as in the ex, he heard."

"Yeah, he heard. I'm sorry Cole. He's coming to pick up Cameron." She glanced at her watch. "Soon."

She said nothing, just stared at him and her eyes said it all. The look caused his pulse to jump and sent a jolt to his heart. "I see," he said, not even trying to hide his anger. Or was it hurt? After putting his coffee mug down, he leaned forward and covered her small warm hands with his large ones. "He shouldn't blame you. I invited Cameron on stage. In hindsight, I shouldn't have asked. I should have realized his father would not approve of him playing with a convicted murderer. How people perceive me is always dead center in my mind, but Cameron's talent blew me away I wasn't thinking there would be consequences. I'm so sorry I've caused you trouble." He went to pull his hands away, but she stopped him.

"No, don't go," she pleaded. "You're right. But you don't know John. He's just doing what he thinks is right. He thinks he needs to protect his son from you, but he's wrong."

This time she didn't stop him when he pulled his hands away, even though losing contact was almost physically painful to her. He ran them through his hair, and she noticed for the first time all the gray hairs mixed in with the blond. It wasn't all she noticed. His hands trembled.

"Tell me Shannon, what does John do for a living?"

Shannon openly cringed at his query and paused for quite some time before she finally answered in a near whisper. "He's a police lieutenant."

Cole closed his eyes, and when he opened them, Shannon witnessed the hurt she caused—correction John caused. "I'm sorry he feels that way, but if he met you, I know he'd change his mind. I know he would," she said with strong conviction, which wasn't easy to do, considering her throat burned as she fought back the panic and tears sure to come. "And I meant everything I said last night," she added with a deep sigh.

He reached over, wiped the single tear slowly trickling down her cheek and then touched his heart. "I know you did, but I'll not be responsible for your ex-husband making your life miserable or causing problems with Cameron." He pushed his chair back and stood to his full height. After clearing his throat, he continued in a quiet voice, "Goodbye Shannon Gallagher, it's been an honor and a pleasure meeting you. Tell Cameron to keep up with his music. I expect to attend one of his concerts someday."

She watched him leave through a haze of tear-stained eyes, and she swallowed the lump in her throat. That's it—done and over before the relationship began. Her hand found its way to her chest, and she'd swear her heart stopped beating.

She watched as Cole briefly spoke with Cameron, who had just come into the restaurant. He gave him a hug and her heart broke, for her son, for Cole and for herself. Damn you to hell and back John for being so stubborn.

By the time she met John in the lobby, anger had over-taken her heartache. She was fuming. It was probably the first time she had barely been civil toward John. She kissed and hugged Cameron. "Keep your studies up at school and behave. I'll be back in one week." She didn't acknowl-edge John's hug or kiss, nor did she speak to him. Which she could tell didn't sit well with him. *Well, that's just too damn bad.*

***

Cole watched the happy family reunion from a chair in the lobby, sitting off to the side so they couldn't see him. The ex was an imposing figure, and he held himself with an air of confidence and arrogance many police officers possessed. He stood tall and fit, his dark hair showing signs of receding. He seemed to care for Shannon genuinely, and he loved his son.

Cole felt a twinge of envy. He'd been robbed a family of his own. Oh, he knew there was still time, but he didn't have any delusions of grandeur. If nothing else, prison life made him a realist and forced him out of the world of songs and music. He now lived in the world convicted murderers lived in. He knew that was always in the back of people's minds when they met him. And he believed, deep down inside, his bandmates and other acquaintances couldn't get it out of their minds either. He didn't blame anyone for believing he killed Lindsey, after all he did the time. Oh, he didn't feel sorry for himself; he was out of prison and things were going relatively well. He felt sorry for Lindsey because her life had been stolen from her, and her murderer left to run free.

As he came to the understanding that he would probably never see Shannon Gallagher again, he thought ahead to the tour. Tomorrow they left Boston for New Jersey. He was skipping New York. He couldn't bring himself to face the city responsible for convicting him. The city he loved beyond all others.

Shannon moved through her day on automatic pilot. The book signing turned out well, but somehow, she couldn't get excited about it. She began plotting ahead to the next two days in New York. She had three different bookstore appearances and a guest spot on *Good Morning America*. During the evenings she would have some time to herself, but her days were tight.

After dealing with John and his stubbornness that morning, she'd decided she would look into Cole's trial. With any luck, she would get to talk to the detective or detectives in charge of the case. She'd use the excuse she was doing a book about the murder of Lindsey Jackson. Of course, that wasn't the real reason—the real one was a selfish one. Shannon wanted to clear his name so she could see him without John hassling her. And put the nagging minuscule amount of doubt in her brain to rest. Maybe she could dig up something everyone missed way back when. She would contact his lawyer, knowing ahead of time that he wouldn't reveal anything confidential, but he may have some helpful suggestions on where she should investigate.

When the signing ended, she walked to a small café in Copley Place and ate a late lunch. Back at her hotel room, she stripped down to her underwear and bra and climbed in bed to take a nap. When she awoke, darkness swirled around her. She wondered how the concert was going for Cole and wished she were there. He'd been incredible to watch last night. His tall, lean, muscular body playing guitar and singing song after song had made her aware of the fact he was all male and she was all female. His blond hair flying, his body dancing and jumping on stage had taken her breath away. The memory had her burning for him now.

How he had treated Cameron as one of the band members instead of the self-absorbed teenager he could be at times touched her deeply. It had shocked her when he told her he'd never been with anyone but his wife. The tabloids had portrayed him as a philandering playboy, even though he was married. What they never said was he had genuine morals. He'd had so many opportunities to trip up in life with his career, but he hadn't. His only real mistake had been to drink himself to the point of numbing his heart and brain from his unfaithful wife.

Shannon could not, for the life of her, understand how Lindsey had turned to other men when she had Cole.

And *why* did she not remember that being a factor in the trial? They portrayed her as the innocent monogamous wife and Cole as the adulterer.

Her mind made up, she would go to Cole and see him once more before they both left tomorrow for different lives. She'd let her imagination run wild last night with the possibility she and Cole could have a future together. Then reality crashed around her. She traveled the country on book signing tours or researching settings or spent time in her office in her bedroom writing. He toured the country in a band and Christ, she didn't even know where he lived. But none of that mattered at the moment. The only thing that mattered was she had to touch him, see him, smell him and taste him one more time. Say goodbye one more time.

Cole was not nearly as nervous for the concert tonight as last night, nor was he as enthused. Shannon and Cameron had added to the air of excitement. Electric currents crackled through the air with her around. Tonight the electric currents eluded him. The surrounding air hung suspended, void of life, choking and suffocating him. Some things would never change though—he still puked in the barrel off the stage before he went on. There was a great crowd again tonight, enthusiastic, energetic and cheering them on, and it wasn't long before they sucked him into their excitement. The band gave it everything they had, and then some. Cole's body and soul were wiped out when the last encore ended. And as with the previous night, he took off immediately, leaving everything once again for AJ.

After he arrived at the hotel, he showered and put on a robe courtesy of hotel management. He ordered up room service, an action flick on cable and settled down for his last night in Boston. Dozing on and off on the bed, he snapped awake when room service knocked on his door. He let them in, signed the bill, and pushed his food around more than he ate. His mind wouldn't get off Shannon. Her sad face when he walked away from the restaurant kept flashing before his eyes. The tears that glistened and flowed gently down her cheeks were tears of pain. Frustrated with the turn of events, he threw his fork down, stripped off the robe and climbed under the covers, only to be tormented once again by her face, her lips and her touch.

Someone knocked on his door and awoke him a short time later. He hadn't the foggiest notion who it could be this time. He tossed the robe on his naked body, peered out the security-hole as an instant jolt woke him up. His hand couldn't turn the doorknob fast enough to let in a stunningly beautiful Shannon Gallagher who looked, to his eyes, uncertain and shy.

"Hi, I hope you don't mind me stopping by."

God, how he wanted her and he could barely hear anything besides his heart pounding in his temples. He scanned her face, her eyes, and he concluded she wanted him too. Words were not needed as he pulled her inside, closed the door, pinning her up against it with his fully aroused body and took her lips with his.

He tasted every speck of her mouth. His tongue tangled with hers. He drank, nibbled and tasted some more while his hands found their way to her firm, round breasts on their own accord. His mind did not condone it because he had no intentions of this going anywhere. He knew, once he sampled her body, really tasted her sweet feminine juices, brought her to orgasm, and he released his seed deep inside her, there would be no leaving her. And he knew he had to leave.

Shannon clung to him. He felt her body quivering and heard her purring, but he had to do it. He would not, could not be selfish with her. She meant too much to him.

He tore his mouth from hers, held her tightly within his arms. When his breathing calmed, and he trusted himself to speak he did, but his voice sounded distant and foreign to his own ears.

"We can't."

Her body tensed up in his arms and he waited for her to speak. And he continued waiting, barely able to breathe.

"Shannon?" he whispered.

Her arms squeezed him tight. So tight he felt her heart beating simultaneously with his. "It's okay, I know, bad timing and all. I just wanted..." She sniffled. "I just wanted to hold you once more." She dropped her arms and Cole stepped back. Before she left, she met his eyes, and he didn't know how she managed it, but she smiled. It didn't reach her incredible blue eyes, but he would always remember that smile.

Chapter Five

JOHN AND CAMERON HAD BEEN AT ODDS WITH ONE another ever since Sunday morning at the hotel. Cameron stayed holed up in his room playing his music and refusing to see anyone since they arrived home. Monday morning came, and John had to leave for work soon, and his house was in shambles. Cheryl was in the bathroom relieving her stomach of her breakfast while their two-year-old son, Matt sat next to her watching with fascination.

Five-year-old twins, Heather and Taylor, were emptying their bureaus, each looking for a favorite piece of clothing, which John knew, would be found in the hamper's bottom. Try as they might, they could not keep up with the laundry. It lived as a bottomless pit, never going away. There were times he swore the clothes were breeding and multiplying. And to top everything off, Cameron's ride would be here in ten minutes and he had yet to leave his room.

. . .

John had the task of dropping the twins off at preschool on his way to work. He'd be late if he couldn't convince them to wear something from the pile on the floor. And if that didn't cause enough stress, they were expecting another baby. He needed his head examined. And never mind his concern about Shannon over Cole Jackson. Christ, he needed a drink. And drinking at seven-thirty in the morning just wouldn't look good. He'd have to settle for his favorite pink drink.

Somehow he survived the morning. Now he sat at his desk reviewing paperwork before heading out on the town in his cruiser, hoping for an uneventful, quiet day. *Like that would happen today of all days.* He gulped his black coffee, trying to perk up as he mused over the Cole Jackson problem. His son and ex-wife were so taken by the man, it got him to thinking maybe, just maybe, the man got a raw deal. John seriously doubted it, but he knew sometimes justice didn't prevail.

Shannon's small shuttle plane to New York's LaGuardia Airport rattled her kidneys the whole way, which didn't help the stomachache she'd had since last night's encounter with Cole. On top of her irritable stomach, her head pounded so badly not even three aspirins had dulled it. She hoped she didn't look as bad as she felt. Because she felt like someone had scrubbed her against a washboard, pounded her against the side of some rocks for extra effort and left her out in the scorching heat of the day to dry. It was not a pleasant feeling.

When the plane finally landed, she thanked God. Although truth be told, she didn't know how she'd get through her busy day. Her agent, Carol Sawyer, was picking her up at the airport, then taking her directly to lunch. After lunch Carol was dropping her off at her first book signing. The signing was in a small independent bookstore in SoHo. It was a quaint, personable bookstore that sold a decent amount of her books. A nice, older couple who always made Shannon feel welcome owned it.

After she finished there, she would take a cab to the Hilton, check-in, and prepare for dinner with her editor, Kevin English. Shannon always looked forward to seeing him. If she timed her day right, she might have time for a phone call or two to start her research into Cole's case.

Later in the afternoon, after a harrowing cab ride across the city, Shannon's nerves were even more frazzled. After scanning her key card, she opened the door and gasped. Sitting on the table which served as a desk, sat two dozen long stem red roses. Mesmerized by the sight of them, she hurried across the room and opened the card. "Shannon, thanks for believing in me. Cole."

She sat down on the edge of the bed and gave herself five minutes to have a good self-pity cry. Whatever happened to the days when you could have a good long cry? Spend all day brooding over your broken heart. Obviously, it was not to be in this lifetime, anyway. She didn't have the time.

After her shower she threw on a robe and called one of the New York police stations. The police sergeant she spoke with was helpful. He gave her the number of the station where the homicide detective who handled Cole's case worked. Sometimes having a well-recognized name was an advantage. He never questioned her motives, so she let him assume it was research for a book.

She dialed the correct station house, but Detective Guy Simone had left for the day. Shannon left a brief message, her hotel and cell phone numbers. Next she would try to reach

Cole's lawyer. His name was embedded in her mind. The case had received so much publicity, and Cole's lawyer had been one of the top defense attorneys in the country. Fortunately for her, he lived in New York. She dialed Arthur Monroe's law office and was surprised to be connected to him. He didn't know how much he could help her. Anything Cole had shared with him was confidential, but he told her what courthouse the trial was held in and she should be able to request a copy of the transcripts. They were public-record since the case was closed.

After thanking him, she hung up and her brain began to hum. Not too bad for today, because now, at least she had somewhere to start. Fortunately, due to the nature of Shannon's work and her love of writing romantic suspense, she knew a few good investigators. Hopefully she might convince one of them to take the case. Especially if she did all the legwork by giving them the court transcripts and internet research pertaining to the case. It might be hard, she mused, since the investigators all lived and worked in Boston, but it was worth a shot.

Shannon, dressed in a stunning black cocktail dress, black ballet flats and a black lace wrap, went down to the lobby to meet her editor. Per usual, Kevin arrived promptly, impeccably groomed and stylishly dressed as always in a dark gray suit, starchy white shirt and muted print tie. He stood no taller than she, so she always wore flats when they dined or went anywhere together. "Kevin, hi." She kissed his cheek and hugged him. "How are you?"

"I'm fine." He stepped back. "Let me look at you." He winked. "You look positively radiant." He looked closer, and his brows suddenly drew. "Your eyes don't look so good, though. Have you been crying?"

Shannon ignored his question and linked her arm through his. "I'm fine. Let's go." She wondered if he'd bring it up again, but knowing Kevin as she did, she didn't doubt it.

Kevin drove a small silver BMW sports car made for speed, but speed was impossible to find this time of day so they drove out of the city heading toward Connecticut at a snail's pace. They went to a small bistro just over the border. Shannon gave him credit, he waited until their wine arrived and after they toasted the success of her book, "Hot Stones," to drop the bomb.

Leaning forward he gave her the look. He had a way of staring at her, making her know he had some juicy information to tell or information he wanted to know. And in this case, she'd bet her life on the fact it was information he wanted to know.

"Rumor has it you were backstage at the BlackJack concert at the Boston Garden and your son performed with the band."

He said it in the nonchalant way Kevin had of pretending he wasn't interested in something, when truthfully, he was dying inside with curiosity. Shannon tried to hide her surprise that he would know this. "The gossip mongers at work?"

Kevin laughed. "No, the internet." He raised his eyebrows inquisitively. "So, tell me, is he as gorgeous as everyone says?"

Playing dumb, she asked, "Who?"

Kevin grinned. "Come on Shannon, you know who, Cole Jackson, that's who."

Few people in the business knew Kevin was gay. Many suspected, but he confided in Shannon one night after he'd had too much to drink and was depressed over a breakup with his long-term partner. Since then, they'd been close. And personally, she thought Kevin liked the mystery surrounding his sexual preference, which stood to reason why he'd never openly come out, so to speak.

"Don't we have business to discuss?"

Kevin laughed. "We already had our business meeting." He winked at her. "We're here to discuss our personal lives as pathetic and nonexistent as they are—or were, if your blushing is any indication." He wiggled his brows. "Do tell."

Shannon took a sip of her wine. Kevin was one person she could tell anything to. John was another, although she would never discuss Cole with John ever again. She ignored the little stab to her heart when she thought about losing John's friendship.

Kevin was an avid listener, so she retold the night's events.

"So, you slept with him didn't you?"

She turned three shades of pink. "You always could read me like a book."

Kevin nearly dropped his wine glass in shock. "Oh God, you did. I was just kidding. Details, I need details," he said excitedly as he leaned in closer. "I need lots and lots of juicy, wet details."

Her top teeth bit down on her bottom lip. "Actually, I didn't and not by my choice mind you. I wanted to. Hell, I threw myself at him. He didn't want to. His life is a mess, and he's not prepared for a relationship."

"I'm sorry. You could have used the sex because you *never* sleep with anyone," he clipped. "In fact, when was the last time you had sex?"

"Kevin, please, enough," she said mortified, wondering how her cheeks could get any warmer.

"Are you sure he's not gay?" he asked with a spark of hope in his gray eyes.

Shannon choked on her wine. "Quite sure."

"I'm really bummed," he said as he held up his hands in disappointment. "I hoped that after spending all those years in prison, he may have reconsidered and switched sides, so to speak."

The waiter arrived with their Caesar salads, causing them to pause their discussion. When he was out of earshot, Shannon remarked, "Sorry to disappoint you, but he's on my side, so to speak."

Kevin frowned. "Well, I can dream, can't I? So, are you seeing him again?"

Her lips tugged down into a frown and her eyes watered. "I don't know. I don't think so. He's on tour for six months. I don't even know where he lives or how to reach him. Besides, John read me the riot act and came to the hotel for Cameron the next morning."

"You don't answer to your prick of an ex-husband anymore."

Shannon's eyes widened. "Since when have you thought John was a prick?"

"Since now." He winked.

He handed her a tissue from his pocket. "Jesus, Shannon, I've never seen you like this. In all the years I've known you, I've never seen you cry. Not unless you were crying from laughing too hard." He reached across the table and took her hand. "What can I do? Just give me the word and I'll go after John. I'll beat him up for you. Hell, I'll even seduce him if it'll help."

Laughter bubbled out of her mouth as she fought to contain her tears. Her hand curled around the delicate wine glass and she sipped, hoping to soothe the fire burning the back of her throat. "Thanks Kevin, but no."

Throughout dinner, she kept expecting him to ask whether Cole had killed his wife and what she thought about it. But she should have known better with Kevin. He would not upset her any more than she already was. And she truly loved him for that.

They drove to her hotel pretty much in silence, listening to Mozart on the car stereo. Kevin knew her well enough to know she didn't want to talk anymore. They pulled up in front of her hotel, and he turned to her with concern in his eyes.

"Do you want me to walk you in?"

Shannon leaned across the stick shift and kissed his cheek. "No, thank you and I'll be in touch."

Once in her room, she ran a hot bath, hoping to soak away the soreness of her day and force her mind to concentrate on what was to come tomorrow. Her agent was picking her up at six and bringing her to the set of *Good Morning America* and from there to two different bookstores and then she was free until her flight the next afternoon to Chicago. For now, she plopped down on the bed with her laptop, powered it up and typed in the name Lindsey Jackson.

Cole tried to relax back in his too-cramped for comfort airplane seat and listen to the music on his phone. There was nothing like a little Led Zeppelin to get you through a flight. Cole, AJ, Ted, Anita, Brad and Dawn were flying to New York and crossing over the bridge to New Jersey while the road and equipment crew went in the band's specially equipped buses. Tomorrow night started their three consecutive nights of shows at the Meadowlands. Then they were taking five days off and meeting up again in Philadelphia, then Pittsburgh and so on across the country.

Ever since his release from prison, Cole hated to travel. He was obsessed with thinking everyone looked at him and saw a man who murdered his wife. AJ thought he was just being paranoid and maybe he should see a doctor about getting on some meds to help his paranoia. Cole rolled it over in his head and thought AJ was probably right. Most people didn't know who he was, yet he still felt uncomfortable around people and in crowds. Felt as though everyone was whispering about him, watching him, judging him.

He never minded the whispering and attention when Lindsey was alive, but now he had such low self-esteem he couldn't get over the stigma of being a convicted killer. He definitely could use a therapist, but he was never in one place long enough to form a bond with one.

Somehow, regardless of the uncomfortable seat, he must have dozed off because before he knew it, they were preparing to land in New York. He told himself it didn't matter. He was on his way to New Jersey.

The band members were caught up in a whirlwind of press and fans at the airport. Cole tried to stay out of the limelight, but since word had gotten out about how successful their Boston shows were, he gave up. He forced himself to be civil for his fellow band members. They'd put a lot on the line for him. Each of them immediately dropped what they'd been doing when he got out of prison so BlackJack could rise again. He felt he owed it to them to put on his acting face and swallow his pride about reporters and about being interviewed. But if just one reporter mentioned prison life or Lindsey's death, he'd walk.

After the first night's show, Cole braved the so-called "backstage room." He wished to God Shannon was there with him, giving him her strength and support. But the quicker he got this over with, the better. However, nothing could prepare him for Kyle Ward approaching and engulfing him in a bear hug, which Cole didn't return. Ward had some nerve coming here.

"You look good, man," Kyle said, leaning close and speaking quietly. "I hope you understand why I couldn't testify at your trial. With my re-election coming up, I couldn't risk it." He paused and glanced around. "I thought after I was re-elected I could help your cause more. You don't know how sorry I was at being unable to help. I hope there are no hard feelings."

"None," Cole forced through gritted teeth. "If you'll excuse me, I must get going."

He made haste to the door before he stayed and punched the lights out of ex-senator Ward. Cole was almost free from the confines of the crowded room when he was stopped by a young, petite, bubbly blonde who shoved a microphone in his face and opened her mouth and let the bomb drop.

"Mr. Jackson, do you have anything you'd like to say about your wife's death?"

He felt as though he'd been sucker punched in the gut—completely stripping his breath from his lungs. Refusing to answer her, he left the room before he had a full-blown panic attack for the entire world to see. Unfortunately for him, the bubbly reporter didn't get the hint. She followed him down the hall. He smelled her overpowering perfume, heard the click of her heels echoing in the hall and her annoying voice repeating her question over and over. He never looked back. He crashed out of the stadium door, climbed into the limo and finally could take a deep breath of relief as it pulled away from the curb. Christ, he couldn't live like this. He had to get control of his emotions and his life. A reporter and Ward in one night. How dare he show up tonight and think they could pick up their friendship where it had ended?

Cole could never forget how Ward had thrown him to the reporter wolves fifteen years ago when he'd been arrested. Not to mention, he screwed his wife. Was there no honor among friends anymore? Obviously not, if he and AJ both fucked Lindsey. AJ, he could forgive. He'd been in love with her. Ward used her shamelessly, and Cole had often wondered if he could have killed Lindsey in a jealous rage over her affair with AJ. Ward may not have loved Lindsey, but he didn't take kindly to sharing her either.

After he exited the limo, he donned Oakley sunglasses and a ball cap and strolled into the hotel bar. His eyes scanned the crowd, and he sighed with relief. No one paid much attention to him. Thank God for dark places. He took a seat at the bar and signaled the bartender.

"What'll it be?"

"Soda water with lime," Cole answered.

The bartender appeared middle-aged, of average height, bald as a cue ball and he didn't give Cole a second glance as he dragged over a bowl of bar mix. He placed his drink on a cocktail napkin and went back to fixing drinks and drafts for the other customers.

Cole absentmindedly munched on the snack as he stared into his glass. Before the woman slipped onto the stool next to him, he'd almost gagged at her overpowering smell. Hadn't she ever heard of subtle perfume? That was twice tonight strong perfume bombarded him. Only after she ordered a drink and didn't make a move to vacate the bar stool did Cole turn his head and look at her. Early twenties, dressed provocatively in tight, low-slung jeans and a clingy sweater that didn't quite reach the top of her waistband. Someone would have to be blind not to notice her cleavage spilling out the top of what Cole was certain would be a miracle bra helping them along. She was pretty with short dark hair, dark eyes and mocha skin. What some would call an exotic beauty?

"I don't mean to bother you," she said with a sexy southern drawl, "but I wanted to tell you I saw your concert tonight and had a blast. My friends and I love your music and were thrilled when New Jersey was one of your tour stops."

Cole turned and peered over his shoulder to her table of friends. There were two men, one black and one white, and two women, both white. He glanced at the woman beside him and wondered how she'd been elected to approach him. He noticed her hands shaking with nerves, which made him smile at her. "Thank you."

"My friends and I are students at NYU. We're broke most of the time, but we scraped up money for your concert. There was no way we would miss it."

Cole couldn't help but warm up to her. "I appreciate it. Can I buy your table a round of drinks as thanks?"

She seemed surprised by his offer. "Um, that's unnecessary, Mr. Jackson."

Cole chuckled. Someone raised this girl properly. "It's Cole."

Blushing and smiling shyly, she said, "Cole."

He signaled the bartender, pulled a crisp hundred-dollar bill out of his pocket, and plopped it on the bar. "Keep the drinks flowing for the lady and her friends."

He slid off the stool, touched the brim of his hat and smiled at the young woman. "Goodnight."

Cole left the bar and went to his room to order room service and a movie. The movie played before his eyes, but none of it registered. His mind was back on Ward. Several years after he'd been in prison a sex scandal had emerged between Ward and a volunteer for his campaign. He may have won the reelection the year he was convicted, but his career ended with a resignation. What did he want from him? There had to be something.

Hoping to take his mind off Ward, he began thinking about the beautiful Shannon Gallagher. He knew little about her, about her past and what she did daily. Yet his whole being craved to know everything there was to know about her.

He wanted to know what her favorite food, drink or movie was. Did his music rate way up with the best of them like Aerosmith, Pink Floyd, U2, and The Rolling Stones? Hell, he sighed, there were so many great rock-n-rollers where did the list end and where did he fall?

Cole wanted to hear about her writing. What inspired her? Who inspired her, and when did the need to write hit her? Jesus, he wanted to know everything. Why the hell hadn't he gotten her phone number before he left Boston? And then he remembered her ex-husband John. He didn't blame John for not wanting Cameron near him, but Christ, the kid had talent and Cole wanted to help him.

There was no doubt in his mind the kid would make it big all on his own someday, but Cole had connections to smooth the way for him. He'd helped no one in such a capacity before, and he desperately wanted to do it for Cameron now.

His last thought before sleep took over was to make some phone calls and find Shannon's number.

Chapter Six

THE MORNING SHANNON PLANNED TO LEAVE FOR CHICAGO, she took a cab to the courthouse and after many tries finally found someone who could get her a copy of the trial transcript. It would take five to seven business days to mail it to her. After giving them her home address, paying the fee for the postage, she headed back to the hotel to grab her suitcase and hailed another cab to the airport.

She slept through the flight to Chicago. It was dark, cold and windy when she arrived, and she headed straight to her hotel room and ordered room service. She was spending three nights here and had a guest appearance on the *Marlene Simpson Show* with two other well-known authors, one mystery writer and one fantasy writer.

On Shannon's second day in Chicago she ate a light supper in the hotel restaurant. Afterwards she took a shower and when she stepped out of the bathroom she froze.

"Hi," he said in his sexy, masculine voice.

She leaned back against the door for support, clutching the fluffy white towel to her damp body as her eyes lingered on Cole. She watched him stroll toward her. He looked uncertain, not sure how he would be received. Reaching out with his hand, he slid it down her cheek and lightly swept his thumb across her bottom lip. "I bribed the maid to let me in."

Shannon thought for sure she would collapse to the floor from his touch.

"Was it all right to come here?"

Shannon beamed at him. "Better than all right, but how did you—"

"I made some calls, booked a room, and I was hoping we could go dancing."

Christ, he stood so close to her she couldn't breathe. He fully dressed, she practically naked. All she wanted to do was drop the towel and make love to him. She saw the lust radiating from his eyes, and she couldn't believe his self-control, his restraint. How did he do it?

Shannon shivered and stepped back toward the bathroom before she embarrassed herself by begging him to make love to her. "Give me some time to dress," she said, sounding breathless to her own ears. "Where should I meet you?"

He jammed his hands in his front jean pockets and tilted his head. "Downstairs. There's a piano bar." He grinned at her and left. Shannon leaned up against the wall and hugged her trembling body. My God! What that man did to her. It was insane.

Thirty minutes later she walked into the dimly lit lounge where a man in a black tuxedo played a baby grand. There were a dozen or so cozy tables encompassing a small dance floor. She didn't see Cole until he stepped out from the shadows, and her heart stopped dead in the middle of a beat. He'd changed. The man loved black and black loved him. He wore charcoal slacks and a black button down dress shirt, his hair held back with a black leather strip.

He was undoubtedly the sexiest man ever, and he'd come to Chicago, *no,* tracked her down in Chicago, to see her. She swallowed the lump in her throat as he strolled toward her.

"You look beautiful," he said, never once taking his smoldering brown eyes off hers.

"So do you."

He laughed out, "I'm not beautiful, but you…" He placed his warm hand in hers, causing scorching heat to dance through her veins. "…my dear, are."

"Cole?" she breathed out. She would not beg him to love her. She would take whatever he could give her and be satisfied.

"Yes?"

"Dance with me."

He smiled and his eyes sparkled. "I thought you'd never ask."

They spent the next three hours in each other's arms. Shannon had never felt more cherished. Cole had a way of making her feel as though she were his entire world. His focus and attention never wavered from her. The hotel could have fallen down around them, and she didn't think he'd notice. She knew she wouldn't.

He danced beautifully. His light feet and grace surprised her. They danced with one of his hands in hers, holding it close to his heart and one splayed against the small of her back. Both burning her skin, causing her body to be aroused and aware of him. The one good thing about being nearly as tall as Cole was his erection hit her where she craved it most. There was no seeking it out. It was there and there was no mistaking he wanted her.

At some point Cole switched her arms, so both were

around his neck and he moved both his hands to her hips, one drifting a little to the right, cupping her bottom, and he pulled her even closer, molding their bodies tighter.

"I dreamed this," he said as he nuzzled her neck and she shivered.

"Dreamed what?" Shannon whispered into his ear.

"This, dancing with you and holding you such," he breathed out.

———

Their hips swayed in sync with the music and for the life of him, he couldn't tell you what the piano player was playing. All his focus centered on Shannon. As far as he was concerned, they were the only two people on the dance floor, and Shannon was the only one who mattered to him.

He pressed his cheek against hers and he breathed in her provocative scent. It was light and floral, possibly jasmine. Whatever it was, he couldn't breathe it in fast enough nor could he get enough of it. Now, not only when they were apart, would he be able to picture her face in his mind, he could conjure up her scent. He swallowed a groan as she set him on fire.

All he could think about was sliding into her sweet body and losing himself in paradise. But not yet, he wanted everything to be perfect when he did. So until he cleared his name, he would have to be content with holding her and fantasizing about making love to her.

When the gentleman at the piano bid a goodnight, Cole walked Shannon to her room and with a restraint worthy of a saint, he kissed her once. It wasn't quick. Oh no, it was long, hot and wet. It was a melt your bones and marrow, shatter your mind and blood vessels kiss that left them both panting and hungry for more. Cole, showing more of his restraint that was killing him, pulled back, winked at her and barely formed the words, which came out deep and raspy. "See you in the morning."

When the wake-up call came in the morning, Shannon wished she were waking up wrapped in Cole's strong, secure arms. But alas, she wasn't. When she'd found him in her room last night, she'd nearly broken down and wept with relief because she had been so afraid she'd never see him again or that she didn't mean as much to him as he meant to her. She would never make that mistake ever again. They may not have made love or expressed their love for one another verbally, but every smoldering look, every silky caress, every graceful dance, every sensual kiss, had spoken volumes.

It shocked Shannon last night when Cole told her he wanted to accompany her to the *Marlene Simpson Show* and the one book signing she had in the afternoon. She was also surprised to find him at her door that morning dressed in jeans and a leather jacket, with his sunglasses as the only deterrent from being recognized. His thick blond hair was once again tied with a string of black leather. And she noticed once again how utterly and completely he took her breath away and caused her brain to fumble for words—coherent words.

Shannon had worn a short black skirt with a matching jacket. Underneath the jacket she wore a cream tank top. She wore sheer silk hose and black leather riding boots.

Cole kissed her quickly on the lips. "You look beautiful."

"Thank you." She winked at him. "So do you, I love men in jeans and black leather."

He threw his head back and laughed, and it thrilled Shannon to see him so relaxed and enjoying himself. Two things he probably had had little of in his life, and damn it, he deserved it as far as she was concerned.

The studio sent a car for Shannon and they drove together. When they arrived, an assistant, assistant, director of something, led them to a dressing room. There was a vase of flowers and a note from Marlene welcoming her to the show.

A short time later, make-up came in, touched up and powdered Shannon's face. During the whole ordeal, Cole sat silently observing her, causing Shannon to squirm in her seat.

It seemed only seconds later when the same assistant, assistant, director of something, came by to escort Shannon to the section of the studio where the taping took place.

Shannon turned and smiled at Cole, hoping he couldn't tell how nervous she was. Television positively paralyzed her. "I'll be back. I don't know how long I'll be. Maybe you could find the cafeteria or something."

Cole got up from the couch and took her hand. "I'm coming with you," he said, surprising her once again.

When Marlene Simpson spotted Shannon, she immediately came over to greet her. "Shannon Gallagher, it's a pleasure to finally meet you. Thank you for agreeing to appear on the show."

Shannon shook her hand. "Hello, thank you for inviting me." She put her hand on Cole's arm. "Marlene, I'd like to introduce you to—"

Marlene took over from there and held out her hand. "Cole Jackson. It's an honor to meet you."

"The honor's all mine. Would it be possible to wait here during the taping?"

Marlene smiled a sugarcoated smile and her face beamed. "For you, anything." She turned her attention back to Shannon. "If you're ready, I'd like to introduce you to Sam Shields and Justin Long."

Shannon turned to Cole. "Will you be okay waiting here?"

Cole pulled her into his arms and whispered in her ear. "I'll be fine. I have a perfect view of the stage and you. Knock-em-dead." He kissed her and for a moment she forgot where she stood and clung to him. He must have known she was lost and had forgotten her surroundings, or maybe he did as well, but eventually he pulled back and rested his forehead against hers, his breathing uneven.

"You better go."

Shannon turned around and found her eyes locked with Marlene's intuitive ones. "Is Cole Jackson open for discussion during the show?"

Shannon glanced back at Cole and then turned back to Marlene. "No."

The taping went great. Shannon had been so nervous at first, but somehow, she relaxed. Her eyes sought Cole's whenever the camera wasn't on her. And respectfully, Cole Jackson's name never came up.

After the taping, Marlene tried her best to persuade him to be a guest on her show. He politely declined but promised her an interview if he ever broke his silence. She seemed disappointed but accepted his answer graciously. She was a classy woman and a respectful one.

Shannon and Cole strolled arm and arm down the street to a cozy Italian Restaurant. They were seated in a warm corner. Cole leaned forward, elbows resting on the table, hands under his chin and his eyes sparkled. "Finally,

I can bombard you with questions." His eyebrows raised. "Personal questions."

Shannon's laughter rang out. "Okay, fire away."

"First ... how long were you married to McKenzie?"

"Five years."

"That long, or not long depending how one looks at it...hmm." He paused and Shannon's heart tripped up waiting for the next question.

"So tell me when did you begin writing and why?"

"Mr. Jackson, is this an official interview?"

"Well, now that you mention it, it could be." He winked. "Answer the question."

"Boy, you're tough." Shannon curled her hand around her water glass and drank a large thirst-quenching sip. "When I was in high school I loved to write, but it wasn't until two years into my marriage that I began crafting short stories, and it took me another two years for bravery to set in before I submitted any to several women's magazines." She reached for her water again, all too aware of Cole's intent interest in her story. Once again he made her feel as though she centered his entire world. He had terrific listening skills.

"I sold the first one," she continued, staring right back at him. "Two years later I wrote my first romantic suspense. It was harder than I thought." She laughed quietly. "Trying to write one hundred thousand words killed me. My first draft hit seventy and I thought, come on, how in the world can I add another thirty? I didn't. I added thirty-five."

Cole broke out laughing. "See, you set your mind to it and presto." His wrist flicked in the air. "You succeeded and surpassed your goal."

"Well, don't get too excited. I ended up taking out about ten thousand words of garbage."

"That's my girl."

She blinked and smiled at his words, *my girl.* "It sold, and the rest is, well, the rest is what you see."

Cole reached out and placed his large hand, cold from his water glass on top of hers. Then he turned her palm over and lightly traced it with his index finger, just barely skimming the surface of her skin. Shannon felt an immediate pull to her stomach, causing her to lick her suddenly parched lips.

"Cole?"

"Hmm." He smiled, his eyes partly closed. "Yes."

"What about you?"

"What about me?"

"Tell me about how your career began."

"Later, I just want to sit here, eat my lunch and watch you. After we eat, I want to take you to this bookstore where I hear there's a phenomenal author visiting today."

Cole poked around the bookstore and the mall while Shannon signed copies of her book for her fans. He'd stayed in the background while she spoke and read a passage, and he couldn't help but swell with pride in everything she'd accomplished in her short life. He was glad for his sunglasses as not one person approached him. Oh, there were some strange looks his way, but no one spoke to him. Once again, he wondered at his paranoia.

They went back to the hotel so Shannon could freshen up before dinner. Cole was sitting on her bed watching television when he heard Shannon's cell phone ring. Without giving it a moment's thought, he answered it.

"Hello, Ms. Gallagher's phone."

"Hi, may I speak to Shannon Gallagher please."

"May I tell her who's calling?"

By this time Shannon stood in front of Cole looking sexy in the thick hotel terrycloth robe, her hair dripping wet. He dipped his head to nibble her neck, but the earth moved out from under him, causing him to sway as he heard a name from his past.

Chapter Seven

COLE'S HEAD SNAPPED UP IN SHOCK AND SHANNON watched in horror as his eyes burned in anguish and the color evaporated from his face. He thrust the phone at her and disappeared into the bathroom, and to shock her even more, she heard him getting sick.

With suddenly trembling hands and a nervous knot in her gut, she put the phone to her ear, though all she wanted to do was run to Cole.

"Shannon Gallagher speaking," she spoke into the receiver."

"Ms. Gallagher, Detective Simone returning your call," clipped a hard voice on the other end of the receiver.

Shannon's hand went to her throat, and the room spun circles around her. Oh God! What must Cole be thinking? Knowing she sounded distraught but not caring, she spoke back into the phone. "I'm sorry Detective, but I must call you back."

With an unsteady hand she knocked on the bathroom door and opened it. Her heart stopped beating. Cole sat on the closed toilet seat with his head in his hands. Tears immediately sprang to Shannon's eyes. This was all her fault. She caused this turmoil she saw him struggling with. Falling to her knees on the cold tile floor in front of him, her hands resting on his thighs and her voice quivering, she whispered, "Cole, I'm sorry." Would he think she overstepped the boundaries in their relationship? Did they even have a relationship? Would he think she had second doubts about his innocence? "I made some inquires. I'm trying to get pertinent information together so I can help you prove your innocence." Why wouldn't he look at her? Panic set in beyond anything she'd ever imagined, and she suddenly thought *she'd* be sick as her stomach revolted. Had she blown it? Would their so-called relationship end before it had the chance to go from seed to seedling to a full-blown plant full of precious blossoms? She sniffled and wiped her tears away with the back of her hand. "I want to help you."

She heard him groan and then he reached for her, wrapping his arms around her so tightly she thought her ribs would break.

"I don't want you to get involved," he breathed into her ear with deep, desperate intensity.

"It's too late. I already am," she said as she pulled away from his embrace, gently placing her trembling hands on his face and bringing his lips to hers.

Shannon tossed and turned most of the night, worried about Cole and frustrated about how to help him. He didn't want her sucked into his past life and trial. Too bad, she already was, just by caring for him now. How could she not help him if she was capable of it? The sound of the lock on her hotel door clicking open had her pulse soaring.

Had Cole bribed a hotel worker to let him in so he could surprise her and finally make love to her?

"Cole is that you?"

No answer.

Sitting up, she came face to face with a tall man wearing a black ski mask. He moved fast, diving on the bed, pinning her and covering her mouth with his hand, blocking her scream in her lungs.

Sick, deranged laughter fell from his lips. "Cole. The murdering bastard. Don't insult me by confusing the two of us. Although you will never make that mistake again since you will be dead. A cool, hard sharp object pressed against her carotid artery."

"Why?" she asked.

"Why you say? Because I fucking hate him. And because I can."

Dear God, please help her. She didn't want to die. Not like this. Not when she knew it would be blamed on Cole. He would go back to jail once again for a murder he didn't commit. Who hated him enough to do this to him?

A commotion outside her door had the man tensing up. He leapt from the bed and flatted his back against the wall by her door. She screamed, "Help me."

The door banged open and in stepped two hotel security officers. Her attacker threw his body into them, knocking them off balance, giving him the opportunity to run. One of the security personnel spoke into his walkie-talkie. She didn't wait to hear what he said, she pounced on her cell phone and called Cole.

"Cole," she said breathlessly, a man just attacked me."

"Be right there."

When he walked in, her room burst at the seams with hotel personnel, but her eyes locked on his worried ones and she waved him over.

"Excuse me." One of the security officers stopped him. "Who are you?"

Shannon watched as his eyes went to her and back to the officer. She could just imagine what was going through Cole's head. He'd say his name and they would instantly believe it was him because of history repeating itself and all. This time, however, she could prove his innocence. Before he could answer the query, she went to his side and placed her trembling hand on his arm. Instantly she felt his tense muscles relax. "This is my boyfriend, Cole Jackson."

"The Cole Jackson?" the officer asked with raised brows.

"Yes," Cole replied with his head held high."

"I'm a fan." He held out his hand. "Nice to meet you."

Cole hesitated then took the proffered hand. "Thanks. Now please tell me you caught the guy?"

"Sorry."

"How did you happen at my door?" Shannon asked.

"One of our room service employees saw him hanging around the hallway before he entered your room and became suspicious."

"Thank God," Shannon said with relief.

"Shannon, was there anything familiar about him?" Cole asked as he slid his arm around her waist and pulled her close against his side. Having his warm body pressed to hers eased her nerves and finally slowed her heart. When the guy had her pinned to the bed she'd thought it would leap from her chest and run away seeking a calmer person.

"No." She shook her head. "I have never heard his voice before, although it was muffled by his mask. I asked him why he was doing this, and he said because he hated you and because he could."

"Damn it." He raked his free hand through his loose hair. "The bastard is after you because of me."

"Why do you believe that Mr. Jackson?" the officer asked.

"Isn't it clear? He wants anyone I love to die."

An hour later, after Cole locked the door and rechecked all three locks, he joined Shannon in bed. He snaked his arms out and pulled her close so her back snuggled up against his chest. "Go to sleep. I have you and I'll keep you safe. He'll not come back tonight and hopefully never."

Shannon believed him when he said he wouldn't be back tonight. But never? Her body shivered. He'd be back to finish what he started she was positive of that fact. The question was when and where? If he wanted her death pinned on Cole, then it would have to be when they were together again. God only knew when that would be.

They went their separate ways the next day at the airport. It was an emotional parting, but a necessary one. It tore at his heart to remember what might have happened last night. Shannon could be dead now. His whole body shuddered at the thought. She promised him she would hire a bodyguard. And he wouldn't rest until she did, and quite possibly not even then. Not until they caught the attacker. Cole knew with every fiber of his being he was the same man who killed Lindsey. Proving it was another thing. The man wanted Cole framed for another murder. If he never saw her again, she would be safe. Was he strong enough to stay away from the woman he'd quickly come to love? If it kept her safe, he could.

Meanwhile, he flew to Los Angeles to check in with his

parole officer, something he could never miss or he'd be in violation of his parole, and they could send him back to prison to serve out the rest of his sentence. And Cole had no intentions of spending another day behind prison walls. Then he planned on resting and relaxing for a few days at his Malibu beach house before he flew to Philadelphia for more concerts, only to fly back here again in a month to see his parole officer once again. His life was one vicious cycle being interrupted by parole officer visits. Would he ever not be reminded of his convicted killer status?

The one good thing that came with all this traveling was he would have no time to see Shannon. And that meant she'd be safe. At least, he prayed she would be.

Cameron sat on a rock in the woods at Wompatuck State Park, drinking with some buddies, still seething in anger at his father. He spoke to him, but barely. Didn't his father have any idea what spending one night with BlackJack had meant to him? His father could be so stubborn and narrow-minded and this definitely qualified as one of those times. Cameron didn't care one way or another that Cole Jackson spent time in prison for murder. It was like, ancient history. The guy was way cool. And Cole liked *his* music, how awesome was that?

But no, his dad couldn't see past his policeman's mind. The mind that said justice prevailed and Cole Jackson deserved what he'd gotten. Boy, wouldn't his dad be shocked if he knew his mom and Cole had been together in Chicago. Cameron found out by accident. He called his mom one night, and he'd heard Cole's voice in the background. She didn't deny it. Cameron laughed out loud, which caused his friends to look at him strangely, which caused Cameron to reach for another beer. Wait until his dad found out. The shit would hit the fan.

Cameron was also royally pissed at his dad for the phone calls coming into the house inquiring about his music. He wouldn't even listen to what the people had to say. His father felt he had the right to interfere with his dream. And shit, it was his dream, his life. His mom, or Cole, would never interfere. He couldn't wait until she came home. He'd had it with staying with his dad. He glanced around at his friends and took another hit of his beer, nearly falling back. Shit, he was *sooooo* past wasted.

John McKenzie sat in his study, trying to think about what to do with Cameron. Everything had been fine until Jackson came into their lives.

"John, the door's locked."

John raked his hands through his thinning hair and went to let his wife in.

She shut and locked the door behind her, eyeing him hungrily, and then she melted into his arms and whispered into his ear. "Matt's napping, the twins went shopping with my mother and Cameron's out with friends. I thought..." She ran her hand down the front of his shirt, and then even lower causing him to take a breath, and she whispered into his ear once more. "We're never alone, not even in our bed at night."

John took her hand, led her to his chair and pulled her onto his lap before he explored his wife's wonderfully pregnant body. Whenever Cheryl was pregnant, she became frisky as hell. And John, always a gentleman, would not disappoint his beautiful wife.

They'd just finished putting their clothes on when the

doorbell rang. John hurried down the hall toward the front door. Glancing through the sidelight and seeing a uniformed police officer with his son Cameron, John closed his eyes and breathed deeply. This couldn't be good.

He swung open the door. "Carl."

"John, we were called to the woods near the high school because neighbors complained of noise. We found a group of teenagers drinking and getting high. Your son here was a little too out of it. I thought I'd bring him to you and let you deal with him."

"Thanks Carl, I owe you one." John stared at his son, who looked a little green around the gills and he thought, here we go, the teenage drinking years are upon us. Shit. He was *so* not ready for this.

Once Carl left, John grabbed Cameron's arm. "Come on, son." He dragged his swaying, limp body up the stairs into the bathroom and flipped the toilet lid just in time for the poison to come up and out of Cameron's body. John gagged. Christ, how much did he drink? John stripped his son naked, put him in the shower and then to bed. It wouldn't do any good to talk to him now. He was too far gone. But shit, John wanted nothing more than to throttle him for his stupidity. Instead, he tucked him into bed, his heart heavy with the burden of guilt every parent felt whenever their children screwed up.

He raked his hands through his hair and swore at himself for it. He would definitely be bald within the year. He'd been tough on Cameron lately, ever since the Black-Jack concert. Hell, maybe he hadn't been thinking clearly. He owed his son an apology, which he would give him, and then he would get the talk about drinking and smoking dope and then the grounding.

As a cop he knew more than most what teenagers truly did these days, and it frightened him to the core. And he wasn't that old that he didn't remember all the things he did at Cameron's age. But times were different now. Drugs were stronger, purer, dangerous and more addicting. And never mind the consequences for kids these days. One screw-up could change the whole trajectory of their lives. Gone were the times when, if they caught you smoking pot on school grounds, you received a week's suspension. Now you were expelled from the school completely. Years ago, if an underage teenager was caught with alcohol, the police would confiscate it and see him home safely. Cameron was lucky the cop brought him home instead of the police station. They lived in a scary time, and the pressure on kids nowadays was phenomenal.

John groaned out loud. What the hell was he thinking by bringing another person into this world he would be responsible for? He could barely handle the children and the responsibilities weighing him down now. He wished she weren't pregnant. "John," came Cheryl's calming voice from the doorway. "Is Cameron okay? What happened?"

Hearing Cheryl's voice caused his heart to lurch more and the guilt to rise. How could he wish she were not carrying his child? A child made from love. God forgive him for thinking such a thing. He wanted the child.

John crossed Cameron's room and hugged Cheryl to his chest. He needed her strength, her calming presence to help him over this hurdle. "He's drunk. I took care of it."

As Shannon drove her Mercedes SUV down her street that ran parallel to the ocean, she lowered the window and breathed in the salty ocean air. She didn't think she could live anywhere not connected to the ocean. It had always been a huge part of her life, and it comforted her knowing within steps of her house she could enter another world. Her long walks on the beach had always done wonders to put her life in perspective when she needed it. She'd created most of her books in her mind during her solitary strolls in the sand. Nothing could compare to the smell of salt water, the feel of the cold, wet sand between her toes and the sound of the surf to inspire her creative juices to flow.

In fact, as soon as she unpacked, she bundled up and headed down to the beach, putting off her phone calls to her family to let them know she arrived home safely. The beach seemed deserted as she knew it would be. She walked over toward her favorite jetties and sat with her legs bent up and her arms wrapped around them to ward off the chilly breeze coming off the water. She stared out into the surf. It rode high on the beach, appearing exceptionally rough, and her mind began to wander.

She needed to plot out her next book. Her agent and editor wanted to see a synopsis within the month. Oh, she had plenty of plots mulling around in her head, she just didn't know which story she would pluck out of her brain. Which story was the one she needed to write next? The character fighting to be heard over all the others would inevitably win. The story and characters would take shape in her mind, much like watching a movie, and she could not think of anything else until she put it down on paper.

The first draft drained her emotionally. She poured her heart and soul into the characters in her story. She laughed and cried with them and fell in love with each and every one, creating just the right mix of personality and emotion to make them interesting and real to her readers. Shannon always strived to make her readers feel connected to her characters and the story of their lives. She wanted them to forget they were reading a book and just become part of the story itself. See themselves as one of her characters. Be one of her characters. Share their feelings and emotions. Weep with them, laugh with them, and feel connected to them as a whole.

When she read someone else's book, and she forgot about everything but the story and the characters and felt connected to it, utterly involved with everything—the humor, the sadness, the terror—then she knew the author had done their job. Anyone could put words on paper, but it took a special someone, a special gift, not to mention a wild imagination, to pull the reader into the story and keep them there. Shannon strived for that in every book she wrote. If she didn't feel the emotional pull herself, how would her readers feel it?

Many times she'd get up in the wee hours of the night and write notes down. Her brain twisted, turned and plotted even as she slept. Often she'd write the last chapter when the book was not even near completion. Shannon had one close friend, an avid reader who dabbled in writing herself, whom she would give the first draft to and hope for a good reception. Her friend had such a knack in knowing good work when she saw it. If it needed more work, she was great with suggestions.

Shannon's relationship with her editor, Kevin, was so good they could always discuss what changes and improvements needed to be made. She respected and admired his ability to know a bestseller when he read one. Not to mention their close personal relationship—a relationship Shannon cherished and never took for granted.

So here she sat on hard, damp, freezing cold rocks trying to pull the plot for her next book out of her creative mind, which felt anything but creative at the moment. The only thing she could think about was Cole and how she missed him terribly and dreamed about when she would see him again. She knew he was in Philadelphia now, and she wasn't positive where his tour went next. She was also anxiously awaiting the trial transcripts, which should arrive any day.

Never mind her terrifying night in Chicago. She'd been on edge, walking around on eggshells, expecting her attacker to appear at any moment. When she'd been on the road, she'd hired a personal bodyguard, but now she was at home and she didn't feel the need. Her address, as far as she knew, was a well-kept secret. Besides, she hated having a big-hulking man following her everywhere. She'd received several calls and texts from Cole, but she knew his tour schedule was crowded and he barely had time to himself. The fact he called her when his time was free humbled her and made her heart sing.

After an hour or so of more daydreaming about Cole, she beat herself up and rose off the rocks, stretched her stiff, sore and cold body. Her bottom was numb and her hands freezing as she made her way back to her house. Five years ago she'd stumbled purely by chance on this beautifully restored Victorian, complete with a wrap-around porch. Some might consider it an upside down house. The first floor boasted three bedrooms and a bath.

The second floor held the large spacious kitchen with white cabinets and black granite countertops. There was a large center island with four bar stools. It was the center of the house. Everyone always gathered around the island. The back of the house, facing the ocean, housed the large family room with a beautiful floor-to-ceiling fieldstone fireplace that held a gas insert sending off instant flame and heat. Shannon had the fireplace on most days from September to May to help with the chill of living in an old drafty house by the ocean. The wall facing the water was completely taken up with windows and the view, breathtaking. She could see Mother Nature in all her glory. And many times since she'd lived here, Mother Nature had tried to come through those windows.

The third floor held her bedroom and office. There was a large bathroom complete with a spacious Jacuzzi tub. The bedroom had French doors that opened up to a small balcony. In the summer it was one of her favorite places to curl up with a good book. A wrought iron bistro set sat on the balcony as well as a comfortable lounge chair. The best thing about it was the panoramic views. At times it felt as though she lived at the ends of the earth. But right now it was time to have her two feet planted firmly on the ground.

John would be by soon to drop Cameron off. She hadn't seen John or Cameron in seven days. She couldn't wait to see her son. John—hell, she was still mad at him and his superior attitude. She had to admit, though, that she and John had a good relationship compared to some divorced couples who shared custody of a son. Shannon knew plenty of divorced people who couldn't stand to be in the same town, never mind the same room as their divorced spouse.

She should count her blessings. She'd been lucky so far. But she still thought John was being unreasonable. He had his lovely wife, three adorable children and one on the way. She was happy for him. Why couldn't he be happy for her?

Cameron went to a private school in Braintree. It made switching back and forth between Hingham and Standish Bay easy. There was a boy nearby in his senior year at the same school who drove Cameron most days. On days he stayed for either sports or a club, she picked him up. When he stayed with John and Cheryl, either they drove him back and forth or a friend did. So far, the arrangements had always worked. And hopefully would continue to do so.

John called last night and told her about Cameron's drinking and smoking escapade. It brought back many memories from her own teenage years, some good and some bad. They both agreed a week's grounding fit the punishment. And when the grounding ended, he had to give them a play-by-play of where he'd be and who he'd be with at all times. They knew it seemed harsh, but with Cameron due to get his driver's license next month, they wanted to make damn sure he would not drink and drive.

John dropped Cameron off mid-afternoon and her heart swelled as it always did when she saw her son. When she saw her little boy, who was not so little anymore. In fact, he stood taller than her by several inches now. Cameron gave her a hug and kiss then went directly down the hall to his bedroom. John came in uninvited, plopped himself down at the kitchen island, and Shannon could tell by the look on his face, he had talking on his mind. She wondered if she should tell him about what happened in Chicago. For the time being she kept it to herself.

Standing with her back against the counter, she studied him. She didn't know when the last time was she eyed him intently and scrutinized every aspect of him, but she did now and was a little disturbed by what she saw. He looked positively exhausted. His deep brown eyes looked almost black with worry. His brows were creased and there were shadows beneath his eyes as though he hadn't slept in weeks. His body was still fit and trim, but his hair was thinning fast and starting to gray around the temples. All in all, he still resembled the handsome teenager she'd loved, although she'd never admit it to him. And at thirty-four, he was still undeniably handsome, but his exhausted and troublesome look deterred from that handsomeness. It was a damn good thing he didn't do it for her anymore, didn't cause her to feel sexual pull or lust anymore, just good old-fashioned friendship.

"What's on your mind John," Shannon finally asked as he still hadn't spoken a word. She wondered if he was scrutinizing her as she'd been him.

"Nothing…something," he stammered as he ran his hands through his hair, clearly grasping for words. "I'm feeling pulled in a zillion directions."

"How about a drink?"

"Water."

Shannon took a glass from a cabinet and filled it with ice and water from the door of her refrigerator and handed it to him. He drank thirstily and sighed. "I can't believe Cheryl's pregnant again. How the hell am I going to handle another kid?"

He looked right into her eyes with his desperate ones, and her heart sped up. He looked on the verge of tears. She hadn't seen him this upset since they divorced all those years ago. Her anger with him over Cole dissolved, and she became instantly worried.

"John, you don't have to handle anything alone. You have Cheryl. Now tell me what's really bothering you?"

His head snapped up, and he nearly smiled. "Damn, you're good."

She grinned at him. "You're damn right I am. Now spill your guts."

"Cameron…and you…I feel as though you're both pulling away from me."

Shannon went to interrupt, but he put up his hand to stop her, causing her intended words to die on her lips.

"I know it's normal for teenagers to distance themselves from their parents and become more independent. I understand that with Cameron, but you've barely spoken to me in the past week."

"John."

"Let me finish. I know we've been divorced a long time and most ex-married couples usually hate each other, but you've been my best friend since middle school. I can tell you things I can't even tell Cheryl, which hell," he snorted, "isn't good. Anyway." He looked at her, his eyes serious, his voice soft. "I'm sorry I was such an asshole."

She narrowed her eyes. "Does this admission of you being such an asshole mean you've reconsidered about Cole?" *She could only hope.*

John got up and started down the stairs toward the door, stopped and turned back, grinning like a schoolboy. "Shit no," he said as he slipped out the door.

She wanted to strangle the man. But instead she went to speak with Cameron and found one boy angry at his father.

Shannon tried to smooth things over without letting her own frustration with John surface. But Cameron bought nothing she said, which wasn't surprising. Her son was no dummy. When he told her about the phone calls coming on John's landline from people in the record industry regarding his music career Shannon saw black. How dare John not discuss this with her? He was only one-half of a parenting team and she intended to have her say in this matter. Christ, what was he thinking? Several talent agents called and two record producers! She was way past upset John had conveniently omitted mentioning it during their talk earlier.

Later in the evening, as Shannon prepared dinner and Cameron did homework behind his closed bedroom door, the bell rang. She wiped her hands on a dishcloth and ran down the stairs to the door, wondering who it could be. As she opened it, her heart pumped wildly. On her front porch stood Cole, holding a backpack and looking slightly frazzled around the edges. One could say he literary looked asleep on his feet. Shannon reached out and pulled him in, wrapped her arms around him for dear life, as if she were in the middle of the icy black Atlantic Ocean clinging to a buoy, the only real lifeline around for miles and miles of raging ocean. He was the last person she expected to see at her door. Was it possible she plagued his mind as much as he did hers? Her mind hummed. How long would he stay? Would they finally make love? Would she tell him she loved him? *Slow down Shannon, slow way down. Start with the obvious.*

"You should've told me you were coming. I would've picked you up at the airport." Then a thought accosted her. "How did you know where I live?"

He smiled. "First." He kissed her lips with a loud smack. "I wanted to surprise you, and second, I called your editor." He kissed her quickly again. "Nice guy." He chuckled. "He actually threatened my life if I didn't take...let's see how he put it? Ah yes, the threat went like this, 'fragile care of your heart, body and soul.' The dramatic type I see."

His bag hit the floor with a dull thud as he pulled her tighter. "I have three days off, and all I could think about was you. I told myself I could wait for you until I cleared my name, but it's a lie. I want you so badly I ache all over from needing you. I told myself I needed to stay away to keep you safe from your attacker. However, I rationalized my decision to come here by telling myself no one would know where I am or where you live."

Chapter Eight

SHANNON DROWNED IN HIS EYES RADIATING LUST, NEED AND desire, and she melted, not giving her safety another thought. Words were no longer needed. Cole possessed her lips, and Shannon lost all coherent thought except for the taste of his delicious mouth. The feel of his warm hard body wrapped around her soft pliant one. Their tongues did the dance of lovers gone way too long without each other's nourishment. Their bodies entwined in desperation, the need for the joining of two lost souls finally coming together as one. His warm hands traveled up the back of her shirt as she heard someone clear his throat. *Cameron*. She'd forgotten about Cameron. Shannon released Cole and turned to face her son.

"Honey," she said a little breathless. "You remember Cole?" She felt herself blush from the tips of her toes to the top of her head. How stupid she mused, of course he remembered Cole. Her nerves were rattled over having her son find her in such a steamy embrace. Not to mention what Cole's kiss had done to her. And his hands, his body. Oh God, his erection!

Cole shook Cameron's hand and smiled at him. "Good to see you again, Cameron. I hope you're working on your music," he said with a deepness to his voice Shannon had heard only a few times before.

Cameron beamed with admiration. "Yes."

"Cameron, why don't you go back in your room and finish your homework," Shannon said, hoping her son got the hint that she wanted some privacy with Cole.

Cameron glanced from his mom to Cole and grinned. "Sure. I'll catch you both later."

Once they found themselves alone, Cole looked uncertain. "Jesus, how stupid of me for not thinking about Cameron. Is there a hotel nearby I can stay in?"

She took his hand in her trembling one and led him up two flights of stairs to her bedroom. After turning into him and kissing him until they were both breathless once again, she looked at him, knowing all her feelings spilled out from her eyes and she didn't care.

"Your hotel room awaits. If you don't mind a roommate?"

He yanked her up against his chest. "Cameron. You mean him right?" he said with a mischievous gleam in his eye.

"If you want to be his roomy, but I had someone else in mind," she said as she held him tightly back, never wanting to let him go. Not quite believing he was here. Whenever she started thinking she'd never see him again, he showed up. Their weird connection coming through.

Shannon left Cole to shower while she finished cooking supper. When she approached the stove, she found the chili boiling hot and ready to eat. Cameron came and sat at the kitchen table, his eyes watching her with a teenager's curiosity. Damn, she could feel herself flush, and it had nothing to do with the spices from the chili she'd just sampled.

After serving up two bowls of chili topped with cheese and heating cornbread in the microwave, she sat down at the table opposite Cameron. His face beamed with exuberance as he babbled on and on about Cole and how cool it was he was staying with them and not to worry, there stood two floors between her bedroom and his, he wouldn't hear a thing.

She dropped her spoon in shock and her jaw opened.

Cameron continued, "Besides, no one can make as much noise as Dad and Cheryl." He rolled his eyes. "She's a screamer and Dad, he howls like a werewolf during a full moon. I'm surprised they don't wake the neighbors. Old Ms. Smart would have a stroke if she ever heard them. The old lady probably never had sex in her life."

Shannon stared at her son in shocked disbelief as he went on and on about John and Cheryl's sex life. She could not possibly be having this conversation with him. And was she not mistaken, but did he just give her permission to sleep with Cole? Not that she needed it, nor was it any of his business. Or was it? Shannon never got a word in edgewise as Cameron talked, ate and left the kitchen for the family room before she could find the words to express her thoughts, never mind, having eaten any of her supper.

Alone at the table, she buried her face in her hands and laughed at the absurdity of their dinnertime conversation. Not a typical mother, father, two-point-five kids and a dog conversation. At least she didn't think so. Sitting at the table and laughing was how Cole found her.

"Care to share the joke?"

She looked at him and laughed more. "Why not, sit down and I'll fix you supper and tell you all about it."

She told him what Cameron had said. He laughed and grinned at her, pinning her with his sexy eyes. "You said Cameron's bedroom is two floors down." He winked. "That might be far enough for what I have in mind to do to you."

She threw her napkin at him, laughing. "You have no idea if I make any noise, and what about you?"

He grinned at her and she melted. "Care to come upstairs with me now, and we'll see who screams the loudest? We can make it a contest to see who can be the quietest. But I guarantee," his voice became soft and downright sexy as sin, "you'll lose."

Oh my God! She tingled all over from his offer. She'd love nothing more than to go upstairs with him, but she couldn't now. Not until Cameron went to bed. And even then, could she? Hell it was only seven—she'd never make it, not with her body burning up. This was something she'd wanted since she first set eyes on him in the hotel suite playing his guitar. His muscles rippling, his intriguing tattoo fascinating her, and oh, she couldn't forget his molten brown eyes sucking her in like sweet, creamy chocolate. Oh, he'd definitely done something to her the night they met, and she'd never been the same because of it. No. Never the same. And at some level that thrilled her. On another level it terrified her as it tore her heart wide open.

While she cleaned up from dinner, she heard Cameron ask Cole if he would jam with him. Cameron went to his room and brought up two acoustic guitars. They spent hours playing together while Shannon sat curled up on a large, overstuffed leather chair beneath a fleece blanket. She listened with love and pride to the two men in her life create beautiful music together. Watching Cole strum his guitar was like watching him make love. He looked all intense and gentle, using his long graceful fingers to make the instrument sing for him. She couldn't wait to be the one his fingers made sing. She fidgeted in the chair as her body craved his fingers on it.

At one point Cameron brought out a pen and paper, and they created a new song together. A beautiful song. The lyrics were potent and sad, causing Shannon to shed silent tears every time Cole glanced her way, which was often. The lyrics were about a boy's lost love and finding her again later in life, only to lose her again to a terrible tragedy. She wondered what inspired her son and Cole in their songwriting. At midnight, she finally made Cameron go to bed. He had school the next day and he would be exhausted.

After he left, Cole looked at her from his position on the couch with his eyes so hot and intense Shannon squirmed in her seat. In that instant she knew he would make her sing tonight. Finally, she would know what it felt like to make love with Cole. And suddenly she couldn't wait any longer. She jumped up and gave him a sultry look that had him following close on her heels.

Once inside her room, she quickly shut and locked the door, then lit several candles on the nightstand. It amazed her she could accomplish the task with her hands as unsteady as they were. She was nervous, anxious and downright burning up with sexual need. And her voice had deserted her.

Cole watched with heavy-lidded eyes and a tightness in his groin as she slowly unbuttoned her blouse. It took longer than it should have, but she finally slid it off her shoulders and Cole sucked in air. Her arms reached behind her back and unclasped the black lace bra she wore, and it joined her blouse on the floor. Once again he sucked in air to his desperate lungs. She was breathtakingly beautiful standing in front of him naked from the waist up. Her blue eyes dark with lust, her skin flush, and her breasts small, round and perfect.

The candlelight flickered around the room, casting shadows, making her seem more erotic. Neither of them moved as Shannon continued to undress down to nothing but creamy white skin causing Cole to nearly drop to his knees as his body went weak at the beautiful, sensual picture she made. He wondered if he touched her just so, would she be wet and warm and waiting for him? *Oh yeah*! Cole undressed, taking his time as he enjoyed the sight before him, a sight he'd waited far too long for. He couldn't wait to taste, touch, love and possess every luscious creamy inch of her.

He stood fully erect ready for the feel of her body sheathing his. Slowly he went to her, not quite believing this was happening and whispered her name, "Shannon." He put his hands on the nape of her neck and kissed her. Slow and teasing. He sucked on her bottom lip and nibbled it. She moaned into his mouth, waiting for him to deepen the kiss. He didn't. He left her mouth to discover uncharted regions. He lingered as he found her pleasure points behind the ear, the hollow of her neck and the spot between her breasts.

"Cole," she purred out.

"Yes, my love?" He didn't wait for an answer as he tore his mouth from her breast and dropped to his knees to explore lower into exotic territory, wet as a tropical rain forest. He parted her thighs with his warm hands and made the most incredible discovery known to man. He discovered the innermost core of a woman's body, the sweet nectar that drove men crazy. He'd dreamed about this. Her taste, her scent, but it paled compared to having the real thing. He drank from her, tasting and teasing with his tongue, unable to quench his thirst. He was like a man gone days in the desert without water, and this woman was his savior. Her fluids were his nourishment. He drank from her deep well and was rewarded when her body trembled with release. He continued to drive her higher and higher until she cried out for mercy and collapsed down to him, breathless and shaking. Cradling her to him, he caressed her breasts as she recovered. And he wondered what he'd done in this lifetime to deserve her?

"Hmm, that feels so good," Shannon murmured. "You have the most talented hands. When I watched you play tonight and you made your guitar sing, I wanted it to be me. I imagined your hands on my body, making me sing."

When she opened her dreamy eyes, they were nearly black and so sensually erotic he knew he needed her now. He laid her back on the floor and groaned out as she parted her thighs in welcome, causing him to nearly lose it at the sight of her. "Condom," he mumbled. Shit, he needed a condom. He scrambled to his backpack and frantically hunted for the box he'd put in there. After putting one on, he covered her body with his and spoke her name as he thrust deep and hard into her wonderfully warm and welcoming body. As they joined as one he knew he would never be whole again without her in his life. This woman he'd known for such a short time completed him. She was the other half of his soul, and he'd been searching for her his entire life.

He moved slowly at first, pulling out almost completely. His eyes locked with her dreamy ones, and he noticed they became a mesmerizing shade of black when she was in the throes of passion. Reaching for her legs, he wrapped them up over his shoulders and buried himself so deep inside her that he thought he would be lost forever. He wanted to be lost forever.

One more hard push and he felt her body spasm around his and she cried out, "Cole," repeatedly. He finally lost it, his body tensed, then trembled as he came, filling her completely. They lay collapsed together, naked, and on the floor. When Cole crashed back to earth, he mumbled.

"Shannon?"

"Hmm?"

"That was better than any dream I'd conjured up these past weeks. But I have something to ask."

"Ask away."

"The floor's hard—can we go to your bed?"

She giggled and kissed his neck. "Why not?"

Cole, in one quick move, scooped her up into his arms and laid her back on the bed, snuggling her into the curve of his body and burying his head into her hair. He loved the way she smelled. He could never smell jasmine ever again without thinking of Shannon. And before he knew what he was doing he breathed out, "I'm so in love with you." Then he drifted off to sleep, for the first time in forever feeling content and loved.

Shannon smiled to herself as she pulled Cole's arms tighter around her waist. Tears pooled in her eyes and her heart pounded with love for him. Never, ever, had sex been like that for her. This was the stuff dreams were made of, and she hoped this dream went on indefinitely. She couldn't believe he loved her. He not only showed her with his body, his actions, his tender touch, he told her as well with incredible words that stole her breath away. She knew it must be hard for him to love and trust after what he'd been through with Lindsey. The fact he trusted her with his delicate, once broken, and discarded heart caused emotions to well up inside her she'd only written about.

She hadn't known she could feel emotions this strong or a love so intense. And to know he felt the same only added to the sensations racing through her veins, causing her heart to swell against the confines of her chest.

Feeling the steady beat of his heart thump against her back, the tickle of his breath on her neck, the warmth of his hard body pressed against hers caused Shannon to slowly drift and join him in contented sleep, not to wake until morning.

Early the next day, Shannon slowly awoke and smiled as she remembered Cole's lovemaking. His warm body still pressed close to hers. He hadn't let her go even in sleep. He still held her possessively and lovingly, making her heart swell. Regrettably, she untangled herself carefully so as not to wake him. After donning her robe, she went downstairs to make certain Cameron was up and getting ready for school. She found him on the couch eating dry cereal and watching the sports channel.

"Are you all packed?"

He hopped up from the couch and put his dish in the sink. "Yup. And, by the way, the milk's bad, and can I have a few bucks for lunch?" he said, his hand in that palm up and out way he did so well when he needed money, which was more times than not. She honestly couldn't remember the last time he didn't have his hand out.

She found her purse on the counter and handed him a ten-dollar bill. "Do I need to pick you up?"

He pocketed the money in his wallet. "Nope, Tom's driving me home."

Just then they heard the beep. Tom arrived on time as usual. "Bye, Mom," Cameron said as he went out the door.

Shannon hummed and danced to a BlackJack tune around the kitchen as she made coffee and toast, then put the fireplace on to shake the morning chill. She curled up on the sofa with her toast and coffee, snuggled under a fleece blanket as she watched a Boston news station. Only the television might as well have been off. Her mind was busy replaying last night in minute detail. It had been well worth the wait. She hugged her quivering body as it reacted to her memory, and her eyes drifted closed. Cole was an incredible lover, selfless, giving, gentle at the right times and not so gentle when she didn't want him to be. It had seemed as if he could read her mind. He knew how to play her body in all the right places, and boy did he make her sing.

As for the noise bet? She definitely lost it. He'd caused her to scream out dozens of times. The only disappointment was she'd not been able to explore his body, and she planned on remedying that the first chance she got. She wanted to hear him yell out as she tortured him with her fingers, mouth and tongue as he'd done to her.

A short time later, she headed back upstairs to shower. She didn't want to disturb Cole, so she crept softly into the room as he slept soundly on his back. One arm out from the covers, the one with the fascinating tattoo, and her heart lodged in her throat at the sight of him sleeping in her bed. She'd dreamed about this for nearly two weeks. It was hard to believe it was real, that their coming together as one finally happened. He looked so young in the relaxing state of sleep that she found it difficult to picture this warm, loving, caring man spending fifteen agonizing years in prison. Her hand clutched her suddenly aching heart, and she wondered how had he ever survived?

Several minutes later, she forced her eyes off Cole and entered the bathroom. She dried her hair and dressed in jeans and a sweater. After putting on a warm jacket, she headed down to the beach, but not before she left Cole a note on her pillow.

"Down at the beach. There's coffee in the kitchen. Love S."

Chapter Nine

It took Cole a moment after he'd awoken to realize where he slept. He spent so much time on the road lately, one hotel room looked like the next, but the minute his eyes focused he smiled and his heart picked up a beat as he knew exactly where he was and whom he was with. *Shannon.* His now wide-awake mind replayed in vivid intensity last night's lovemaking. He felt his blood flowing to the one special place south of the border, and his cock strained against the covers. It wanted out. It wanted Shannon's delectable body wrapped around it. It throbbed for her and her alone.

He groaned and turned toward her side of the bed, his hand reaching out and finding it cold and empty. After spotting the note and reading it, he smiled again, then got up, showered, dressed and went out on the balcony to look for her. His eyes scanned the beach until he spotted her down on some rocks, looking deep in thought. He frowned, hoping she was thinking good thoughts and not having any regrets over last night.

Grabbing his beat up and battered black leather jacket

he'd had forever, he meandered down to the beach. The closer he got to her, the faster his pulse soared. When she looked his way and saw him approaching, she climbed off the jetties and her face broke out into a beautiful smile. Instantly putting his runaway thoughts to rest.

"Good morning," she said, her face flush from the cold and her eyes warm with love. Cole walked up behind her, wrapping his arms around her waist, and held her tight. Shannon leaned back against his hard chest and placed her arms on his. He kissed her neck and spoke softly into her ear. "Good morning to you. It's beautiful here. How long have you lived here?"

"Five years."

"I thought you hired a bodyguard. I don't see him. Is he that good at his job he stays hidden amongst the sand dunes?"

Her body flinched. "I did while I traveled. I don't believe I need one here. I had no privacy."

"You need one. Especially when I'm around you, he will not attack when I'm gone, only when I'm with you. He wants to accomplish two things. The first one is your death, and the second is my going back to prison. Please let me make a call?"

"No. I'll call the same agency I dealt with before."

"Today."

"Yes. I'll call today."

"Now that that's settled, please tell me, besides your ex, do you have family nearby?" he queried as his warm breath tickled her ear, causing her body to tingle from head to toe and everywhere in between.

"My parents live on the Cape, my two sisters both live

here in Standish Bay and my brother lives in Back Bay. I'm the oldest."

She stood there enjoying the feel of Cole's arms around her and the sound of the surf. *Can life get any better than this?*

"What about your family Cole? You've never spoken about them?" He never had, and she was a little more than curious—very curious actually.

She tried to be patient as she waited for his answer. It paid off when he finally spoke.

"My father was an American who fell instantly in love with my mother during a backpacking expedition across Europe. They married three weeks later, and my father took his new bride back to California with him. One year later I was born, four years later, my parents divorced and my mother took us back to Wales, to her family. My father stayed in California. I never saw or heard from him again. I don't honestly know if he's alive or dead. I had a stepfather, but he died when I was seventeen. My mother died when I was in prison. I have two younger sisters who live in Wales. They've never left Great Britain and I've not seen them in, oh God, in well over fifteen years. I'm not sure I would recognize them if I saw them."

She heard him sniffle and then clear his throat.

"I wish I could go home, not to my house in Malibu, but to my home back in Wales."

"You can't?"

He groaned. "No, not while on parole. I can't leave the country. My lawyer's been trying to work out something, but, well it isn't happening. My sentence was twenty years. I served fifteen and got out early for good behavior. I still have five more years of parole until I'm truly free."

"Thank God you got out for good behavior or we might not have met."

Cole closed his eyes. Yes. Thank God, or they wouldn't have met. The thought sent a chill up his spine and he snuggled Shannon closer to make it go away. He opened his eyes and watched the surf crash on the beach and the seagulls hunt for their breakfast. They were nasty creatures as they fought and nipped each other while fighting over the same dead crabs on the sand. Then he reached for her hand and led her back to the warmth of her house.

Cole wanted to make Shannon one of his special omelets for breakfast. Few people knew it, but he was an exceptional cook. However, when he looked into her refrigerator, he outwardly cringed. One sniff of the milk and his nose wrinkled up. The eggs were old, the shells probably so thick they would never crack open. The onions appeared frozen and the peppers she had in the vegetable crisper were rotten and moldy and had seen better days. "I think you need to go shopping and buy some edible food," he said, shaking his head in disbelief.

"I know. I will later today. We won't starve. We have bread for toast and leftover chili for lunch." She walked up to him and kissed him, long, wet and hot enough to engulf him in flames. "Besides." She winked. "We have each other." She went to move away, but he pulled her back and gave her his most provocative grin. "Not so fast, I'm starving." He crushed her mouth to his and feasted to his heart's content. Even nibbled her ear and neck for a little extra nourishment. "Hmm, that should do me for a while."

"Hmm, you think?" she countered.

"Actually. No," he replied, slipping her sweater off in one quick swoop. "I think I missed a few spots."

Before she knew it, he swept her up into his arms and gently laid her down in front of the fireplace. They had breakfast, lunch, dinner and dessert all in one sitting.

Shannon finally got to explore every incredible muscular inch of Cole's body. And when she took him into her mouth, she took great pleasure in causing him to squirm. And when he fed her, she didn't miss a single drop.

Snuggled under a fleece throw, satiated from love-making and enjoying the heat from the fireplace, Cole and Shannon talked about nothing and everything until the doorbell rang.

Shannon sprang up. "Shit! What time is it?"

Cole forced his eyes away from her naked body and looked at his watch. "Eleven, why?"

"Oh my God! I forgot my sisters were coming by."

She ran around like a madwoman gathering Cole's clothes and throwing them at him. She quickly dressed, running her hands threw her mussed hair as she ran down to get the door.

When she opened it, her two younger sisters stepped in with bags of food. Rachel was the first to go up the stairs chatting away. "We brought food because we know what you're like, there's probably not an ounce...oh."

She stopped dead in her tracks, and Shannon could well imagine what Rachel was thinking. "Who is this gorgeous man with long blond hair, jeans slung low on his narrow hips and a Rolling Stones T-shirt showing off well-formed muscles in her sister's kitchen?" If it wasn't for the shopping bags Rachel carried, Shannon imagined her sister wiping the drool from her mouth.

"Hi," Rachel said in her usual deep, hoarse voice she perfected years ago, knowing it drove men crazy.

"Hello."

"Oh my God, what a voice," Rachel crooned.

By now, Bridget stood beside Rachel, staring at Cole as well. He quickly and carefully took the bags from their arms and placed them on the counter before they dropped them on the tile floor. Shannon joined Cole at the counter gently touching his arm.

"Rachel, Bridget, I'd like you to meet Cole Jackson. Cole, these two women staring at you with their mouths open are my sisters. Please forgive their manners," she added with lightness in her voice.

He held out his hand and Rachel took it first. "Nice to meet you Cole. Are you *the* Cole Jackson?"

He laughed at her query. "The one and only…I think."

He shook Bridget's hand next. She stared with detached interest and more than a little contempt. Cole got the impression this sister didn't like him much. Some people had strong preconceived notions about him, and this little lady was one of them. And he knew from experience nothing he did or said would change those preconceived feelings just like Shannon's ex. But what the hell, he could try.

"Nice to meet you, Bridget," he said with a warm smile hoping she couldn't tell was forced.

"Glad to meet you Cole. I'd forgotten you and my sister knew each other."

Glad, Cole mused, that's a good one. She was anything but glad to meet him.

Shannon gave Bridget a warning look as she emptied the grocery bags. Rachel stepped up to help as Cole excused himself and went up to Shannon's bedroom.

He stepped out on the balcony, sat on the chaise lounge and froze his ass off. He wanted to give Shannon time alone with her sisters, and he didn't want to hear what they had to say. Rachel wasn't a problem, but Bridget was not too happy to see him here. Could he blame her? Hell, if one of his sisters started dating a convicted killer, whether or not he claimed innocence, he'd be none too thrilled either.

Being able to see two sides of the coin didn't lessen the pain and anger he felt when people disapproved of him or were truly afraid of him. Afraid he might kill again, even though he never killed in the first place.

He groaned out his frustrations and once again proved to himself he should have waited until he cleared his name before seeing Shannon again. But shit, there was no guarantee he'd ever clear his name. So what was he supposed to do? Put his love life on hold because some people didn't approve of him dating her? Hell, all that mattered was Shannon's opinions and feelings for him. Fuck everybody else's. If only it were that simple. Cole cared what people thought of him, which angered him even more. He wished he had enough confidence and self-esteem that nothing anyone said would ever bother him. But no, he had a soft heart and a caring nature, and what people thought about him mattered. It may not have during his heyday, but it did now. And he didn't want to add more problems to Shannon's life. Her ex-husband being dead set against him caused enough trouble. Her sisters were another. How could they have a relationship with so many people trying to pull her away from him?

Once Cole was not within hearing range, Bridget let Shannon have it as Shannon knew she would. Out of the three of them, Bridget was the opinionated one, and she sometimes spoke first and thought later. She was thirty-one years old and never been married. Bridget was the petite sister with short blonde hair, green eyes and an incredible body. She worked in Plymouth at a fitness and tennis club as a personal trainer. She was secretive about her dating life. Shannon had no idea if she had found *the one* yet.

Rachel, on the other hand, stood tall like Shannon. She had black hair at the moment and green eyes. She was twenty-seven and worked in a small beauty salon in town. Also single, but as long as Shannon could remember, she had a string of guys vying for her attention. She was probably the prettiest of them all, but sometimes it was hard to tell with her constantly changing hair color, excessive makeup and unusual style in clothing. But, she was a sweetheart, and a little on the flaky side. Shannon sometimes referred to them as, Shannon the introvert, Bridget the serious one and Rachel the flake.

They got along fairly well, mostly. It hadn't always been that way when they were growing up. They had the typical sister squabbles, but they didn't last long since Bridget was only fifteen and Rachel eleven when Shannon got married. Their brother, Mitch had been thirteen. God, it seemed like a lifetime ago since they all lived in the same house with their parents. Shannon often wondered if she hadn't gotten pregnant and married so young, would her life have turned out much differently? That was a question she would never know the answer to.

"What is he doing here?" Bridget asked in her most demanding voice, pulling Shannon out of her reverie.

Shannon took her sweet time answering, knowing Bridget's anger would simmer under the surface, and if she didn't like her answer it would bubble over. She didn't feel like having one of Bridget's confrontations. And Shannon knew her sister all too well, nothing she said would change her mind about Cole. Hoping to stall for time, she quietly put the food away, except the chicken salad and rolls.

She finally faced her sister. Hell, she was the older one,

why should she have to make herself accountable to Bridget or John or anyone else. This was her life, and she was in love with Cole, and nothing anyone said would change her mind. Absolutely nothing could change her feelings for him, feelings which just ran too deep. They were now a part of her.

"He's here because we're friends, and he came to stay for a few days between concerts." Shannon stared at Bridget, daring her to question her answer.

Bridget gave her the look she had been famous for since she was ten years old and thought she ruled over everyone. She pursed her lips, narrowed her eyes and stared until for some unknown reason you had to buck up, tell the truth, and come clean. Her kids, when she had them, would be doomed.

"Friends," she said, emphasizing every single letter.

Shannon looked at Rachel, pleading for help. Rachel shrugged her shoulders. "Hey, don't look at me to come to the rescue. I'm dying for juicy details. He is," she sighed and fluttered her lashes, "sexy as hell. If you don't want him, I'll take him."

Now, Bridget shot Rachel the look.

Shannon loved her sisters, but they were nosy. She didn't pry into their love lives, did she? Well, maybe she did occasionally, especially Bridget's, as she was so tight-lipped.

"Okay, okay, we're." Lovers. In love. Made for one another. Screwing each other's brains out? Okay, a little crude, but true as of last night. "I guess you could say we're dating." Could she possibly hope that would be the end of the discussion on Cole as she turned her back and made up three sandwiches? She would make one fresh for Cole when he came down. And she had the feeling he wouldn't until her sisters left.

After carrying the food to the table, she sat down to eat. Bridget and Rachel joined her, bringing bottles of water. The next question had her nearly choking to death on her sandwich. As close as her sisters were, they rarely discussed the intimate details of their relationships.

"Well. Are you having sex with him?" This interrogation came from Rachel, her supposed ally.

Shannon could have killed her traitorous body for blushing and her hands for shaking so badly she had to drop them to her lap.

Bridget gasped. "How could you have sex with him? Need I remind you he spent years in prison? Do you *know* what happens in prison? He could have any number of sexually transmitted diseases, including AIDs. And let's not forget to mention why he was there in the first place. Such as the fact he *killed* his wife. What were you thinking?" Her voice rose several octaves on the last sentence.

Shannon looked from Bridget, whose face flushed red with anger, to Rachel. Rachel looked a little sympathetic toward her. *Thank you Rachel!*

Before she spoke, Shannon steadied her voice to keep out her growing frustration. "What I think is, it's none of your damn business. Now, I'm going to eat lunch and you two are more than welcome to stay, but the discussion about what's taking place between me and Cole is over. I *will not* discuss it again."

She was so thankful when her sisters gathered their things to leave. As much as she loved them, the relationship between her and Cole was still new and fragile and she wanted to spend what little time they had together with him alone, without the interference of her beloved but opinionated and nosy sisters.

Bridget gave her a hug. "I hope you know what you're doing."

Rachel hugged her next. "Sorry, you know how Bridget can be. Will we see you at Mom and Dad's on Sunday for Dad's sixtieth birthday?"

Shannon couldn't help groaning, knowing her family would give her an earful that day. "Yes, I'll be there. Who do I owe for the present?"

"Mitch," Bridget replied. "He bought a really nice bird bath at this garden shop. We each owe him forty bucks." Even though Mitch was the only male among her siblings, he always seemed to take care of the details when it came to present buying or parties. If he settled down, Shannon knew the woman he chose would be lucky as hell.

When Shannon closed the door after her sisters, she leaned back against it and tried to breathe steadily. She felt as though she'd gone ten rounds in the ring without her boxing gloves. Ten long rounds being beaten to a bloody pulp. Why was everyone so quick to judge Cole before they got to know him? The sound of her phone chiming away on the counter had her running up the stairs to the kitchen.

"Hello," she said as her finger slid the arrow.

"Hey Shannon, how's it going?"

She smiled and sank onto a stool. "Hey Kevin, why do I feel this is not a business call?"

Well for starters," Kevin said and she could picture his shit-eating grin from ear to ear. "A certain male with a sexy-as-sin voice called me recently. Want to tell me about it?"

Shannon laughed and was glad he called when he had. She needed this light, teasing banter they did so well. "Think you can handle it?" she goaded.

"Well maybe, just don't shock me. Seriously, is he there in your home?"

"Yeah," she breathed out, her heart going still. "He's here, thanks to you giving him my address."

"Don't mention it. Do me a favor and tell him I said hi."

Shannon laughed once again. "Sure, I'll tell him. But you do remember what I said?"

"And what would that be?" he teased.

"He likes women."

"Oh, that," he croaked out. "I know, I can dream, can't I?"

She giggled. "Sure Kevin, you can dream. I, on the other hand, *have lived* the dream."

"You loose woman you. Oh shit, I have to go...love you. Don't do anything I wouldn't do."

"Now why would I do that? Bye, love you. Oh, Kevin? Thanks for looking out for me?"

"Anytime sweetheart. Anytime," he replied.

As soon as she hit the end button, she ran up the two flights of stairs to her bedroom to find Cole. When she caught sight of him, her heart melted. He'd braved the freezing cold balcony, lying in a lounge chair, looking uncomfortable as hell. His teeth chattered loudly, and his lips were tinged blue.

"Are you coming in? You look frozen," she asked, concerned for his health as he wasn't used to New England weather.

"Come out," he said, sounding and looking defeated.

Shannon grabbed the quilt off her bed and joined him. He opened his legs for her to sit between them and wrapped his arms around her as she covered them with the quilt. With her help, it wasn't long before he burned hot against her.

"I'm sorry," whispered Shannon. "My sister Bridget can come across a little harshly."

She felt him take a large breath, his chest rising and falling with it. "You have nothing to be sorry for. They are your sisters and obviously Bridget loves you and is concerned about you. There was a time when I was proud of my name and who I was and what I had accomplished in my life." As he spoke, his voice became melancholy. "By twenty-three, I'd had it all. And believe me, I'd worked fucking hard for it. But the most pathetic thing about it was that I didn't appreciate it at the time. I never thought it would end so quickly and so badly."

"When I was arrested, I believed in the judicial system, innocent until proven guilty." He gathered his thoughts. "Boy, was I wrong. Was it because of who I was, or what I represented? Why did everyone despise me? I will never forget the contempt and hatred vibes I felt coming from the jurors from the beginning of the trial. They were biased from the get-go. But, stupid me," he snorted. "I still believed I'd be found innocent. How could I be found guilty when I didn't do it?"

Shannon hung onto every word Cole said, and she wept for the young man he'd been and for his idealistic beliefs. Then he continued, his voice just as mellow. "When they read the verdict, I thought I'd die on the spot. I physically felt the thrust in my heart shattering my world, my beliefs that justice would prevail. I cried for Lindsey because I loved her regardless of our unconventional marriage and because the person who had killed her would go unpunished and free." He tightened his arms around her, buried his face in her hair and breathed.

"When my appeal got denied, I died. When I was in jail waiting for my trial, I knew it would only be a matter of time before I was free," he huffed. "Could I've been more wrong? The day I arrived at the maximum security prison after being convicted, I really didn't care whether I lived or died. There were many days I prayed for death."

He sniffed and cleared his throat. "Then one day I'm in the shower. It's amazing what your mind can overcome and the strength your body possesses when there are those trying to violate you."

A groan escaped Shannon's lips, and she held her breath, waiting for him to go on as her heart broke apart for him.

"Needless to say, I spent more time in the beginning in solitary confinement. Which, trust me, I preferred. Eventually I gained the other inmates' respect, and they left me alone. And I'm relieved and so thankful to say my sexual experiences in prison were limited to my own lonely, over-worked hand."

Shannon swallowed, trying to cool the fire burning in her throat from her tears. "Cole, you don't have to tell me all of this. I love you anyway."

"I know, but I wanted to tell you. There's more." He shifted in the chaise lounge and continued, "I became addicted to books, my music and songwriting. It killed me. I didn't have a guitar, but fortunately for me, I could hear the music in my head. I thanked God every day I hadn't lost the sound of the music. Anyway, AJ, once a month, sent me a package that contained books and other such things that were allowed. He mailed me every one of yours, among other authors. I spent so much time reading your books over and over. I would stare at your picture endlessly—I swore I could feel you looking at me, smiling at me. Before I even met you, I felt a connection." He laughed nervously. "I think I was halfway in love with you before we even met, weird huh?"

Shannon laughed nervously. "Not so weird, I felt the

same way about you. Every time I saw you on television, in the paper or in the gossip magazines, it was like you were looking inside me, and I could see inside you. There was a connection. There *is* a connection. How else can we explain how and why we met and came together? And I had strong feelings for you, feelings for a total stranger I'd never met. But when I met you, the connection was instantaneous. It was real, it is real and powerful."

Cole traced little circles with his fingers on Shannon's arms, causing her body to quiver and her pulse to soar.

"When I received early parole, the first thing I did was hire an escort to spend the whole night with me. I needed to feel like a man, to be with someone who would not judge me, and to be held through the night. Fifteen years is a long time to sleep on a springy mattress in a cold cell with nobody to hold on to but yourself."

Shannon sat up and shifted her body so she straddled him. She needed to look into his eyes, his golden brown eyes shining glassy with tears.

"Cole?"

He put his finger on her lips. "Shh. I want to clear the air and I don't want your pity. I didn't tell you for the pity. I told you because I wanted you to know. I don't want you having questions or wondering about things and being afraid or embarrassed to ask. I need to clear the air between us." He placed his warm hand on her cheek and she leaned into it. "As the woman I love, I wanted you to know."

Shannon closed her eyes and let her tears fall as everything he'd just said registered in her brain. When she finally opened her eyes, she smiled with all the warmth, compassion and love she could muster. Then she lowered herself down and kissed the tears from Cole's face. Salty tears from pain. Tears from loneliness. Tears from love.

"I love you Cole," she choked out.

He slid one hand up to the nape of her neck and brought her lips down to his, reveling in the sensations ricocheting inside his body. There was a connection all right. The joining of body, heart and soul. What stronger connection could there be?

Shannon adjusted her body, lay down with her head on his chest and Cole knew the moment she drifted off to dreamland. Her breathing slowed and her body relaxed and became heavier. He relaxed back himself and smiled at how lucky he was to have found her, and he joined her in sleep, enjoying every minute of holding her and feeling her head and hand on his heart. The heart that belonged to only her, now and forever.

That night Cole cooked his famous omelet for Shannon and Cameron. And afterwards they sat in the family room, fireplace roaring, and Cameron and he played guitars while Shannon sat curled on the chair, eyes and ears transfixed on the two males in the room.

Cole spent the latter part of the evening making love to Shannon, and then he held her through the night, content once again to sleep soundly. Reveling again in the love she so freely lavished on him.

Shannon and Cole awoke the next morning to the sound of a door banging and a loud, angry voice yelling, "Shannon, I'm coming up." Her pulse instantly soared and she sat up, clutching the sheet to her bare breasts as she listened to her ex-husband stomping, none too quietly, up her stairs. What the hell did he think he was doing? She'd had just about enough of his meddling in her life when it came to Cole. And she could just imagine how he came to find out Cole was here. *Bridget.* Wait until Shannon got a hold of her tattletale of a sister.

Cole immediately jumped out of bed and had just pulled on his jeans when the door burst open and John stood there face red with anger, hands fisted at his sides and the veins pulsing at his temples. The three of them stared at one another, eyes switching from one face to the next until Shannon couldn't take it anymore and broke the silence.

"John, what are you doing coming in here like this, acting like a lunatic?" She didn't bother keeping the anger out of her voice.

John stood speechless as he took in Shannon's appearance. She'd let the sheet drop and her breasts bounced, exposed to his gaze. He swallowed hard. He had forgotten how beautiful she was. He quickly looked away, trying to calm his suddenly pounding heart. Christ, he had no business seeing her like this. And he would not acknowledge the fact it turned him on by the sight of her nakedness. And definitely would not acknowledge the sudden strain against the front of his jeans.

"Shannon, for God's sake, cover-up," he growled out at her.

He'd seen her naked before, so the hell with him. She climbed out of bed and heard John curse as she grabbed her robe off the back of the chair and wrapped herself into it. She was still tightening the belt when she turned to face her ex. She promised herself she would not lose her temper. It would solve nothing. So she tried to fight back the anger trembling inside her, trying to explode like Mount Saint Helens on a terrible day.

"You coming in here was wrong. What I do with my time, my body and my life are none of your concern. I want you to leave."

John was pissed beyond reason and he glared at her. "It is my concern. You're the mother of my son and whether or not you like it, it gives me a say in your life." His temper snapped, and he went for Cole, who'd stood in the background watching the exchange between the once married couple.

"You murdering son of a bitch, stay away from my family," John yelled as one hand closed around Cole's neck. He had him shoved up against the wall before Cole clearly knew what hit him. Shannon's eyes widened with surprise and shock at John's behavior.

It didn't take long before Cole wrestled away from John's death grip and threw an uppercut into John's gut, sending him down on one knee, coughing and wheezing. He didn't stay down long though before he charged Cole again. They went at it for a time, each one getting their punches in, and it would have gone on for a lot longer if Cameron hadn't come into the bedroom.

"Stop it, stop it," he yelled at the top of his lungs, and Shannon froze at the anguished expression on her son's face. Cole and John ignored him. He finally got their attention with his next sentence.

"Cut the fucking shit, now!"

Chapter Ten

Both men froze in their tracks and turned around to face an extremely upset Cameron. John was bent over at the waist, his hands on his thighs as he sucked in air. Shannon could see the blood clinging to his nose and lips. He mumbled something unintelligible and booked it into the bathroom.

Shannon broke out of her spell when she heard the bathroom door slam and she hurried to Cole's side. "I'm sorry about John. I don't know what got into him." She reached up with her trembling hand and gently brushed his hair out of his eyes. She cringed. "You're going to have quite a shiner and your lip is split."

Then to her surprise Cole laughed, he hugged her to him and laughed harder. "I don't think I've fought over a girl since I was thirteen." He pulled back and smiled at her, then flinched. "Ouch, my lip hurts. Who do you think won?"

Shannon couldn't help but smile at his boyish question. "I think it was a draw. Cameron, I realize you're upset with what happened here, but please go downstairs and make some coffee while I have a talk with your father?"

Cameron looked from his mother to Cole then to the bathroom door. He shrugged his shoulders and said, "Sure Mom."

Cole moved to leave with Cameron, but Shannon reached out her arm and stopped him. "Please stay."

How could he resist the pleading in her eyes and in her voice? He would stay and confront John reasonably this time with words instead of fists. That all depended on John and if he could be reasonable. Cole didn't think he could be when it came to Shannon.

Cole finished dressing and sat down in a chair while Shannon dressed quickly before John came out of the bathroom. She sat, back straight as an arrow on the bench at the foot of the bed and waited. When John finally came out of the bathroom, he didn't look any better than Cole did. In fact, he looked worse. Good, she thought. John deserved it the way he came barreling in here like a madman. Cole didn't deserve it though. Anger twisted around inside her stomach, causing it to ache. She reached out and patted the bench beside her. "Come, sit down John and we can talk like the adults we are," she said as calmly as she could because she refused to have a repeat of what just happened.

John sat down next to her on the bench and exhaled loudly. "I'm sorry I came in here like that. It wasn't my intention for things to become physical. But I have something to say to you, and I will only say it once. If you continue seeing…" He glanced in Cole's direction. "…that man, I will fight for Cameron. I will not tolerate him being around my son." When Shannon tried to interrupt, he put up his hand. "I told you once before I didn't want him near Cameron and you ignored me like I had *no* say, well guess what?" His voice became low, deep and menacing. "I *do* have a say. A huge say in my son's life, and you can choose either…" He pointed across the room. "…that man or Cameron."

Shannon, too shocked to answer right away, sat on the bench while a battle raged out of control inside her. Her throat burned, and tears, against her will, leaked out of her eyes and streamed down her cheeks onto her lap. Her trembling hands clasped together and her insides shook like California experiencing an earthquake. A catastrophic earthquake. When had John become such a tyrant? He used to be a practical man and so considerate of others. Oh yeah right, he used to be, about a million years ago during a previous life. Now he was nasty and mean and trying to control her life and make her choose between her son and the man she loved. A love that went beyond any other she had ever felt and she would surely wither and die without it. But she would die an even more slow, painful and horrendous death without her son.

She would never have thought John could be so cruel as to take Cameron away from her. But she wasn't so sure anymore. This was a side of him that frightened her. He could persuade a judge to see his side. He had connections with everyone because of his job. She hunched her shoulders in defeat and sobbed into her hands, hoping John suffered tremendously for putting her through this torture.

After a time of complete silence, except for the sound of her crying, Shannon finally looked up to Cole and saw by his expression he knew what her decision was and he understood. He closed his eyes and nodded slightly then got up and went into the bathroom.

Once inside the bathroom, Cole slammed the toilet seat closed, sank down on it and breathed deeply, fighting the pain in his chest and the lump in his throat. John was a son of a bitch. How could he treat Shannon like that? How could he play their son against her? Didn't he know she would choose her son over him? Cole snorted. Yeah, he knew. And that's why he gave her the ultimatum.

John only saw what he wanted to see when it came to him. He saw in black and white only. What he saw was Cole, a convicted killer and ex-con on parole for the murder of his wife. And there was nothing gray about it. Shannon, his heart constricted when he thought of her, saw all shades of gray. She saw the good in him and she knew he wasn't capable of killing anyone. She loved him as he loved her, but he wouldn't put her in the position of losing her son. He wasn't a quitter, definitely a fighter, but sometimes the stakes were too damn high. For now, he would step aside. But there would come a time when he and John would have it out, and he would come out the victor then. Shannon was worth too much to him to lose her. His heart was worth too much to be broken for a lifetime. Her heart deserved to be whole. She deserved her lover and her son.

Cole leaned over the sink and splashed icy cold water on his face, wincing at the stinging of his lip, and then stepped out of the bathroom to find Shannon alone, looking out the French doors to the ocean beyond. Her arms were wrapped tightly around herself and she looked defeated. His chest constricted and his legs appeared suddenly void of all strength as he walked up behind her, enveloping her into his arms and burying his head into her hair. He cleared his throat to enable himself to speak. "I'm leaving now," he said with a quiver to his suddenly hoarse voice. "I love you."

She pivoted around, put her unsteady hand on his cheek and looked at him with all the anguish of a thousand souls riding on her shoulders. "I'm sorry," she said in a defeated whisper.

He took her hand and kissed the palm. "Don't be. Your son *should* be the most important person in your life. I just wish John didn't see in black and white only."

She broke down then, clinging to him, sobbing and shaking. He held her until she quieted down, and then he walked out the door with one last look back as he picked up his bag. His insides burned from the spears of a hundred flaming arrows. He ran down the stairs and glanced once at Cameron who sat at the kitchen counter looking stiff and uncomfortable. Cole forced a smile and a wink and he mouthed, "See ya, kid."

He found John standing outside by his rent-a-car. No big surprise there.

"Don't get your piss in an uproar. I'm leaving."

John looked at him with eyes blazing. "Stay away from my family."

Cole couldn't help the snide remark that came out. "Last I checked, you gave up the right to call Shannon family after your divorce. And by the way, does your current wife know you're still in love with your ex?"

Before he heard John's reply, Cole climbed in the car, turned the key, and hit the gas. As he headed toward the highway, he decided to drive all the way to Pittsburgh. He needed the feel of the open road to soothe and lick his wounds.

After John watched Cole drive away, he reentered Shannon's house hoping to make peace with her and his son, whom he knew would also be angry at him. But nothing prepared him for Shannon's words. She stood there, looking like the wrath of hell herself, her hand held out.

"Hand it over."

John tilted his head as he did not understand what she wanted him to hand over.

"My house key," she said. "Hand it over."

"Shannon that's ridiculous, I've always had one of your house keys."

She wasn't caving on this. She didn't start the war, he did, and she meant to finish it. "You're no longer welcome in my home. When you come to pick up Cameron, you will stay outside and beep the horn. I never want to speak to you or see you again unless it has to do with our son. You ruined our friendship when you barged in here this morning interfering with my life and my happiness." She tried to keep her voice calm, but it got harder by the second.

"You had no right to do what you did. Cameron and I are perfectly safe with Cole. That's right. I said his name! *Cole Jackson* is more of a man than you'll ever be. He has suffered more than you will ever know because of narrow-minded, self-centered people like yourself and I want nothing to do with you anymore. I loved you once and continued to love you long after our divorce." She saw the confusion on his face so she clarified. "I loved you as a friend, but it's over and done with. I'll never forgive you for making me choose my son over the man I love. How would you feel if I suddenly felt Cheryl wasn't fit to be around Cameron and made you choose?"

"It's not the same." he snapped out.

"The hell it isn't," she yelled. "In my eyes and in my heart, Cole has done nothing wrong. So it *is* the same. Now, I will say it once more. Give me my house key."

Damn her to hell and back for this. John fumbled with his suddenly trembling hands to remove the key from his key ring and reluctantly handed it over. It was not a sign of defeat. He would not give up the battle yet, just put it on hold for now. He stormed out of the house and sat inside his car shaking at the words she'd spoken to him and at the words he remembered Jackson had spoken just as he left.

He scrubbed his hands down his face. Jesus, was Jackson right? Was he still in love with Shannon? Was it okay that he'd gone on with his life, but he didn't want Shannon to go on with hers? Couldn't bear to see her in love with someone else? Damn them to hell and back for putting thoughts in his head. He loved his wife, Cheryl, not Shannon. And to prove it he drove home, stopping along the way for flowers, and the minute he stepped inside the door he swept Cheryl off her feet, brought her to their bedroom and locked the door. He pulled her into his arms and kissed her senseless.

"John, the children," she reminded him.

"They can wait. I need you."

AJ awoke in a cold sweat from a deep sleep. He rolled over and looked at the clock, four in the morning. He rarely dreamed about Lindsey anymore, but with Cole out of prison and the band back together, AJ's guilty conscience was getting the best of him. Every time he looked at Cole, guilt and shame churned inside him. Maybe if he'd spoken up about Lindsey's infidelities with him and the many other lovers she'd had, he could have kept his best friend out of prison.

But he'd been too ashamed to have fallen in love with his best friend's wife. He and Lindsey had spent two years together, stealing moments of pure carnal pleasure whenever the opportunity presented itself. And it presented itself often, with Cole seemingly uninterested in his own wife. But that didn't make what he'd done right. What he'd done with Lindsey would never be justified. He'd coveted another man's wife.

He wanted to tell Cole about his relationship with her. He needed to clear his conscience. He supposed it was selfishness on his part in telling him now, but he had to.

AJ had already checked in at the hotel in Pittsburgh where the band would stay during their concert tour. He came early. He hadn't wanted to go home. He had a small condo in Los Angeles but he hadn't felt like going there, and besides, his real home was in Scotland with his wife Elizabeth and their three children. After Lindsey's death and Cole going to prison, AJ, brokenhearted and dejected, went back to his homeland to make a new life for himself. He'd set himself up on a horse farm. Breeding and raising horses had become his life. He'd married Elizabeth Walsh, whom he'd known most of his life. He didn't truly love her, not with all his heart, but he loved her as much as he could love anyone after Lindsey.

Elizabeth was kind, and she truly loved him. She was easy to be with. He missed her terribly, and he couldn't wait for the concert tour to end so he could go home to her, his children and their horses. He loved the quiet, hard, busy life of the farm. He had loved the life of a rock-n-roller when he'd been younger, and he was not ready to give it up, but he needed his downtime and his family. But before AJ could truly be happy and content with his life, he needed to speak with Cole. There were many things that needed to be said and should have been said ages ago.

Cole drove straight through to Pittsburgh from Shannon's house. And as he drove, his mind engaged in a constant battle with itself about how things were left. He'd let John simmer down a bit, but he had no intentions of letting Shannon slip through his fingers. His heart and soul and every other part of him was now a part of her too. It hurt too damn much to contemplate life without her.

Christ, what had John been thinking barging in on them like a crazed lunatic? He'd upset Shannon and Cameron. Didn't he care the two of them probably hated his guts right now? Hell, he did. Shannon was an adult, she could handle it, but he didn't need to alienate his son. Cole ran one hand through his unruly hair, frustrated beyond belief with worry about his life and Shannon's. Add to that he now worried about John and his relationship with Cameron. John, who didn't deserve a thought in his head, but somewhere in the back of Cole's mind, he truly believed John was a decent guy led astray by his emotions.

And since Cole never knew his real father, he hated to see any man, even John, mess up a relationship with his son.

Okay, now that he'd worried about John and Cameron's problems, he needed to think about his own.

He planned on calling every private detective in the

New York area the minute he arrived in Pittsburgh. There had to be something or someone who could help him dig up the past. He realized a lot of time had gone by, but there had to be someone at the hotel who saw something. They probably didn't even know what they saw was important but it could lead to Lindsey's killer without tarnishing her reputation. Even after all this time he still didn't want her parents and her siblings to know what Lindsey had turned into.

Yeah right, he was desperate and grasping for any tiny crumb. Crumbs that had been examined time and time again and led nowhere. Jesus, he was screwed. And really, why had he kept silent about Lindsey's affairs? Because his lawyer advised him that the prosecution would use the information as motive, which could have led to premeditated murder and a murder one conviction.

His mind drifted back to Cameron. What a talented kid. He wanted to help him and work with him. He believed he needed someone because he could see John being the type of father who built a life on reality, not dreams. And it would be a crying shame if he killed Cameron's dream. Some musicians had the voice, some had the song writing ability and no voice, some wrote the melody and not the words, others wrote the words and nothing else. Cameron had it all and then some. He fit right in the musical world. He had fit right in with Black-Jack when he was on stage with them at the Fleet Center.

He had such incredible talent, stage presence and style enough to go a long way in this business. And it would please Cole to no end if he could be a part of his life while it happened. They had clicked which wasn't easy. Cole didn't connect with just anyone. In fact, during his whole life there had been few people he could think of he'd connected with enough to call them friends. He'd had Lindsey, AJ, Ted and Brad.

He'd clicked with Jerome. An old man who'd spent most of his life in prison for killing a couple during a home invasion. Cole had looked past his guilt and found a lonely, old man who regretted that one terrible act. They'd bonded during the first six years Cole had spent in prison. Jerome was an uneducated man who had grown up on the streets of Harlem. At the tender young age of eighteen he'd committed such a heinous and unspeakable act of violence, he landed himself in prison for life. He was fifty-two when Cole met him, but he looked about eighty. He'd died during Cole's seventh year in prison from lung cancer, and Cole missed him terribly during the rest of his time spent behind those concrete walls.

Cole pulled up to the hotel and the first thing he did was hit the suite and play his guitar, which thanks to the equipment manager always arrived before he did. Playing was his life, his love, but it also served as his therapy. And if he ever needed a little therapy, it was now. He was playing and singing the song he and Cameron had written together when AJ came into the suite, took a seat and listened.

When Cole finished playing, AJ spoke, "Wow, it's great. When did ye write it?"

"Actually, Cameron and I worked on it together. We wrote a few others as well."

"Aye, it's good." AJ smiled. "That kid is something else. He reminds me of ye when ah first met ye."

AJ got up and walked to the door and locked it. Cole watched with curiosity, wondering what was up. On close inspection, his friend looked restless and tired as though something weighed heavily on his mind.

AJ sat back down again and said, "Cole, there's some-thing ah want tae tell ye. Way back when Lindsey was alive," he paused, cleared his throat and lowered his gaze toward the ground. "Ah...um...we...Ah mean Lindsey and me. I'm sorry."

"I know."

AJ's head snapped up, and he looked Cole in the eye inquisitively. After several moments he replied, "Aye, ye knew."

"Yes, I knew. I was drunk and high a lot but not blind or stupid. I know it went on for over a year."

"Ah dinnae understand. Why didn't ye say anything? Did Lindsey know ye knew?"

Cole rubbed his eyes with the heels of his hands. He was tired and didn't feel like getting into this now, but he supposed it was long overdue.

"I said nothing because Lindsey and I were...I don't know." He shook his head. "Things were weird. When I found out she was sleeping around, I never touched her again. She must have known I knew, how else to explain my never wanting her."

"Ah'm sorry," AJ mumbled.

Cole studied his friend. He looked awfully pale, and he felt sorry for him. "I know you loved her, but I'm not sure she was capable of love. Maybe she was, but she didn't know how to be faithful." Cole's voice lowered. "Did you know there were others?"

AJ groaned. "Aye, only ah dinnae ken who they were. Well, not entirely true. Ah had my suspicions. What ah dinnae understand is if ye knew she was having affairs, why didn't ye say something during the trial?"

There were many days when rotting in jail he'd asked himself the same question. "Since the prosecution had no knowledge of it, my lawyer thought it could give them more ammunition to use against me. It could really have gone either way. The jury could have sympathized with me for having a cheating wife or they could have condemned me because they finally had their motive and might put me away for murder one. Put me away for life without parole. In the end, however, they hated me anyway and I believe it would have hurt my case even more. Either way, I was doomed."

"Who do ye think killed her?"

Cole looked at AJ. He knew AJ could not have done it, but he didn't want to share his suspicions as to who he thought it was. Or the attack on Shannon. So he lied. "I don't know, and I'm thinking it doesn't matter anymore."

"Aye, it does. He went unpunished. He was free tae live his life while ye could not. He killed her. Ye did not. Aye, ah'd say it matters. It matters a whole hell of a lot."

Chapter Eleven

On Sunday morning, two days after John dropped the bomb, Shannon walked like a zombie through her house. She'd never felt more empty, hollow and alone. Oh, she knew Cameron was there, but suddenly it wasn't enough. She wanted and needed more in her life. Her heart ached and her head hurt. Truth be told, everything down to the most insignificant and smallest muscle and joint in her body screamed in pain. And she wondered if it were possible to die of a broken heart?

Cameron moped aimlessly around the house, sighing loudly and banging cabinet doors and drawers, looking for God only knew what. Did he miss Cole as much as she did? They had bonded quickly, and she was afraid that's what was bothering him. That, and the fight she'd had with John, not to mention the fight John had with Cole. And poor Cameron, stuck in the middle of a war zone, being pulled every which way without having a say in the matter.

After forcing down two pieces of buttered toast with strawberry jam, Shannon went upstairs to shower and get ready to drive to the Cape for her father's birthday celebration. She prayed her sister, Bridget, would not make a big to do about Cole. Shannon didn't think she could handle it today. One wrong word from someone would cause her to breakdown and cry. She hoped that didn't happen because she didn't want to spoil her dad's big day with her problems.

The day turned out to be a rather chilly one, cloudy, but not raining. Shannon and Cameron had always played a game of trying to guess the number of boats on the Cape Cod Canal when they drove across the Sagamore Bridge. Cameron was getting too old for it, but she was glad when he made his guess.

"One boat."

Shannon didn't think it was a good day for boating. "I'd say none."

As they crossed the bridge, Cameron leaned up in his seat, scanned the dark choppy water on both sides of the bridge and groaned. "All right, you win." Then he spotted a lone fishing vessel coming out from under the bridge. "Huh, one boat, I win!"

Shannon laughed for the first time in days, and her jaw muscles ached from under use. The pain associated with it was one she didn't mind feeling though. She needed to laugh and smile and feel good again.

When they pulled into her parent's quiet neighborhood, Shannon smiled, impressed with the way it looked. Everyone took such pride in their homes and yards, including her parents. They lived in a large, sprawling ranch. The house was full of palladium windows and cathedral ceilings. Everything was on one level, which she supposed was nice for her parents as they got older. They lived in a golf course community with every street named after a professional golfer. Their backyard was the ninth fairway. It was almost as nice as the ocean, but not quite in Shannon's mind. But considering both her parents were avid golfers, they had chosen well. Not to mention there were dozens of beaches within a short drive.

Shannon and Cameron had just stepped out of their SUV when Rachel and Bridget pulled in behind them. Shannon noticed her brother Mitch's BMW parked on the street. Mitch drove the BMW during the winter. His vintage corvette was the pride of the summer for him. Such was the life of being single. And it made her wonder if either of her sisters or her brother would ever settle down and get married. She hoped so because she realized these past few days how lonely life could be. Having someone to love and share your life with was the greatest gift of all time. She herself had not realized what she missed until Cole walked into her life.

Her brother was twenty-nine and a pilot for a large, successful company with offices all over the world. He piloted one of their company jets, and he had flown the world over and then some. He'd graduated from the Naval Academy, and after becoming a pilot and serving his time, he decided he wanted civilian life again. He bought a townhouse in the Back Bay area of Boston and continued with his dream of soaring in the air.

He stood tall and handsome and had beautiful thick wavy brown hair. When he was around his family, he relaxed and had fun. He loved throwing the football back and forth with Cameron. But she knew another side to her brother, the Naval Academy side. He may not be in the Navy anymore, but he had the charisma, confidence, self-control and impeccable manners of a Navy man. She knew she thought it often enough, but the woman who finally hooked Mitch Gallagher would be a lucky lady indeed. It was not prejudice on her part because she was his sister. It was the truth because in her experience he was a rare man.

Shannon greeted Bridget and Rachel. They each hugged and kissed Cameron, and bearing the food they brought, they went into the house. As with all Gallagher family gatherings, everyone began talking and laughing at once.

"Happy Birthday Dad," Shannon said as she kissed her father. She turned to her mother and kissed her. "Dinner smells great. What are we having?"

"Your father's favorite—roast beef," her mom replied.

Mitch came over and hugged Shannon. "How's it going, sis?" he said with a twinkle in his eye as he looked at her. Heard you've had some excitement in your life lately —namely a man."

Shannon hated her brother for causing her face to heat and to feel the twinges of heartache down in the pit of her stomach. "How are you? Have you forgotten how to use a phone?" It had been weeks since she last heard from Mitch and she felt guilty about it. She talked to Bridget and Rachel nearly every day, but Mitch? It wasn't his fault he was a guy. They remained close, just not as close as the three Gallagher gals.

Mitch laughed. "Come on, I have someone I want you to meet."

He led Shannon over to a young woman, and *young* being the operative word. The *girl* looked like a Barbie Doll. She was done up perfectly without a lock of bleached blonde hair out of place. Her makeup was flawless, and she dressed impeccably.

"Brittany?" Mitch queried for her attention.

Shannon had to fight from rolling her eyes. *Brittany*, it figures.

"This is my sister Shannon. Shannon I'd like you to meet Brittany Evans."

Brittany stood up and started *talking* nonstop about how much she loved her books, especially her latest one about the jewel thief. Shannon tuned her out. God, what did her brother see in this bimbo? Could it be her perfect body, with her large perky breasts, small waist and long shapely legs? Her perfect face with its perfect small features. *Please*, no one was that perfect without a little help. When she focused back on the bimbo, she saw her brother roll his eyes and mouth to her, "I'm sorry." Thankfully, she was saved when her mother announced dinner was ready.

Dinner conversation around the Gallagher table began in the usual way. What had everyone been up to? How was work going? Everything appeared to be going along just fine until Cameron dropped the bomb.

"Hey, Uncle Mitch, did you know Mom is going out with Cole Jackson from BlackJack? Or rather was until my father interfered. They had this huge fight. Dad gave Cole a black eye and a fat lip. Cole gave Dad a fat lip and I think he broke his nose, only Dad won't admit it's broken. I don't think my father likes him very much, and he threatened Mom about seeing him again. I sure hope she doesn't listen to him. I think Cole's great." All this was relayed on one gulp of air, leaving Cameron gasping.

Mitch's fork stopped midway to his mouth, and he glanced at Shannon and then back to Cameron. "Yes, I heard about the dating. I think it's great about them going out. Your mother never dates and she should. But I didn't know about the fight. It's none of John's business what your mother does. I for one think Cole is incredibly talented." He looked at Cameron and winked. "Like you."

Cameron beamed. "When he stayed with us he

jammed with me and we wrote a few songs together. He's the greatest."

Shannon struggled to fight the unbearable pain in her chest and the tears stinging her eyes. When Bridget went to open her mouth, Shannon silently pleaded with her not to and she snapped it shut. Her dad though, had quite a few questions of his own. After he drilled her about her relationship with Cole, he said he sure hoped she knew what she was doing.

Brittany squirmed in her seat and didn't look like she could contain her excitement any longer. "You date Cole Jackson? I can't believe it. I was young when BlackJack first hit the music scene, but I love them now. Cole is like, wow, gorgeous. Actually, they're all quite handsome. Are they all single?" she asked, her eyes wide with interest.

Shannon's jaw dropped as she looked at her brother whose mouth stretched tight causing her to smile to herself. Served him right for dating someone practically still in high school. Maybe he should try finding someone his own age for a change. Or at least date someone a little less shallow. Maybe she gave great head? Yeah, that must be it, because he wasn't thinking with the right brain.

"They are all married," Shannon finally replied with a smirk.

"Happily?" Brittany queried breathlessly.

Oh God, this was too much.

"Yes, I suppose so." Shannon didn't give her another chance to speak. "Mom, dinner was delicious, as usual. I'll help you clean up." She rose from the table and went into the kitchen, keeping Brittany from asking any more asinine questions.

Dad, Mitch, Brittany and Cameron went for a walk around the neighborhood while Mom, Shannon, Bridget and Rachel cleaned up the kitchen.

"Tell me about this man, Cole is it?" Alberta Gallagher asked her daughter.

Shannon stopped loading the dishwasher and leaned her back against the counter, her arms hugging herself. Her mother would be blind not to see the sadness and longing radiating from her eyes.

"He's wonderful, sensitive, caring, shy and oh, yeah gorgeous. Cole and Cameron get along so well, and they are so much alike it's amazing."

"I can see you love him," her mother said with a concerned expression on her face. "I'll try not to pass judgment because of his past." Her mother glanced at Bridget and then back to her. "He sounds wonderful. And as old as I am, I have heard his music. Some of it I even like, and Rachel told me he is sexy."

Shannon looked over at Rachel and laughed, contradicting the tears streaming down her face. "Oh, that he is." Then she hugged her mother. "Thank you. Now what creation did you whip up for Dad's birthday cake?" she asked as she dried her tears with a napkin.

"Wait until you see it. I had to make your father's favorite Boston cream pie, but I also made a cheesecake. It's a new recipe I got, and it looks sinful. Bridget honey, would you please put the coffee on and Rachel, put the kettle on for tea while Shannon and I set out the desserts."

When the walkers returned, they sang happy birthday and opened presents. Shannon thought the birdbath Mitch picked out for their father was beautiful and their mom gave him a new watch. He needed a new watch practically every year with all the gardening and golfing he did. He either took it off while gardening and lost it or smashed in the face playing golf. Nobody could understand how he did either, but he did.

Shannon, glad to have seen her family but glad it was over, breathed a sigh of relief as she drove home alone. Her brother had offered to drop Cameron off at John's house, saving her the trip. Cameron was spending the week with him while she worked on the book she was supposed to be writing and under an approaching deadline. But try as she might, the words just wouldn't come out of her head. She had never experienced writer's block before, and she wasn't at all sure she liked the experience one bit. She felt as though she'd lost the touch, and her head was void of her usual wild imaginings.

The internal dialog she usually had with her characters had disappeared completely. Her head was empty, and it was frightening. It petrified her that the stories would never come back. What would she do if they didn't return? More to the point, who would she be? Hoping to soothe the ache, she put the newest BlackJack CD in the car stereo and hoped to use Cole's magical voice to calm her. It had the opposite effect. Deep volcanic sobs vibrated up and out causing tears to blur her vision, forcing her to pull over at a rest stop in Plymouth.

Once home, she took a long soak in her Jacuzzi tub with the lights off and several aromatherapy candles lit for calm and relaxation. Closing her eyes, she dosed for several minutes until startled awake to what sounded like banging on her door. She reluctantly dried off, pulled on flannel lounge pants and a T-shirt and went to answer the door.

Mitch stood on her front porch, which shocked her. It had probably been months since he'd graced her door. When she studied his face and his eyes, her heart paused at the concern she saw, so she tried to make light of things.

"Well, what brings you here? Barbie…oh…I mean Brittany have an early curfew?"

Mitch swept past her, the concern on his face gone instantly as he gave her the evil eye and ran up to her kitchen to put the teakettle on. "Hilarious," he mumbled as he found her mugs and tea bags. "I love this cook top. Boils water faster than I can get things ready." He fixed everything and carried two mugs to the coffee table by the couch. He flipped the switch for the gas fireplace. "It's freezing in here." He sat down on the couch shivering, and he gestured for her to join him.

"So I spoke with John when I dropped off Cameron. Want to talk about it?"

Shannon picked up her mug and leaned back against the cushions, enjoying the warmth on her hands from the heated cup. "I don't know what to say."

"Why don't you start from the beginning? I find it's always a good place to start."

She told him everything up until the morning John came storming into her house and made a mess of her life. He'd already heard about that encounter from Cameron.

"If it's any comfort, John's suffering too. He feels bad for how he behaved. And you can feel hell freezing over when Cameron and he are in the same room. I think Cameron's quite upset with him. Actually, I can think of several more colorful words to describe what Cameron is feeling, but I'll be good."

"He should be upset. You should've seen John. He was a madman. He had no right to come barging in my house and order everyone around. He sits in his house with Cheryl and their children, living the grand life, all cozy and happy, while I have lived alone for eleven years. How dare he interfere with my happiness now?" She couldn't fight the tears. One would have thought there would be none left to shed, but she guessed not. Mitch reached out and put his arms around her, pulling her close.

"Don't cry. I hate it when you cry," he laughed a little, "when all women cry. If it's any consolation, I gave John a piece of my mind for you. I'll be dammed if he thinks he can control your life. But you know John, the control freak. I truly think he's concerned for your safety and means well with his warped, unreasonable standards."

Shannon pulled away from his arms and glared at him coldly.

He held up his hand. "Woo, let me finish. I know you're a good judge of character, although we must excuse you for marrying John. Which I might add was a *bad* choice."

She raised an eyebrow.

"Well, I'll admit he's a good friend but not worthy of my favorite sister's love."

She smiled. "Are you trying to make me feel better?"

He winked at her. "Is it working?"

"A little, thanks."

"Now, here's what I think we should do."

"What do you mean we?"

"Okay, here's what I think you should do," he amended.

"Better."

"Let John think you've stopped seeing Cole, but you could go to him. If you truly love him, don't let him get away."

"I've a better plan. I've been doing research into Lindsey Jackson's murder. Cole has as well, in hopes of finally clearing his name. I'm going to hire detectives right along with Cole."

"Good. How can I help?" Mitch asked.

"You can't. I need to do this alone. It'll give me something to do while Cole's on tour for the next five months." She hugged her brother close and suddenly realized how much she missed him. He led such an exciting and busy life. Sometimes they would go months without seeing each other. "So tell me what's been going on with you." She tried not to feel guilty for not telling her brother about the attempt on her life in Chicago. Not only did she not want to worry her family, she didn't want them to suspect Cole. She knew it wouldn't matter what she said, they would have their suspicions. She also didn't want to remember that night. It wasn't real if she didn't let herself think about it. Not a smart thing to do, but she did it anyway.

He gave her the once over. "Nice PJ's, are they supposed to turn Cole on?"

She threw her head back and laughed. "Cute. And I suppose all your women wear little black lace teddies."

"Mostly." He grinned and his eyes sparkled. "Some wear see-thru red."

"Well then, Cole's luckier than you are, because I usually wear nothing when he's here." She laughed again and was glad to see that shut him up. "Okay, you're not leaving until you tell me something about your personal life. You can't make me believe that with your career and your good looks, there isn't someone, anyone, besides Brittany, that's in love with you or you're in love with."

It hit her at precisely that moment. There was someone. Someone he cared about and cared about deeply if his look was any indication. And he shocked her when he admitted it.

"There is this one woman."

Shannon fluttered her lashes. "Do tell."

He hip-checked her, nearly knocking her off the couch. "Shut up."

"Okay. I'm sorry. You looked so serious I was trying to lighten the mood. And I'll tell Mom if you try to knock me off the couch again." She laughed. "Do you remember the time you shoved Rachel off the couch and broke her collarbone?"

He groaned. "Yeah, I felt like shit. Remember Mom thought she was being a baby. It wasn't until Dad got home, examined Rachel and convinced Mom it was broken that they went to the hospital."

"Oh yeah, she wouldn't get the Mother of the Year Award for that."

"Right, but any other year she would. Can I tell the story now?" he said.

"Go ahead, tell away."

"Thank you. There's someone I care very much for. I've never dated her nor have I asked her out. Can you believe it?" He inhaled deeply and exhaled loudly. "I'm afraid of being rejected."

She put her hand on his. "Mitch."

"Men have doubts too, you know."

"I know." My God, she never in a million years would have thought Mitch insecure when it came to women. She must be special.

He combed his fingers through his hair. "Well, I've secretly been in love with her for a year now. She's a vice president for Brentin International. I only see her at the times when I pilot the jet she's traveling in, which is at least twice a month. When she travels with me, she sits in the cockpit and acts as my copilot. Believe it or not she also has her pilot's license." He ran his hands through his hair once again. "Hell, I don't think there's anything the woman can't do. She's amazing. She grew up in Texas in a large family on a humongous ranch and learned to pilot helicopters and small planes when she was in her teens. She graduated from the University of Texas and received her MBA from Harvard and the rest is history."

"How old is she?"

He snorted. "I only know because I had to check her pilot's license the first time we flew together. She's thirty-two. And I know what you're thinking after meeting Brittany today. You're thinking it's about damn time I dated someone my own age."

"Well, if you don't mind me pointing it out, she's actually three years older than you."

He laughed. "Oh, yeah, I know. Last week I flew her home to Texas for a vacation, and I spent the night at her family's ranch outside of Dallas. You wouldn't believe the size of the place. It's incredible. And I was taken completely by surprise when she invited me to spend the night at the ranch instead of at a hotel by the airport."

He had Shannon's undivided attention now. She stared intently at him, waiting for more. No, not waiting, hoping for some juicy details. Christ, she was like a little kid. "So," she blurted out, encouraging him to go on.

"So nothing. It was nearly dinnertime when we arrived so we drove straight to the ranch and had dinner with her family."

"Yeah and don't tell me you didn't make a move?"

He smiled and actually blushed. "After dinner we went for a ride out on the ranch in the moonlight. It's a good thing I know how to ride a horse or I'd have made an ass of myself. She's one hell of a natural rider. We stopped and sat along this river for a while. I don't know which river? Hell, I know nothing about Texas, except compared to Massachusetts, its one big ass state." His voice suddenly softened. "Did I tell you she's beautiful?"

Shannon smiled. "No, you didn't." Why was she impressed that he just now mentioned her beauty? Usually it was the first thing Mitch remarked on. That alone spoke volumes about his true feelings.

"She is. She has the most gorgeous, long, deep auburn hair. It's so thick and soft I could lose my fingers in it for days. She has the cutest mouth and the most perfect nose splattered with freckles. Her green eyes are as deep as the deepest part of the Atlantic." He paused and chuckled. "Listen to me. I sound like some lovesick teenager. She's the tiniest thing. Barely hits the top of my shoulders. Sitting with her on the banks of the river with the moonlight streaming down on us was the perfect setting. I wanted her so badly, I ached."

Mitch groaned out and Shannon saw him blush. "I can't believe I'm telling you all this."

Shannon tried not to feel offended. "Why not?"

"Because guys don't talk about this shit. Well, what I mean is we talk about sex and women with other guys. We joke around and embellish stories. But we rarely discuss feelings. And I've never had a lover or girlfriend that I discussed my innermost feelings with. It's something I've never felt comfortable doing."

Shannon felt sorry for her brother for never having had that type of relationship with a woman before.

"Mitch, John and I used to discuss our feelings all the time. Cole has told me things I never believed he would. Someday you'll meet someone you want to share everything with, and you will share because it will seem like the most natural thing to do, like breathing air. When you meet a woman who makes you feel that way, never let her go. Hang on to her." She looked at her brother, her brows raised in silent question. "Could this Texas beauty be her?"

Mitch laughed. "Her name is Lynn Montgomery." His

face took on a dreamy, faraway look for a moment then he shook if off. "Yeah, she could."

"So tell me, did you kiss her?"

He smiled and his eyes sparkled. "Oh yeah, and then some." He shook his head and snorted. "I can't believe we made love on the banks of the river." He paused to intake his breath. "She was like molten lava in my hands—all hot, wet and fluid. She burned me with her touch. We were on fire. It was insane. Afterward, she seemed embarrassed, and I stumbled around apologizing.

"It was awkward as hell. I don't know if she felt as moved by our lovemaking as I did or was she appalled by it. Jesus, I hope to God it's the first one and not the latter. Anyway, she wasn't up the next morning when I left. I think she was avoiding me."

Shannon's heart went out to her brother for the agony she heard in his voice and the pain she saw in his face. And she prayed Lynn was just surprised by the intensity of their sexual relationship and only needed time to adjust.

"When will she be back?"

Mitch looked at his watch and groaned. "Shit, it's midnight. I have to go. I fly out in the morning to pick her up and fly back the following day." He scrubbed his face and sighed. "I'm afraid to see her. Wish me luck."

Shannon hugged her brother close, feeling the pounding of his excited heart against her chest. "Luck."

She locked up after him, and not wanting to face her empty bed, grabbed a fleece blanket and crashed on the couch. Staring blindly into the fire, she contemplated her life. Why was it so complicated? Cole loved her. She loved him. So why weren't they together?

Her brother Mitch loved a woman named Lynn. Did Lynn have secret feelings for him? Shannon sure as hell hoped so. She'd never seen him like he was tonight. Vulnerable, anxious and nervous, not to mention his eyes positively glowed with love. She just hoped his heart didn't get stomped on because there was no pain, and she meant *no pain*, in the world that compared to the piercing pain from a shattered heart. And Shannon should know.

She pulled the covers up under her chin and felt her body relax. Soon her mind emptied of all thoughts as she drifted off. The sound of the waves crashing on the beach and the hiss from the fireplace became her world. And slowly, ever so slowly, her heart beat soft and steady, her eyelids too heavy to keep open, and she floated into sleep.

Her dreams plagued her with crazy images, images of Cole, John and Cameron swirling around in the air over her head. They were like ghosts flying, yelling and fighting all around her. She couldn't understand what they were saying, but she didn't need to hear, she knew. They were fighting about her. She awoke with a start, drenched in sweat even with the nighttime chill hanging in the air.

She stared out the windows and watched the stars twinkling in the dark sky as her heart settled down to a reasonable beat. The clock glowed three-twelve in the morning, and suddenly she was wide awake and wondering what Cole was doing?

Something flickered directly outside her house and the silhouette of someone moved. Shannon dropped to the floor, her heart exploded, and she gasped for air. She hated that man in Chicago for making her afraid of her own shadow. It could be anything or anyone out there. It didn't mean the man was here to kill her. Hadn't Cole said he would only kill her if it could be pinned on him? Inhaling deeply, she held her breath and rose up to her knees to peer out. She dropped back down, wrapped her arms around herself and groaned.

"Shit, shit, shit." She looked around for her phone and spotted it across the room. She crawled across the floor and cradled her cell phone to her chest for a moment then called 911.

"I'm sorry, Ma'am," one of the uniform officers said. "There's no sign of anyone outside, although there are plenty of footprints. But to be honest, they could belong to anyone. Do you have reason to believe someone is out to harm you?"

Good question. What did she say? She panicked and said, "No."

"To help ease your mind, we'll beef up patrol in the area for tonight. Don't hesitate to call us again if you feel threatened."

For the rest of the night Shannon sat on the floor trembling, trying to convince herself she'd imagined the whole thing. The light could have been anything, and the shadow the play of the moon's rays. She'd hit the ground so fast, she wondered if she'd gotten a good enough look. And she admitted to herself she hadn't. But she knew what she saw, and it brought back memories of Chicago. She would be much more aware of her surroundings from now on.

In the morning, Shannon lazily walked the beach and sat on the jetties. She even skimmed rocks into the water, anything to occupy her time. Occupy her mind. This time next week, she would be out on the West Coast, traveling from Washington State to Southern California, then off to Las Vegas. She would be gone two weeks and had been looking forward to it. But now she didn't know if she had the strength or energy she needed to sustain such a hectic schedule. After the events of last night it would be good to get away. Would a crazy murderer really follow her across the country? Probably not.

The other thing she had to look forward to was she would be away from John. She could contact Cole and hopefully...hopefully what? Hell, she didn't know. She knew if she told him about last night, he'd come running. So okay, she would make the call and hire a bodyguard. If nothing else, it would put her mind at ease. Being jumpy and anxious as hell was detrimental to her health.

After acknowledging several joggers on the beach, she went back to her house just as the mail arrived, and the thought of making the phone call vanished. Shannon stood frozen in fear as her heart pounded against her chest, threatening to break through. The court transcript had arrived, and she suddenly felt terrified to read it. What if there were things in it that shocked her and changed her mind about Cole's innocence? She truly believed he was innocent, but should she risk opening Pandora's Box? Feeding that one little percentage of her brain constantly nagging maybe, just maybe he did it? You bet, and she tore it open immediately.

After brewing a fresh pot of coffee, she spent hours reading through everything. And it was not the most pleasant of reads. She spent hours switching from anger, to pain, then back to anger. She had read court transcripts before, but these shocked her to the core. They were a joke. The judicial system railroaded him. They had nothing on him, circumstantial evidence at best, which was probably why the judge had been lenient on his prison sentence.

Cole had never taken the stand in his own defense. Probably a mistake, she mused, but it was too late. They would never know one way or another. Her heart bled for him all over again. Imagine being twenty-three and alone. His wife was murdered by someone else, and he was blamed, tried, and convicted. My God, the despair he must have felt when they'd read the verdict and led him away to a maximum security prison. Actually, she knew how he had felt as he'd told her, but she could understand more now after reading this. And hell, she had watched most of the trial on television, but reading it now pained her to her core. She was emotionally involved now, and she hadn't been then because she hadn't known him then, hadn't loved him then.

From what he had told her, surviving prison hadn't been easy. But the main thing was he had survived. And he was thriving again and doing what he was born to do, making incredible music.

Shannon picked up the phone to call him. Her hands shook so badly she replaced the receiver. What could she possibly say? Sorry for the way he had been treated. Sorry he spent fifteen years of terrible loneliness, anguish and torture for a crime he didn't commit? What she wanted to say was she loved him and she needed him. In the end she didn't call. She took out a notebook, put on a warm jacket and went down to the beach. Pen in hand, she began making an outline of the case including a list of suspects and motives. Depending on how many guys Lindsey had slept with, there could be many suspects with many motives. When she completed her list, she felt the familiar tug of her creative juices flowing. She had never written a nonfiction book, but Cole's story was begging to be written, and she started making notes of everything she knew and everything he'd told her.

Someday, with his permission, she would like to tell the world his story. Let them meet and get to know who the real man, Cole Jackson, had been and was today. She became lost in her writing, writing page after page, her hand flying at top speed, out of control and barely keeping up with the words exiting her brain. She reveled in the wonder and exhilaration at finally having so many words to put down on paper.

If it hadn't been for darkness descending all around her, she would have continued. When she stepped inside her house, it hit her how tired and chilled to bone she was. After turning up the fireplace, she lay down on the couch under a fleece throw and contemplated the fact she never called for a bodyguard—first thing on her *to do list* tomorrow. Exhaustion overtook her, and she slept soundly until morning. She never heard John's frantic message left on her answering machine or the one from Cameron. She never saw the man watching her sleep from her back deck.

Chapter Twelve

SHANNON AWOKE THE NEXT MORNING STIFF AND SORE FROM sleeping on the couch, but all that aside, she felt rested and ready to charge forward on a new day. She planned to do more work on Cole's case and the book she hoped to write someday with his blessing. She sat down with her first cup of coffee to read over her writings from yesterday when the doorbell rang. Who could be here on a weekday? Wasn't everyone she knew working? She combed her fingers through her mussed hair and opened the door to the last person she expected to see there. John. Before she slammed the heavy wooden door in his face, he stuck his foot out and stepped inside uninvited and unwanted. It was then she noticed the worried lines around his mouth and forehead. The dark circles surrounding his eyes casting deep shadows. The anger and hurt from last week melted, and she reached out with her suddenly trembling hand to touch his arm. "John, what's wrong?"

He folded Shannon into his arms and cried out, "Cameron's gone. He ran away."

Shannon choked back a sob, her knees buckled,

refusing to carry her weight. Fortunately for her, John supported her and carried her up the stairs to the couch. She clung to him and cried as he told her what he knew, which didn't amount to a whole hell of a lot.

Cameron sat curled up in the last seat of the bus, hugging his coat close to himself as he tried to sleep. The bus was nearly empty, cold and smelled like exhaust fumes, but he didn't care. It represented his ride to freedom. He was still too upset at the turn of events of the past twenty-four hours to sleep. His brain buzzed along running a marathon, but his body had been left behind at the starting line. So what if his father caught him getting high in his room, no big deal? But to Lieutenant McKenzie it was a big deal. His Dad, *Saint John*, like he never got high when he was his age? *Please*. What did he take him for, an idiot? But that was just the beginning. He tore through his room spilling drawers, emptying the closet until he found his stash.

Okay, so he had some pot, a pipe and some pills in his closet. It wasn't like he would turn into a drug addict or anything. His father had gone on and on about how he was turning into a derelict and going down the road to Nowhereville. That had stung. Cameron couldn't ever remember his dad speaking to him so hurtfully before. He had taken his best and favorite guitar and smashed it against his bedpost over and over until it splintered into a thousand pieces. Then Cameron saw the look on his face and was afraid of his father for the first time in his life. He thought for sure he would hit him. His father's eyes were black and glazed over, his face beet red, and Cameron could see the muscles tensed up in his neck and his veins bulging in his forehead. His hands were fisted tightly at his side and Cameron could tell he struggled for control. Cameron wiped the tears pooling in his eyes as he remembered it.

The only other time he had ever seen his father so upset was during the fight with Cole. He'd never been like that with him before, and he'd never said such hurtful things to him before either, not to mention the fact he ruined his favorite guitar. And that was the problem. His dad didn't understand him.

Couldn't understand him.

Didn't want to understand him.

He shouted at him, asking why he couldn't be like most sixteen-year-olds, thinking about sports, working a job or planning for college. Why did he just sit in his room writing music and lyrics and playing his guitar? And oh, don't forget about getting high. His father told him he was throwing his life away. Well, guess what Dad? It was his fucking life to throw away if he wanted to and his father be dammed.

That night he packed his backpack and his old guitar and waited until dawn to sneak out the door. He'd left a note for his father and a message on his mom's answering machine. He crashed in the woods near the bank, waiting for it to open. He withdrew everything he had. It was quite a bit, he had eighteen hundred dollars, and it would get him far across the country until he decided what to do from there.

After hitchhiking his way to the Braintree T-station, he took the subway to the bus depot and bought a one-way ticket cross-country to Los Angeles. He figured he'd look Cole up when he got there, and maybe he could live with him for a while. He knew his mom would be really sad.

First she lost Cole, then him, but this was something he had to do.

All this thinking caused his chest to ache, but at least it took his mind off his rumbling stomach. He couldn't remember the last time he'd eaten, and he hoped the bus stopped at a rest area soon.

Cole entered the hotel room at midnight after another sold-out show in Philadelphia. Pittsburgh had also been a sellout, and he still tingled numb over it all. Tomorrow he flew to California for a parole check, then off to Chicago. He tried not to remember the last time he visited Chicago. The ache in his heart was excruciating. He tried not to think about the deranged killer's attempt on Shannon's life but the good things they shared. Shannon, God, how he missed her, missed being with her, missed her laugh, missed her smile and everything else about her. He had spent the last half an hour in the bar downstairs staring at a glass of Jack Daniels while he sipped a soda water with lime.

It had been tempting. Oh, so tempting. He didn't know what he was trying to prove to himself. That he had restraint and self-control? Or was he trying to slide into self-destruction mode and ruin his life all over again? He finally got up and left disgusted at himself for his self-pity. Enough was enough. He had to stop. So what if he had been dealt more raw deals than most people? *Get over it.*

He dreamed during the night of the early days with the band, before Lindsey's affairs, before his self-destruction tendencies. Those had been the days of his innocence and youth. Those were the days of loving Lindsey, his music, AJ, Ted and Brad.

Why and when had things gone so terribly wrong?

AJ awoke to his heart pounding like a runaway freight train heading for derailment. He fought with all his might to breathe in through his nose and out through his mouth, hoping to calm his heart rate and bring it under control. After he succeeded, he sat up in bed, turned on the bedside lamp and tried to remember what he dreamed about.

Lindsey. He'd dreamed about Lindsey. But there'd been more. Flashes and bits and pieces of the past. Some of it coincided with his memory, but some of it was strange and foreign to his mind. There was yelling and fighting between him and Lindsey which was odd as he never remembered fighting with her.

Aside from the dream, the most bizarre thing of all was the cryptic message he'd received that morning. Someone accused him of killing Lindsey. The no-name person claimed he was hiding in the Jackson suite at the time and saw him, yes him, stab Lindsey. AJ's whole body shivered in dread. *"Could it be true?"* And why after reading the note, which had an unusual odor, did he feel lightheaded and strange?

"Where could he have gone?" Shannon asked as she paced the floor of her living room for the hundredth time since learning of Cameron's running away. Nobody answered her, which she'd expected, because nobody knew the answer.

Her body twitched and her heart raced from all the caffeine she'd drunk and poisoned her body with. She paused and looked out the windows. Mother Nature was in a rare mood. The clouds hung low, dark and menacing. It would only be a matter of time before the rain pelted them in wind-driven sheets. Gusts howled, and the waves were a surfer's dream come true. The ocean looked like one large endless white cap after another.

The weather could not have depicted Shannon's mood any better. As she turned her back on the windows and surveyed the gloomy faces of her family, she wondered what the hell she was doing here. She should be out looking for her son. It had been two days, and they had heard not a single word from him.

When she craved his voice, she listened to his message on her machine. "Mom, I'm sorry but I can't take Dad anymore. Don't worry about me. I love you." She had sat in the dark the first night she'd found out he'd run away and listened to the recording over and over, at least fifty times. She finally had to stop as her grasp on sanity hung tenaciously by a thread. If she hadn't stopped, she would have lost it and who knew if she would have come out of it.

Shannon had not seen nor spoken to John in two days. Every time she called, Cheryl told her he was locked in Cameron's bedroom. He wouldn't come out, nor let anyone in. *Jesus John, a fine time to fall apart.*

So, to take matters into her own hands, she called anyone Cameron was even remotely friendly with, and unfortunately no one had seen or heard from him. She called the bank and knew he had cleaned out his account. Shannon had felt a small, short-lived relief knowing he at least had money on him. The next thing she did was call her private detective friend, Scott Danvers and hired him to find Cameron. And so far she had heard nothing from him. They couldn't trace his phone because he'd left his cell at home.

Her brother Mitch arrived with takeout, jarring her out of her thoughts. She'd not had time to speak to him in private about the vice-president lady he was in love with to find out what happened when he went to her home in Texas to fly her back to Boston. Shannon hoped he had something good and juicy to tell her because she needed a break from the constant state of worry and doom her life had become. She knew at some point she needed to confide in her family about the incident in Chicago, but they had enough to worry about with Cameron without adding that to the mix. So once again, she put the danger to herself into the recesses of her mind to be visited later.

Ever since John told her about Cameron, she felt as though something physically squeezed her lungs, choking off her air supply. Add to that the walls were moving in, and she had to constantly stand on her porch gulping air as her pulse raced and her head spun. It was not a pleasant feeling, and she didn't see things changing anytime in the foreseeable future, unless she heard from Cameron.

She loved her family dearly, but their hushed voices and their eyes constantly following her everywhere, expecting her to break down any minute, was not helping her anxiety attacks any.

"Shannon, honey," said her mom in her placating tone. "Come eat while the food's hot."

She walked over to the table, sat down and stared at the food on her plate. Eggplant Parmesan, pasta and garlic bread sticks, her favorite food from her favorite Italian restaurant. If only she could stomach it. Even sitting here smelling the food was too much for her tonight. She went for the wine her brother poured for her instead and downed every last drop. Perhaps if she got good and drunk, she'd pass out.

Glancing around the table, she realized this picture was not your typical Gallagher gathering. No talking, no laughing, no jokes, and no wild storytelling. The only other time

Shannon remembered such a somber dinner happened the day she told her parents she was pregnant. And oh God, what an awful day that had been as her mother cried all day and her father couldn't look her in the eye as though he were ashamed of her. Ashamed of what she had done with John. She could read her father's thoughts—How could his little girl have sex?

All she had to say was thank God they'd liked John. It had made it a little easier for them to handle the fact their oldest daughter was pregnant and getting married at seventeen. And now here they were some seventeen years later. Her mother trying hard not to cry and her father once again having a hard time meeting her in the eye, but she knew it was because he felt helpless to solve the crisis. Bridget and Rachel were quiet, not like themselves at all. And not once had Bridget made a comment about Cole. *Thank you, God.*

Now—Mitch—God love him, sat in his seat and tried his hardest to act normal, but he couldn't do it alone. He had taken several days off from work and had moved into her guest bedroom while her parents were sleeping at Bridget's house in her extra bedroom.

She appreciated her family wanting to be close to her, but at this very moment she needed space, she needed air. She heard herself mumble something unintelligible, and then she left the table, grabbed her jacket and ran down to the beach. The rain had finally begun, and in no time her hair stuck plastered to her head and she couldn't tell whether it was her tears or the rain blocking her vision as she stumbled down toward her favorite jetties. Or what was left of them because the tide had risen so much higher than normal thanks to the storm.

Shannon stood shivering on the rocks, battling the wind and trying to keep her footing on the slippery surface while the spray from the ocean beat against her face. The wind whipped her body from every direction, the waves crashed and churned out in the ocean while the rain flew sideways, pelting her from every conceivable angle.

Everything happening around her was also happening inside her body. Never had her insides hurt so badly.

Before she knew it, she threw her arms out, lifting her face up to the sky and screamed, "Cameron, where are you?" Her screams were swallowed up by storm sounds surrounding her and her heart bottomed out. How would he ever hear her?

"John, you can't stay in there forever," his wife said through the closed bedroom door. He could hear the concern laced in her voice, making him feel worse.

"I'm coming in."

Cheryl opened the door slowly. At least she respected him and didn't turn on the light, taking away the darkness. He needed the darkness, and he belonged in the dark for what he'd done to his son.

"I brought you something to eat." She placed the tray on the night table then sat down on Cameron's bed and peered intently at him through the dark.

John sat on the floor, his back up against the wall, his legs out straight, and he held a picture of his son in his quivering hands. His eyes burned dry as he'd already shed all the tears humanly possible for one day. His heart hurt and seemed to hardly beat as he felt scarcely alive. Nothing anyone had ever told him could have prepared him for the emotions churning inside him. Since Cameron ran away, a dark abyss swirled all around him, engulfing him within its obscurity. The bottomless pit built on guilt, anguish and pure, stark terror.

Cameron was a smart, streetwise kid, but there were always decisions to be made, and it would only take him making one wrong one to cost him his life.

He'd sat for two days in the dark gloom, torturing himself with:

What if I'd done this?

What if I'd said that?

It was not helping the situation, but shit, he just couldn't move. He kept remembering Shannon's face when he told her and her collapsing and sobbing in his arms. And for the first time, she hit him and lashed out at him. Oh, he knew it was because of the anguish and heartbreak she felt, but she'd frightened him with the wild and unfocussed look in her eyes.

She had said things to him he would likely never forget, wanted to forget, but probably wouldn't nonetheless because it all rang true. He was a control freak and a self-centered bastard. And he didn't understand Cameron's need for music.

It was the same with her writing. Shannon always told him it wasn't *what* she did. It was *who* she was. It wasn't as if she'd chosen to be a writer, it had chosen her with the endless stories running rampant in her brain and needing to be told. It had gotten to where she couldn't ignore them anymore. He came to understand her need for writing, so why couldn't he understand Cameron's need for music and songwriting?

Probably because he was terrified he would end up like —all right—like Cole Jackson. Someone so smart and talented that they threw it all away for the lure of drugs, alcohol, fame and sex. How many great ones had self-destructed to the point of death? Great ones like Jim

Morrison, Jimi Hendrix, Janice Joplin and Kurt Cobain. He realized it was a different time and era, but that didn't matter. It was what he remembered. Now if he took in the whole picture, there were a tremendous amount of highly talented musicians who led fairly normal lives. So why did he always remember the tragedies instead of the success stories?

A pessimist, never an optimist that was him. Yeah, he was one of those people who saw the half-empty glass. Shannon, and Cheryl for the matter, saw the glass half full. So why couldn't he learn from them?

Glancing at his beautiful, pregnant wife, he actually felt his heart pick up a beat. *So he wasn't dead after all?* A damn good thing considering he had four children and another on the way. If only he didn't feel eighty-years-old instead of thirty-four.

He finally resigned himself to getting up and out of the room, but as he stood he grabbed for the wall to steady himself. Having no food for almost twenty-four hours was not necessarily a wise decision. His body ached as he walked toward Cheryl with a numb butt and legs. Sitting down he held out his arms to her and thank God, she melted into them, laid her head on his chest, and as always, had the patience to stay and give to him her understanding, her love and the comfort of her body.

Burying his face in her hair he breathed in the scent of her shampoo, freesia, her favorite. And since John didn't care what he smelled like, he used her shampoo. Maybe he did it on purpose so when they were apart, his own scented hair reminded him of her.

John would never forget the first time he set eyes on her. He'd been on routine patrol and had come across a beat-up old Mustang with a flat tire and a young blonde cursing up a blue streak and kicking the tire out of frustration. It was obvious immediately to John that she was having some trouble changing the tire herself.

Now, it was one of those ninety degrees, hot and humid summer days when the last thing he wanted to do was get out of his air-conditioned cruiser. One step out of the car and he knew what waited for him. Instant suffocation would come. The weather reports had said the air quality was poor and would make even the healthiest of people gasp for a decent breath of cool, dry air. And the weather reports were right. The air sucked.

But he climbed out of his cruiser and went to do his civic duty. He fully intended to ask if he could call a service truck for help. But one look at her pretty face, red from the heat, her tank top clinging to her small firm breasts, her barely there jean shorts, frayed at the bottom, showing off incredible legs and pink flip-flops bringing out the pink polish of her toenails, and he'd lost all capability to breathe or speak.

He'd grabbed the tire iron, changed her flat and replaced it with her spare without so much as saying a word. Cheryl had gone on and on, but John did not understand what she said, all he could think about was sex and what a great time to be thinking about sex. What was he, some kind of pervert? He'd come to the aid of a stranger and could think of nothing but doing it with her.

After completing the tire change, they went their separate ways. However, two days later, while sitting at his desk, working on his never-ending paperwork pile, he glanced up to the sound of a woman's voice, a voice that sounded vaguely familiar, and he stared into the prettiest amber eyes he'd ever seen. The voice and the amber eyes belonged to the pretty blonde whose flat tire he had changed.

Today she wore a sleeveless, short sundress and instantly his stomach tightened and his blood pumped in a southerly direction. Damn, she made him think of sex. *Christ John, think of something else and quick before you have to stand up and shake her hand,* her small hands full of something wrapped in tinfoil.

"May I help you?" he said in his calm, patrolman's voice, though he felt anything but calm.

"Yes, I...my name is Cheryl Bradford, and I wanted to stop by and thank you for changing my tire the other day." She paused, held out her hands and blushed. "I brought you something I baked."

John took the foil-wrapped package from her, his fingers lightly brushing her soft delicate ones. "Thank you. What is it?"

She smiled, bringing John's attention to her full, pink and kissable lips, and he again thought of sex. *Oh Boy! He was in trouble.*

"It's blueberry bread. I made it for you and picked the berries myself." She paused and suddenly looked uncertain. "I hope you're not allergic to berries?"

John barely comprehended what she said as his focus centered solely on her mouth and what pleasure it could bring him.

"Are you allergic?"

John coughed and averted his eyes from her lips to the bread he carried. "Um, no and thank you. I love blueberry bread."

She shifted on her feet, suddenly seeming at a loss for words. "Well, I better be going. I don't want to keep you from your work."

Think John? And think fast. Don't let this incredible woman slip away because if you do, you may never see her again.

"I was just leaving. I'll escort you to your car," he lied.

He wasn't going anywhere until his paperwork pile disappeared.

There was a moment or two of awkward silence when they reached her Mustang. And to John's surprise, she reached inside her car and handed him a business card. "Bradford's Bakery." He stared at the card, bewildered. Was there a business purpose to this? Or could he hope it was personal and he hadn't misinterpreted the silent interested looks she'd thrown his way—still throwing his way now.

"You're a baker?" How stupid of him, of course she was, the card said so.

Her laughter was light and nervous. "Yes, but it's not why I gave it to you."

John raised his brows in silent hope. "It's not?"

She blushed, and it made her look about sixteen, not that she was probably much older than twenty, anyway. Hell, he'd only just turned twenty-five himself.

"No," she replied and vanished inside her car. He continued standing there staring at her car like an idiot as she exited the parking lot. Why hadn't he asked her out? She all but told him she was interested. He knew why though. He was out of practice. Way out of practice.

John spent the rest of the day struggling with his feelings. He had been divorced from Shannon for two years. There should be no guilt in wanting to date another woman. Just because he hadn't yet didn't mean he couldn't —or wouldn't.

However, until this point, he'd yet to meet a woman who interested him. Someone who intrigued him to the point he wanted to pursue her. A woman who attracted him physically sent his libido into overdrive and made him realize how long it had been. Made him yearn for the intimacy two people shared. Shit! Cheryl did it all. Made him want all and believe he could have all.

He had tried his hardest with Shannon. He had loved her beyond reason at seventeen. Had done right by her and married her when she became pregnant. He loved his son, but unfortunately, their marriage never progressed forward. They'd been too young, but nothing, and he meant nothing, would ever make him regret what happened. He had a beautiful seven-year-old son and an ex-wife he still loved as a friend. Yet, there was something missing, the emotional and physical attachment with another human being.

His fingers absentmindedly toyed with the card. Maybe it was time to move forward in his life. That evening he called her because if he didn't do it then, he would lose his nerve, never call and always wonder what if? And what ifs were never good.

They met the following night for dinner and eight months later—they married. That had happened nine years ago, and she still made him ache for her constantly. His body, heart and soul needed her, loved her.

"I'm sorry I shut you out."

"John..."

"No, let me finish." He looked at her, and she was still as pretty as ever. The years had been kind to her. She still looked twenty-three, the age she had been when they met.

"I don't know what I would do without you in my life. You are everything to me." His trembling hand slid gently over her belly. "Our children are my life. And I know you love Cameron, even though he's not biologically your son, and you're hurting and frightened for him." John sniffed and wiped the tears from his eyes.

"I shouldn't have shut you out, but I had to be alone. To think...hell," he snorted, "I wanted to sink into the dark underground of blame and shame knowing he ran away because of me."

"Oh honey," Cheryl said as she placed her soft, warm hand on his cheek.

"I'm okay now. I'm ready to go downstairs, join the world and fight for Cameron." He squeezed Cheryl as tight as her expanding belly allowed. "Fight for all our children. I'll never let you down again. Or shut you out. I promise."

After John spent the day with his wife and three small children, he drove to Shannon's house, ready to face the consequences for everything that happened. He was ready to face Shannon and apologize for his behavior of late. But before he left, his son, Matt needed to go number two, and for some reason he always wanted his dad to wipe him. Matt said Mom was a girl and boys went to the bathroom with boys.

As John stood outside the bathroom waiting for the words, "I'm done," from his son, he leaned against the wall and closed his eyes for a moment. Damn, he was asleep on his feet. The first stop, once he left his house, would be Dunkin Donuts for a large black hazelnut coffee.

John stood, and stood, and stood, waiting for Matt who could take ten minutes or longer to go. Today, however, John had neither the patience nor the time and he barged through the door. His feet froze in place as he looked at his son. John didn't know whether to laugh or whether to yell at him.

There was his son sitting on the toilet seat, his pants down around his ankles, oblivious to John's presence as he plunged his face with the red rubber toilet plunger.

"Matt," John yelled, struggling to stay in control.

Matt dropped the plunger and John swallowed a laugh.

A bright red circle outlined his son's face from where the plunger had sucked on it for quite some time.

John fought disgust and laughter at the same time. It had to be the most disgusting thing John could think of to put on your face. Christ, didn't Matt know what they used it for? After John scrubbed his face three times with anti-bacterial soap, he left his noisy house and was now alone in his car driving down Route 139 toward Brant Rock, laughing his ass off so hard his eyes watered. Matt was a nut. What the hell would possess someone to plunge his face?

God, it was disgusting when you thought about where the plunger had been. But putting all grown up thoughts aside, to an almost three-year-old, it probably looked like a fun way to kill time while he waited for his shit to come out. Well, no more toilet plungers inside the bathroom. Matt needed toys to play with to occupy his toilet time, or a book. Yeah, a book would be good. Anything would be better than a plunger. What a story to tell Matt when he grew older, and they both could have a good laugh. John could also bribe him, but good, with threats of divulging the details to his friends, or worse, a girlfriend. John laughed again, wondering if Matt would ever remember doing it.

A short time later he pulled up to Shannon's house, turned off his ignition and counted the cars in her driveway. Shit! The whole Gallagher family appeared present and accounted for. Just what he needed, the ex-in-laws giving him the evil eye and judging him.

The Gallaghers wove a tight group. One he had been part of once. He'd had no complaints about his in-laws, they were great. They had always been good to him, but because of his own insecurities about knocking up their teenage daughter, he'd never felt comfortable around them.

He knew he probably read things into it that didn't exist. He also knew there would be no evil eyes or accusations, but he just couldn't help feeling like he deserved them.

His heart hammered around inside his chest as he waited for his knock to be answered. It was finally by Mitch, who immediately let him in and shook his hand.

"Where's Shannon?" John asked nervously as he listened for voices.

"Asleep in her room. She hasn't slept in days, and it finally caught up with her."

"Is everyone here?" *As if he needed to ask.*

"Yeah," answered a solemn Mitch.

Chapter Thirteen

SHANNON WASN'T ASLEEP, ALTHOUGH HER EYES WERE closed and her body relaxed from sheer exhaustion. The ache in her heart kept her awake. Many scenarios kept playing in her head and they were all bad. There were times she damned her creative mind because the things she conjured up were far-fetched and not realistic.

While she continued driving herself crazy with her imagination, she welcomed the interruption of the phone ringing. It was her detective friend, Scott, she'd hired to find Cameron, and he had a lead. Someone with Cameron's description had bought a bus ticket, but the older gentleman who sold him the ticket couldn't remember if he bought a ticket to California or Chicago. Scott would dig deeper and he told her not to lose hope. He would find him.

Before he hung up, she confided in him about her incident in Chicago and asked if he would please look into that and Cole's case as soon as they found Cameron? He agreed, although it didn't make her feel any less burdened right now.

Unfortunately, Shannon knew it wasn't easy to find runaways if they didn't want to be found. So she prayed Cameron would want to be found once he had time to calm down and think sensibly. Being on your own at sixteen was not only lonely, it was scary. And thank God he'd taken his guitar. He would be all the easier to trace because of it.

When she heard John's voice inside her house, she tensed and then realized how hard this must be for him as well. And she tried her hardest not to blame him or resent him because of the circumstances. Deep down in the bottom of her heart, she knew John would never intentionally cause harm to their son.

The past two days she'd fought an overwhelming urge to call Cole. She needed to hear his voice and let the sound of it engulf her and soothe her, but instead she played his music and thought of him. She must have dozed off because the rain stopped, the wind no longer howled and she could make out moonbeams shining through the breaks in the clouds. The BlackJack CD had also ended. All was quiet, too quiet, and it pricked her nerves how silent her house appeared to be.

Had everyone left?

Did they all fall asleep?

Shannon dressed and descended the stairs to find Mitch and John, sitting side by side on the couch watching television. Darkness had swallowed the house except for the glow from the fireplace and the light from the television.

"Hi. Did everyone leave?"

Mitch and John looked at her both looking weary as hell and showing every bit of their ages. It was amazing what stress and worry could do to people. And she could only imagine how badly she looked right about now.

It was Mitch who finally answered her.

"Yeah, they left." Mitch went to get up. "Can I get you anything?"

"Sit. I'm perfectly capable of taking care of myself." She poured a glass of juice and curled up in the oversized chair with a blanket, then looked speculatively at John. "Shouldn't you be home?"

John looked at her and shrugged his large shoulders. "Yeah, but if you don't mind me crashing in Cameron's room, I'd appreciate it."

"Cheryl won't mind?"

"She'd rather I stay here than crack up the car."

John unfolded himself off the couch and walked to the patio doors, his head and shoulders hunched down. "What are we going to do?"

The way John said it grated on Shannon's nerves, and all the pain and heartache he had caused her lately bubbled up to the surface. She didn't even try to hold it down. She let loose.

"We? What do you mean we? You spent two days locked in a bedroom sulking like a baby because your son hates you so much he ran away."

By this point both John and Mitch stared at her, their mouths open in shock, their eyes wide in disbelief.

Shannon now sat, perched on the edge of the chair, her back ramrod straight, and her eyes nearly black with anger. "I'm trying to feel sorry for you, John. But I'm having a difficult time with it considering the circumstances leading up to this. When you barged in here that day, did you ever take in anyone's feelings but your own?" She jumped up to her feet. She rarely lost her temper, and it felt good to lash out at John, even though, in the back of her mind she knew she would regret it later and owe him an apology. But for now, she'd let him have it.

"Did you ever think for one second your son might care for Cole, and that you were hurting him and not just me and Cole?"

"Shannon I..." John tried interrupting, suddenly looking pale and uncomfortable.

"Let me finish." Her eyes darted from John to her brother who also looked uncomfortable. "If you're worried I'll embarrass you in front of Mitch, don't be. I already told him everything."

John groaned, looking even worse if that were possible.

"Cameron saw me happy with Cole and he was glad for me. He could see what most people like you can't, he saw another human being. Cameron saw a person with flaws like everybody else, but a man with strong convictions and strong morals. Cole has a genuine kindness to him, and he shares it with anyone willing to give him the time of day. He's also highly talented, intelligent, shy and embarrassed about his past. Embarrassed about the truth and the untruth, he has one hell of a conscience."

Shannon caught her breath. Her heart pounded ferociously and her whole body trembled. "Did you know his wife cheated on him for years, and he never once broke his marriage vows?"

John and Mitch both continued to stare at her, words lost to both of them as they let her vent.

"That's why he drank. It humiliated him. But you know what? He has more love and compassion and goodness in his heart than anyone I know. I also know we're not here to discuss him, but I wanted you to understand how much he means to Cameron—" She stopped and her hand flew to her mouth as she struggled to keep the sob from escaping. "How much he means to me." Her eyes suddenly flared. "And how could you break your son's favorite guitar? I gave it to him for his thirteenth birthday. You had no right—"

She collapsed on the chair, buried her face in her hands and cried. Mitch approached her, but John waved him off. This was his doing, his fault and his problem. He hunkered down in front of her and swallowed his pride. He'd been a jerk and he shouldn't have interfered, but he had been frightened. Frightened of losing Shannon and losing his son to a man who could open doors and give him the world, the world of his dreams, and the world of music. Something he could never do and it burned inside him, eating away at him, and he wasn't proud of it. He wasn't proud of his thoughts of jealousy and hatred toward another human being.

Yes, damn it, he was jealous, and he behaved spitefully and no one would ever know how sorry he was for it. He'd made a huge mess of everything and because of what? His male ego and pride felt bruised. He would have to share Shannon and Cameron with another man. He had behaved selfishly and childishly and it was time to correct it. He took a deep cleansing breath and forged on.

"Shannon. I'm sorry. Sorry for everything."

She lifted her face and wiped her runny nose with her sweatshirt sleeve, and it nearly made John smile. He took her hands in his and looked her in the eyes, her stunning blue eyes, filled with teardrops waiting their turn to fall down her beautiful face. How could he have intentionally hurt her? His heart split in two for her, for him and for their son.

"You're right. I was an asshole. Not fit to wipe the dirt from the soles of your boots. I regret everything. I was jealous, afraid and...hell...just really stupid," he groaned. "It's your life. I shouldn't have interfered." He cleared his throat. "Now, can I repeat my question from earlier without you jumping down my throat?"

That brought the tiniest smile to her lips. "Sure."

John let go of her hands and sat back on his heels. "What are we going to do?"

———

Shannon closed her eyes for a moment to bury the problems of the past several weeks with John. And when she opened them up she once again thought of him as her best friend since their days in school.

"I hired Scott Danvers. He's a private detective I've worked with in the past. He's tracking down Cameron as we speak." She told John and Mitch what she learned earlier in the evening from Scott. "I didn't make the connection until now, but Cole lives in Malibu. Cameron knows that. Do you think?"

"Maybe; it's worth a shot," John said as he stood up and stretched. "Will you call him?" he asked hopefully.

"What time is it?" she queried.

Mitch looked at his watch and replied. "It's almost midnight."

Shannon picked up the handset on the house phone and dialed Cole's cell phone number. The phone rang until his voicemail message came on, and the sound of his voice had hers nearly fainting.

"Hi. It's me, Shannon. I need to talk to you. When you get this message, I don't care what time it is, call me."

She pushed the off button and glanced at John, her body wearier than ever. She needed sleep to re-energize and think clearly. She opened her mouth to speak and had to force the words out, "What now?"

"We get some rest and call your detective friend in the morning." John kissed Shannon quickly on the forehead and bid her and Mitch goodnight.

Cole's long fingers gripped the armrest on his seat like a vise as the plane rocked from some of the worst turbulence he had ever experienced. At one point the plane had taken a sudden nosedive. It lasted probably only a few seconds, but to anyone on the plane it seemed like an eternity.

Would they crash?

Die?

Survive?

It went through his mind and he was sure it went through everyone else's on that plane bound for LAX. First class had been full, so Cole sat in coach and he could hear the screams of the children. It tore his heart out at how terrified they must be as the drinks and peanut packages flew everywhere.

He himself had just ordered a coke, and it had landed in his lap. The flight attendant, a male, probably somewhere in his late twenties, had landed in the woman's lap across the aisle from him. Now the flight attendant was safely buckled in his pull-down seat. Cole peered through first class and stared at the locked cockpit door wondering what was going on up there.

Cole was not afraid to fly, nor was he afraid to die. It was just he had unfinished business and now would not be the most convenient of all times to die. Just then the captain addressed them over the plane's intercom.

"This is Captain Gauthier, we're experiencing extreme

turbulence and for the time being no one is allowed out of their seats. Please observe the seat belt sign. I'm sorry for the recent sudden descent. I don't expect it to happen again. If anyone needs assistance, please let your flight attendant know. Please try to relax and enjoy the rest of your flight."

Enjoy. Was he kidding? There wasn't a single soul on this plane who would relax or breathe easy until they landed safely, including himself.

The turbulence didn't let up, in fact, Cole thought it might be getting worse, and he wanted to do something, anything to ease the fear plastered on the passenger's faces. He glanced up to the overhead compartment holding his guitar. If he could get it, he could play and maybe he could take some people's minds off the rattling and banging of the plane.

Cole looked toward the flight attendant. "Excuse me, do you think I could play my guitar? It might help calm some passengers."

The attendant looked confused and uncertain. "It's not something that's usually done, but under the circumstances, I don't see why not."

Cole sat in the front row on the right side of the plane. The one seat next to him was empty. He quickly unbuckled, reached over his head, unlocked the compartment and pulled down his guitar case. Once he removed his guitar, he shut the case back inside the luggage compartment.

When he buckled back up, he played. It felt awkward playing on a plane, and he wondered how many people could hear him. He played a soft, soothing ballad he had yet to record. Halfway through the song he became so engrossed in his music he never noticed how hushed the plane had become.

When he strummed the last chord, the passengers

clapped and Cole's heart dropped. He asked if anyone had a request. A young mother several rows to his left, flying with her two young children, requested a hymn.

Fortunately for Cole, his mother had been a Christian, and he'd gone to church regularly growing up. As he played, it all came back to him, including the words, and the young mother sang along with him, surprising him with her lovely voice.

Cole continued to play until the turbulence faded and the seat belt sign blinked off. He replaced his guitar and went to the bathroom at the back of the plane. They reserved the one closest to him for first-class passengers only. On his way back, many people thanked him for what he'd done and Cole's face warmed with every compliment.

The young woman, who had sung with him, hugged him, and he found out she sang with a famous choir. She introduced herself as Katie Devers, and she didn't bat an eyelash when he introduced himself as Cole Jackson.

"It's a pleasure to meet you, Mr. Jackson. I love your music. Thank you. My children were truly frightened and your playing helped calm them immensely."

Cole smiled at her. "I think it was their mother's voice doing the calming. You have the voice of an angel. If you ever care to work with me, please call me."

She seemed embarrassed and surprised by his offer.

"Thank you. God bless you for what you did for everyone on this plane."

He shrugged his shoulders because to him it was no big deal. He did what he could do to help. Anyone else would have done the same in his place.

Later that evening, Cole sat on his back deck while the sun set over the water. Every shade of yellow, orange and red imaginable radiated in the sky, not to mention the pinks mixed in as well. No wonder people lived at the ocean. The serenity of it was incredible.

After he downed his soda, he strolled back inside. His internal clock ran on east coast time and exhaustion crept up on him fast. He had a meeting first thing in the morning with his parole officer. He'd been summoned to meet with him, and Cole suppressed worry over why as it hadn't been a month yet. Depending on the outcome of his meeting, he had a plane to catch to Chicago. But now it was off to his large empty bed alone.

"No," AJ yelled as he awakened from his nightmare. He sprinted into the bathroom and puked up his dinner. It's not possible? No way? He couldn't have? Never would have? His legs gave way, and his body crumpled to the unforgiving cold, hard tiled floor. The painful pounding of his heart beat against his chest. Everything appeared hopeless as he realized the implications of his dream. Was it a dream or was it reality?

He curled up into a fetal position, his body raked uncontrollably with pain, sorrow and shame.

What had he done?

Lindsey?

Cole?

God help him. What had he done?

Why after all these years were the events of that night returning to him?

The reasons were Cole's return to the world of the free and Ward trying to suck up to them for his past mistakes. AJ always had a niggling feeling Ward had a thing for Lindsey. Had they engaged in an affair? Lindsey admitted to seeing others besides him. Was it Ward? It made sense since Ward had been reminiscing about earlier times when she lived. He'd also stated he'd seen him and her together the night she died. It was true, they'd been together, but not intimately. They'd had their first real fight, and over something ridiculous. But AJ would swear his life on a Bible she lived and breathed when he'd left the hotel room.

So if it wasn't him or Cole who committed murder? Thinking about it made him even more nauseated. Perhaps his memory and mind was playing tricks on him?

———

Cole swore as he reached around in the dark for his cell phone. What the hell time was it, and who the hell would call him at this hour? He found his phone just as it stopped playing the obnoxious ring he had it set on. After turning on the light and wincing at the time on the digital clock, Cole scrubbed his face with his hands, trying to wake up. Then he glanced at his phone and the missed call from AJ. Why would he call at this hour? Hell, it was even later in Chicago or earlier depending on how you looked at it. He called him back and waited two rings before AJ picked up.

"Hello."

"AJ, it's Cole. Did you just call me?"

He heard AJ clear his throat. "Aye, ah...um...had this weird dream about Lindsey, and ah didn't know who else tae call."

Cole heard something in his tone of voice that made him wake-up and pay more attention. "Okay, you want to tell me about it?"

"No, not really, it just freaked me out. Forget about it. Go back tae sleep."

Before Cole replied, AJ disconnected the phone. That

was, without a doubt, the strangest phone conversation he'd ever had with AJ.

He headed into the bathroom to relieve himself and then climbed back in bed. Wide awake now, Cole reached for the television remote and turned it to HBO. He finally dosed off only to be woken up a short time later, his heart pounding, his body drenched in sweat as he sat up and hugged his knees to his chest.

Damn, he thought he'd finally broken free from his nightmares. Shit. This nightmare didn't relive his prison life. It was about Lindsey and AJ, and the trial. It must have been the call from AJ that triggered his mind to conjure up images of Lindsey in his sleep.

Christ, would he ever lead a normal life?

He doubted it.

He swung his legs off the bed and resigned himself to hitting the shower. Sleep would not revisit him tonight.

To soothe his frayed nerves, he let the hot water pelt his face as he thought of Shannon. He could picture her perfectly in his mind's eye. How she looked the first time they met. How her eyes glazed over when she came for him and the love that shone from her cobalt eyes when she thought he wasn't looking. Which was rarely when they were together as he had trouble keeping his eyes off her.

Then his heart clenched as he remembered what she'd looked like the last time they'd been together. He saw her tears in her defeated eyes, skin as pale as the moon and her body trembling as though it were below zero in temperature. He pounded his fist into the shower wall. Lucky for Cole, it was fiberglass and not tile. Fiberglass had give, but he still flexed his fist open and closed. Fiberglass or no fiberglass, it hurt like a son-of-a-bitch.

Cole honestly didn't know how much longer he could go on without Shannon. She had become his other half, and he needed her, wanted her and craved her. He wanted her more than ever and continually had trouble concentrating on his concert tour as his thoughts drifted to her. He had finally found the love of his life and wouldn't you know it, the relationship was doomed from the beginning. He was cursed. No doubt about it. There was no other explanation. His whole life had been cursed.

Chapter Fourteen

CAMERON SAT STARING OUT THE BUS WINDOW AT ALL THE miles and miles of farmland as cornfields flanked both sides of the road for what seemed like forever. Would he ever come out the other side of the maze of green, yellow and brown that defined the state of Kansas in his eyes.

Today, he didn't feel well. His stomach protested something he'd eaten. He'd already used the bus's closet-sized bathroom three times during the past hour, and he needed to use it again. He was doubled over with unbelievable cramps that stole his breath away, causing him to take short, shallow breaths. He prayed the pain would subside and he'd make it to the toilet in time because he couldn't get up just yet as another wave of excruciating pain hit him.

He tried hard not to groan out too loudly as the pain seized his stomach, but he knew he did as this girl several rows in front of him kept looking back his way. And by the look on her face he knew he wasn't successful in being quiet. *How embarrassing.*

The pain suddenly eased, and he ran into the john,

pulling his pants down just in time as whatever caused him agony left his body. God, would it ever stop?

Weak and shaky, Cameron washed his hands and splashed cold water on his face, hoping to stop the spinning in his head. As he stumbled back to his spot, he used the backs of the tall seats to keep him upright. After collapsing into his, he hugged himself, fighting the dizziness and sweat and chills plaguing him. He'd never felt this bad before. His stomach seemed to have turned inside out and his ass hurt something fierce. If he had to crap one more time, he didn't think he'd survive.

"Excuse me." He looked up to see the girl standing beside him in the aisle. She cleared her throat and seemed somewhat hesitant and nervous and then she asked, "Are you feeling ill?"

Cameron looked her over with as much intensity as a sick as a dog sixteen-year-old could. She was maybe a year or two older than him, petite and dressed as a Goth. She was pretty, but all her eyebrow piercings and nose rings took away from it. Cameron never did care much for body piercing, except maybe the belly button. She wasn't rail thin, nor heavy, but she was stacked.

"Yeah I am," he groaned out, clutching his stomach as the cramps hit him again. *Not now Jesus, not now.*

She held out a bottle of pink stuff, causing Cameron to smile. The pink stuff his father lived on. But he hesitated, looking at her speculatively.

"It's not open." She held it closer. "Take it. You'll feel better." Her face broke out into a warm smile, and Cameron knew he could trust her. Reaching out, he took the bottle from her, read the directions, fumbled to open the children's safety cap and poured the desired amount into the measuring cup.

"Thanks." He went to hand it back, willing his hands to be steady.

She shook her head, causing her jet-black hair to sway. "You will need it." Then she left him and went back to her seat. Cameron smiled as he lay down as best he could on the bus seat and prayed for sleep.

Maybe if he slept for a while, he'd wake up feeling normal. He hated being sick, and if he wanted to be truthful with himself, he wanted his mom or Cheryl, or even his dad when he felt like this. Someone had always been there for him when he was sick, which wasn't often, but still, someone was always there to make him comfortable. Make him soup, check his temperature and watch a movie or play video games with him. You name it, they'd done it for him.

He rolled onto his side, curling into a ball, and felt the first tears dampen his face. He swiped them away in disgust. Damn, he wished he'd brought his cell phone with him so he could call one of his friends. Running away seemed like a good idea at the time, but now, he was lonely, sick and tired. Sleep. He needed sleep and then, when he felt better, he'd make friends with Goth Girl.

When he finally woke up and wiped the sleep from his eyes, he noticed the bus sat motionless, parked in a rest area and the sun crept low on the horizon. By his best estimate, he'd slept for about four hours. The cramps in his stomach had subsided for now, but it still felt odd. He didn't know whether to risk food or just get a soda. He'd play it safe and get off the bus and buy a Coke. But as he gathered his stuff together the driver and several passengers returned. Damn, it was too late. He'd have to wait for the next stop.

Goth Girl approached him carrying a plastic convenience store bag. She hesitated, smiled shyly, and then kept on approaching.

"You're alive," she whispered.

"Hmm, barely," he replied."

She gestured to the seat beside him. "Can I sit?"

Surprised, Cameron replied, "Sure." He scooted over to the window seat and moved his belongings to the floor to make room for her.

"Is that your guitar?" she asked, pointing to the case on the aisle seat opposite him.

"Yeah," he answered."

Her eyes widened, and he noticed she had pretty deep blue eyes. "Do you play?"

Cameron rolled his eyes, suddenly feeling better. Was she for real? "No. I just lug it around with me for the hell of it." He regretted his sarcastic tone immediately because she blushed and looked embarrassed.

"Oh, I mean. I figured you played, but you know, some people play, and some people *really* play."

"Uh huh, well I'm one of those who *really* play."

Her eyes lit up, and she glanced up the aisle. "Do you think anyone would mind if you played now?"

Cameron shrugged his shoulders. "I don't know. I could start, and if someone complains I'll stop."

She removed his guitar from the case and whistled. "Nice guitar—top quality."

"Yeah." Cameron tilted his head. "How do you know?"

She handed over the instrument. "My old boyfriend's in a band. I used to sing for them."

"Cool."

She blushed. "Yeah, well, no big deal. They aren't very good, neither am I."

Cameron began playing. His hands were unsteady

from being sick, but the more he played the steadier they became. He glanced up now and again at Goth Girl who sat, smiling and moving in her seat to the rhythm.

He sang, softly so not everyone could hear, and he became lost in his music. It became his world. So tuned into his music he forgot where he was, who he was with and where he was going and why. His music turned all encompassing. He became one with his guitar, nothing else mattered but the sound emanating from him. And he truly did not understand how beautiful it sounded to those around him.

After playing nonstop for about thirty minutes, he paused and looked at Goth Girl, who just stared in awe.

"What?"

She shook her head. "Shit, you're good, better than good."

He threw his head back and laughed. "Yeah well, I told you I could play. And if you think I sound good on an acoustic guitar, you should hear me on an electric one."

"I know you told me you could play, but shit man, you can *really* play." Her eyes widened again with awe and he felt a strange sensation in his gut. She reached down for her bag. "Oh...I forgot. I bought you crackers and a soda for your stomach."

Cameron's heart lurched at her thoughtfulness. She may dress oddly, and look odd, but she seemed nice. He took the food from her. "Thanks. How much do I owe you?"

"Nothing, besides you can buy me something at our next stop."

He smiled at her and again felt his insides do something weird, and it had nothing to do with having been sick. "Sure." After he polished off the crackers and downed the whole can of soda, he suddenly realized he couldn't exactly call her Goth Girl to her face.

"I'm Cameron." He put out his hand, waiting for her to take it.

She paused then smiled and damn she looked pretty. "I'm Amber."

Cameron suddenly felt his face heat up as he realized he still held her small, warm hand. He let it go.

"Are you going to LA too?" she asked as she twirled a lock of her dyed black hair that shone blonde at the roots.

"Yeah," he replied a little hesitant.

"Why?"

"Is this the Spanish Inquisition?"

She laughed. "No, the Amber Inquisition. Obviously, you seem like a rich kid so if you're traveling somewhere you'd fly. Are you running away?"

He glanced at her, his guard suddenly up. "So what if I am?"

"Don't be mad." She paused and bit her lower lip. "I thought we could travel together and be friends."

Cameron regretted snapping at her. "I'm sorry. And you're right. I took off." He shook his head, took a deep breath and expelled it. "My dad's a cop, he doesn't understand me."

She snorted. "That's tough. My dad's a lawyer."

Cameron snapped his head toward her. "No way."

She rolled her eyes. "Yes way. My mom died last year and since then he's buried himself in his work. I thought…" She gestured toward her hair and face piercing. "If I drastically changed myself, he'd notice me." She hugged herself and her voice quivered. "He didn't."

"I'm sorry." Cameron's throat scorched as he fought back his own tears while Amber's silently travelled down her pretty face. "My parents are divorced. My mom's a writer and my Dad remarried and he and his wife Cheryl are expecting baby number four. Sometimes I feel like an intruder in their house. My dad has this whole other family, a whole other life. I feel like I'm only there because my mom travels a lot, and there's nowhere else for me to go."

Amber reached for his hand and held it. "How old are you?"

"Sixteen. And you?"

"Seventeen last July. I'm a senior this year."

"Junior," he added.

"Where're you from?"

Cameron liked the feel of her hand in his. He moved and entwined her warm fingers together with his. "Massachusetts and you?"

"Newport, Rhode Island."

"Why are you going to LA?" he asked.

She shrugged. "I don't know. It seemed like a good destination. I've never seen the west coast and thought I'd like to." She studied him with her deep blue eyes. "What about you?"

"I'm looking for someone."

She tilted her head and her eyes sparkled with interest. "Who?"

Cameron laughed and shook his head. "If I told you, you wouldn't believe me."

She narrowed her eyes. "Try me?"

"Cole Jackson," he said with a resigned sigh.

"The Cole Jackson," Amber said, her voice raising several octaves, "from BlackJack?"

"Uh huh," he grunted.

"Do you know him?"

"Yup," he mumbled.

"Isn't he on a tour or something?"

"Yeah he is, but I know for a fact he flies home once a month to check in with his parole officer."

"How do you know that?"

Cameron frowned and sighed as he remembered the last time he'd seen Cole. What a mess his dad made of that day. "My mom used to date him."

Amber sat up straight and inspected him. Tall and thin with long, thick brown hair curling up at his neck. His deep hazel eyes made him look cute as hell. Loose fitting faded jeans and black Nike T-shirt looked good on him. The big question was, was he telling the truth, or just being a typical teenage asshole trying to impress her? Somehow though, she thought he was being straight with her. She hoped so anyway because she liked him.

"Your mom dated Cole Jackson?"

"Yeah, sounds hard to believe, but it's true. I even played with him on stage at the Boston Garden."

She remembered hearing something about some gifted musician playing with BlackJack. That was Cameron? She shifted in her seat, leaning closer and tightening her grip on their still entwined fingers. "Get out. What was it like?"

Cameron's face lit up and Amber smiled. Damn he was cute.

"It was incredible, even better than incredible, more like awesome. Being up on stage with thousands of screaming fans listening to you play was strange. I don't know how to describe it except to say it's indescribable. I always dreamed about it, but my dreams didn't even come close to the real thing."

"What's Cole like?"

"Not like you'd think. He's quiet, protective of those he

cares about and treats me as an equal." Cameron's face lit up again. "We've written several songs together and man, oh man, he's talented. He wrote all the music and lyrics to every song BlackJack has ever recorded."

"I didn't know that." Amber suddenly became quiet, and Cameron thought she looked sad.

"What's wrong?"

Amber pulled her hand from his. "Do I look ugly to you?"

"No. I think you're pretty."

Her eyes flew to his and widened with hope. "You do?" She hoped he was telling the truth because she found him hot.

"Yeah, I do."

"What about my nose rings and my eyebrow studs?"

"They're okay."

"I hate them—the piercings. I only did it to get my dad's attention, and to tell you the truth...I don't think he even noticed. Other people notice though, they stare at me, at them, even you did."

She removed two nose rings, several eyebrow studs and placed them in her pocket.

"I like the way you look without them," Cameron said as he smiled at her shyly.

"Cameron. There's barely anyone on the bus and it's dark. Would you have sex with me?" she whispered.

Cole's morning went like clockwork and after meeting with his parole officer he drove straight to LAX and boarded his flight to Chicago's O'Hare Airport. Boring as hell was all he could think. Where were the heavy traffic and delays when you wanted them? The flight was even boring and so was the drive to the hotel. Almost too calm, too boring, too easy and it unsettled him. Something didn't feel right in his bones.

He found Ted and Brad in the suite next to his room. The puzzled expressions on their faces had Cole stopping dead in his tracks. Also present was Ward, who Cole glared at. Did he really think they wanted him here? What did he hope to gain by latching onto them? It wasn't as though they could help him with his destroyed career, nor was Lindsey alive for him to have an affair with. Oh, shit. Was he having an affair with Ted or Brad's wife? He'd think about Ward later. Right now he needed to help AJ.

"What's wrong?" he queried.

Ted and Brad exchanged looks, then Ted talked and what he had to say didn't sound good. "AJ's acting weird man. He won't come out of his room."

"What do you mean he won't come out of his room?" Cole said as his skin prickled.

Brad interrupted, "Just that. He refuses to leave his room. He orders room service and won't let anyone else inside."

Cole's stomach churned as he remembered AJ's strange phone call from the night before. Something had to be seriously wrong for him to act this way. AJ was the most reliable, down-to-earth, head-on-straight person he knew. This behavior was so not like him. Could there be a problem with his wife and kids back in Scotland? Cole ran his hands through his hair in total panic and frustration. Jesus, all AJ had to do was come to him if he had any problems. Cole went to AJ with his problems all the time. So did everyone else in the band. Didn't he know he could do the same?

"Hey Ted, how much time before we have to leave for the show?" Cole asked anxiously.

Ted glanced at his wristwatch. "Two hours at the latest and that's pushing it."

Cole grunted a reply and went out into the hall and knocked on AJ's door. By this time his heart vibrated in his chest and his hands shook from worry. Didn't he think earlier in the day that things were going too smoothly? Now he knew why. This behavior was so totally not AJ, not like him at all. He was everybody's rock, everybody's anchor in a storm.

He raised his hand and rapped his knuckles on the door. The door with the *do not disturb* sign hanging on the knob. An unintelligible muffled answer came from the other side.

"AJ, it's me Cole. Let me in."

Still no reply came forth that Cole could fully comprehend.

"Hey man. You're scaring me. Let me in or I'll get housekeeping to do it."

Finally he heard AJ answer.

"She won't let you in. Ah paid her big bucks tae keep her key tae herself."

That wasn't good, and he sounded like crap. In fact, he sounded drunk or high or both. Cole leaned his weary body against the wall and exhaled loudly. Think man, think. AJ called last night talking about Lindsey. Hell, maybe he missed her, but come on, enough to push everyone away? It made little sense. But shit, what made sense in this world lately? *Absofuckinglutely* nothing made sense, that's what.

"Come on AJ, talk to me. Tell me what's bugging you?"

No answer.

"Come on. It's me. We can tell each other anything. We're like brothers man."

Cole waited, feeling more and more unsettled with

every unanswered question. So unsettled his body shivered from the inside out and his knees threatened to buckle.

"AJ shit, talk to me. I can't help you if you don't talk to me."

"I can't," came through the door in what sounded to Cole like a sob.

"You're scaring me here. I don't do scare well and you know that. Do you want to do the show tonight?"

"Aye, go without me. Ah promise tae be there on time."

Cole tapped his head against the wall numerous times in frustration at being unable to help his friend. A friend who never needed his help before now, and he really didn't know what to do. It scared the shit out of him to hear AJ like this.

"AJ are you sure?"

"Go," he growled out. "Ah'm fine. Leave me be."

Cole hated to leave him to his own devices, but what could he do? He swallowed the lump in his throat and went to his own room to prepare. Christ, as this tour continued on and on he found himself less liking it and wanting to go home. But where did he call home?

Ten minutes before the show was to begin, AJ showed up looking like he crawled out of a cave after a three-day bender. His clothes were dirty. His hair looked in desperate need of a wash and comb. His eyes were bloodshot and sunken and his hands, Cole noticed when he went to pick up his guitar, trembled.

Damn, he looked like hell and Cole wondered how he would make it through the concert. Somehow he did. He never spoke to him, or to anyone else. He played like a machine, inhuman. AJ played like a man dead in his soul and in his heart, but his body was very much alive and going through the motions, just like a well-oiled robot. Cole didn't know what to think about it or what to do.

And when Cole had gotten a good look at AJ's eyes, they looked glazed over and void of life as though there was nobody home. Shit. Something had a hold on him and it was squeezing the life out of him. Cole could relate. He'd probably looked like that fifteen years ago.

When the concert ended, AJ fled without a word. A chill swept up Cole's spine and he once again felt weary, worried and unsettled. Something in his gut told him a violent storm brewed inside AJ and nothing good would come of it. A major catastrophe threatened him, and Cole was damned because he didn't know how to help him or how to reach him and snap him out of his trance.

And then a selfish thought occurred to him. Who would deal with the radio DJs and television reporters backstage if AJ didn't? Shit. It looked like he would be. Whether or not he liked it, he would be the band's spokesperson tonight.

A wave crashed inside him, threatening to take him under and never release him. That was how terrified of reporters he was, and it embarrassed him to no end to admit it. But it was the truth.

After he showered in his dressing room and changed into clean jeans and a T-shirt, he looked at himself in the mirror and gave himself a pep talk. Whether it helped remained to be seen. He just had to focus and block out the words, *murder, wife* and *Lindsey* and he'd be fine. *Yeah right, keep telling yourself that and maybe you won't puke your guts up.*

Pausing outside the door, he took a deep breath, clenched his teeth shut and walked inside. His first thought was who the hell were all these people? His eyes darted around and it wasn't long before people recognized him and crowded his personal space. And Cole considered anything within ten feet of himself his personal space.

He tried to be pleasant and answer questions and sign autographs for fans. It went okay until this guy shoved a microphone in his face and asked the question.

"Did you kill your wife?"

Just like that he asked it, like it was no big deal, like he asked it all the time, as though it was nothing more than casual conversation. Cole froze on the spot. His pulse soared and the room tilted as black spots flashed in his eyes. He mumbled something even he couldn't understand. Thankfully, someone grabbed his arm tightly and led him out of the room, down the hall and into a deserted unlocked room.

Whoever rescued him pushed him gently onto a sofa, forced his head down between his knees and held him in that position. Then he heard the woman's voice.

Chapter Fifteen

"BETTER?"

"Hell no," Cole spat out.

"Sometimes it takes a few minutes to get your bearings back," the woman said in a calm, soft, comforting, and strangely familiar voice.

"You can take your hand away. I'm okay now."

"Oh, sorry." She snatched it away.

Once her hand left his head, Cole reclined back on the couch and looked at his savior. It was none other than Marlene Simpson, the talk show host he'd met when she'd interviewed Shannon. His body tensed and his guard went up. What could she possibly want? As if he didn't know.

"If you're hoping for an interview, I already told..."

Her hand rose up, palm out. "No. I respect what you told me before. But I suppose you're wondering why I'm here?"

Cole raised a brow and when Marlene smiled at him he relaxed. For some unknown reason he suddenly felt as though he could trust her.

"I came for the concert. My daughter and her friend

are backstage waiting for me. I told them I could introduce them to you, but I saw you panic at something the reporter said, and the next thing I knew we were in here."

Cole slid across the couch and invited her to sit down. It was the least he could do after she saved him from embarrassing himself in front of all those people by having an anxiety attack or worse, hitting the floor from fainting. He studied her and assessed her. She appeared to be in her mid-forties, of average height, nicely built, and attractive. He was not the least interested, but she was nicely put together. Cole cleared his throat.

"I owe you a thanks. I almost lost it. I thought I was going to pass out in there," he snorted and put his hands up. "I can see the headlines. 'Cole Jackson, after having drunk himself into a stupor, collapses after a concert.'" He pulled the leather strap out of his hair and combed his fingers through it. "I'm nobody. Why does everybody bother me?"

"Cole?"

He felt her warm hand on his knee, and he knew it rested there purely for comfort and nothing else.

"You are somebody. You're a talented, handsome man who piques the interest of everyone around you because of your past. You're an enigma, which only makes people push harder to know the person behind the screen. And I speak from experience when I say it will not stop until you tell your story. And even then there are no guarantees it will stop."

Cole knew what she referred to. Even though he'd been in prison at the time, he remembered Marlene making headlines a few years back. Her second husband had been arrested and convicted of statutory rape. He had sexually assaulted her daughter and some of her daughter's friends. He supplied them with alcohol and drugs then had sex with them. It took a long time for the media to stop hounding her about it. Finally she'd gone public with her side of the story. But Cole didn't know if he could.

"I can't give an interview." The words struggled to come out of his mouth because he felt so deflated of energy.

"Why?"

"That's a damn good question." Cole looked over at Marlene and was shocked to see a genuine concern for him reflected in her eyes. He didn't even know this woman, so why?

"I can't give an interview. You saw what just happened. The bastard asked if I killed my wife and I lost it. It would be one thing if I got angry, but I nearly blacked out. I would have blacked out if you hadn't come to my rescue." He paused and looked right at her. "By the way." His face softened, and he smiled. "Thank you again."

"What if you did the interview with...say...me?"

He narrowed his eyes at her, his guard back up. He should have known it would come up.

She put up her hand, the concerned look still there. "Hear me out. It's just a suggestion. Say I interviewed you and promised not to bring up Lindsey. We chat about your life now. Your music now, and only, and I mean only if you bring it up, do we discuss it."

She appeared so sincere Cole almost wanted to agree. He smiled at her. "You're a nice person Marlene." He shook his head, disgusted in himself. "I'm thirty-eight, a big guy, a tough guy. You'd think I could handle it."

Everything she said about reporters hounding him rang true. He'd been out of prison for more than a year, and still, he couldn't shake the press or his past. It was probably better to go public with his story once and for all.

And Marlene would be the only one he'd go public with. What he said next shocked her and he liked that.

"I have another concert tomorrow night. How about tomorrow, early afternoon?"

It took her a moment to find her voice. "Perfect."

"I want it to be informal, and I want to see the questions you will ask me ahead of time."

"No problem."

He figured she'd agree to just about anything to get her interview. "And you promise not to ask me if I killed Lindsey?"

She put her hand on her heart. "You have my word."

"Good enough," he resigned. "I'll do it tomorrow at your studio and oh, one more thing, no questions from the audience."

"We won't have an audience. It'll just be the two of us."

"Even better," he murmured.

Cole sent Marlene to get her daughter and her friend, and they enjoyed a bite to eat at a small out-of-the-way diner that served breakfast all day and night long. Cole indulged himself with eggs, bacon, and home-fried potatoes. He couldn't remember the last time a meal went down so smoothly. Well, actually, he could remember the last time he'd been with Shannon. But so as not to spoil the night, he pushed all thoughts of Shannon out of his head until later when he relaxed in the privacy of his hotel room.

"Lindsey, ye don't mean that?"

"Yes, I do. It's over. I want to go back to Cole. He needs me and I really love him."

"Ah can't accept that. Ah love you. Ah know it's not Cole ye love. There's someone else, isn't there?"

"Get out."

"Lindsey, please?"

He begged. It was the most humiliating thing he'd ever done, and for what? A woman who'd suck any man's dick that struck her fancy? But he loved her, God damn it, he loved her. Something inside him snapped.

Hating himself, hating her, he slapped her, then he saw something metal in her hands and there was a struggle for control.

AJ flew out of bed in the middle of the night, ran into the bathroom and dry-heaved again. It seemed to be all he did lately. Sitting on the cold tiled floor, he hugged himself as he rocked back and forth and hummed. Had he lost his mind? He probably lost it the night Lindsey died. The night he killed her. How else could he explain never having remembered it until now? His dreams and memories had progressed, so he knew most of what happened but not all. Some of it seemed a little sketchy, like the actual stabbing part. He didn't remember that at all. Nor did he remember seeing her dead body. Why were those memories lost to him?

Christ. He killed her. He'd killed Cole's wife, Lindsey Jackson, his lover. How could he have done it? Never mind not remembering it until now? He didn't even know what he'd done with the knife or his clothes. There must have been blood.

"Oh God, Lindsey," he sobbed out. "Forgive me. Please, please, please forgive me for taking yer beautiful life."

He couldn't go on like this. AJ couldn't go on living a

lie, living in hell on earth. The guilt, the pain, the realization of the unimaginable. He found himself perched tenuously at the edge of a stone cliff, and the stones and dirt were giving way beneath his feet. Did he dive to the ground and save himself? Or throw himself off the cliff into the raging river below and end his torture?

What would happen to his wife, Elizabeth and his children? He moaned louder and louder as his insides twisted in silent agony for the pain and shame this would cause them. Oh God. He rose off the floor and stumbled to his bed. He'd not eaten in so long. The lining of his stomach was in the toilet, and he was so weak he collapsed onto the bed. "Please, God," he mumbled. "Let me die. Let me die. It's what ah deserve. Please take my life."

When AJ woke and saw the sun the next morning, he cursed out at God as his heart pierced with pain. "Why didn't ye take me?" he yelled out as he fell to his knees and pleaded with God once again.

"Ah dinnae deserve tae live, tae breathe. Ah dinnae deserve tae see the sun, or the moon, or the stars. Why dinnaeye take me?"

Cameron had trouble sleeping on the bus after Amber asked him to have sex with her. On the bus, was she serious? He couldn't do it on the bus, and to her disappointment he told her so. But he'd also mentioned getting off at the next stop and renting a motel room for a day or two. He still didn't feel all that great and needed—no wanted solid ground beneath his feet.

So here they stood in front of a rundown roadside motel in the middle of nowhere. The only other building in sight was a roadside café, its parking lot jammed with eighteen-wheelers. Besides that, there was nothing around but miles and miles of mundane blacktop twisting and turning, with beautiful mountains all around them. He had to admit, the mountains took his breath away.

His stomach still felt like shit from being sick, and now it also ached with nervousness. He'd never rented a motel room before and didn't know what to expect. He hoped he didn't have to show a license or something because all he had on him was his school ID.

The door to the office squeaked when he opened it, and he stepped inside and faced an ancient lady with wrinkled skin. She wore the ugliest purple dress or bathrobe he'd ever seen and purple fuzzy slippers. Her eyes were glued to the television, and she never heard him enter. He cleared his throat.

"Excuse me."

"Rooms are sixty dollars a night. Cash only." And still she didn't look at him.

"Okay, I'll take one for two nights." He slid the exact amount over the dirty, sticky counter, and still she didn't look at him.

"Room four. Sign the register and if you break anything you pay for it."

Cameron scribbled his name on the register and then realized too late he'd signed his real name. *Good going moron, you're supposed to be incognito.*

Before the lady looked at him, he grabbed the key and left. He signaled Amber and held up four fingers then pointed toward the room.

After they were inside, Cameron lay on the bed looking around and became nervous as hell because, oh shit, he was on the only bed in the room. While Amber took a shower, he curled up on his side and was nearly asleep when she came out of the bathroom. He swallowed the lump in his throat as his eyes followed her across the room. Amber's dyed black hair hung long and dripping wet. The T-shirt she wore clung to every curve and Cameron felt himself harden as he stared at the puckered nipples straining against the thin cotton. His heart pounded as his eyes roamed lower to where the shirt barely covered her ... his breath came faster as he glimpsed her curly pubic hairs.

Christ. He'd never seen a naked girl, except in dirty magazines and some "R" rated movies, but never up close and in person, and how humiliated he felt suddenly for still being a virgin.

"I...um...I'm gonna shower." He slid off the bed, grabbed his backpack and locked himself in the bathroom. Before he got in the shower he sat on the closed toilet seat and willed his pulse to slow down. Once it had, he stepped in the shower and paid meticulous attention, soaping up every speck of his body. After he washed his hair, dried off, threw on shorts, he brushed his teeth and placed his shaky hand on the doorknob. Shit! He was about to have sex for the first time and he felt like throwing up. *Not good Cameron, not good at all.* He released the knob, went to the sink and splashed cold water on his face and stared at his reflection in the mirror. The person staring back at him was someone he saw all the time, yet something appeared different. He looked different. He shook it off and before chickening out and curling up on the bathroom floor for the night, he opened the door and found Amber sitting in bed watching television. Maybe he was wrong, and she didn't want sex after all? He didn't honestly know if he felt relieved or disappointed. As he walked toward the bed, his knees wobbled and his heart hammered triple time inside his chest.

He nonchalantly—and boy was that hard to pull off—stretched out on the bed, flat on his back, his arms behind his head, and asked, "Anything good on?" like he didn't have a care in the world.

Amber replied, "Soap Operas and talk shows. What's your poison?"

"Whatever, I'm gonna sleep anyway."

Amber scooted closer to his body and snuggled against him, one leg thrown over his legs, and he hardened instantly as he felt her warm vagina make contact with his thigh.

"Amber?" Christ, he sounded nervous.

"Hmm," she mumbled.

Cameron took a deep breath and blurted it out before he lost his courage. "I've never done this before."

She raised her body and looked at him with a smile curving her lips, and he felt his face burn up.

"Sex, are you telling me you've never had sex?" she asked, her expression one of surprise.

His stomach knotted and then dropped as he shook his head.

"Oral sex," she questioned.

Again he shook his head and suddenly felt so out of the loop. Most of his friends had had sex already, and it wasn't as though Cameron hadn't wanted to. He just never had the opportunity to—until now.

He knew oral sex was like, the thing to do these days. He'd heard about these parties where the guys line up and the girls go down the line giving blow jobs. It was called a train or something like that. He'd always been too busy with his schoolwork, his music and shuffling between his mom's house and his dad's to go. But now he wished he'd been to one of those parties so he'd, like, have some experience.

"We need a condom," she blurted out as she rolled off the bed. Cameron sucked in his breath as he got a good look at her naked butt when her shirt rode up to her waist. He gawked as his pulse roared. Amber fished inside her bag, turned to him holding up a foil-wrapped condom with a shy smile plastered across her pretty face.

"We have one. Actually, I have a whole box."

Cameron physically felt his blood pumping through his body and settling in his dick as she climbed back onto the bed, onto her knees and peeled off her shirt. Christ, she was stacked was all he could think about as he reached out with his trembling hands and cupped her heavy breasts.

Amber showed Cameron what he'd been missing for the rest of the afternoon. And by the day's end, there wasn't much in the way of sex, oral or otherwise, Cameron hadn't experienced firsthand.

Chapter Sixteen

SHANNON AWOKE IN THE MORNING TO HER HOUSE PHONE ringing. She dove off the bed, not wanting to miss the call. Her heart pounded in hopes it was Cameron as she pushed the talk button on the fourth ring.

"Good morning," she said as she held her breath.

"Good morning to you."

"Cole," she breathed out and her heart fluttered even faster. "Hi, you got my message?"

"Yes. Is something wrong? You sounded anxious on the voicemail. I would have called last night, but it was late when I realized I had a message."

The concern she heard in his voice warmed her heart, even if it was broken at the moment. "Cameron ran away."

"What?" Cole responded loudly into her ear.

"He ran away four days ago. I think he might be heading to California to find you."

"But I'm in Chicago."

"Oh." She had hoped he might be home even though she'd known the chances were slim to none he would be. Hell, he was on tour. What did she expect?

"I leave for Detroit day after tomorrow, but I'll cancel and go try to find him."

The man's unselfishness never ceased to amaze her. His career was just getting back on track and he was willing to cancel a concert engagement for her and her son. She'd never loved him more she mused as tears escaped her eyes and trickled down her cheeks.

"No, don't do that. I just need your address so I can send the detective I hired to stake out your house and hope he shows up."

"It's 1210 Malibu Road. Are you sure about not needing me to go there?"

"Yes. Cole?"

"I'm here."

"I'm scared. I want my son back." She sniffled and wiped the tears from her cheeks with her free hand. "I miss him, and I keeping thinking up all these horrendous things happening to him. Oh God." She sobbed into the phone. "I'm so afraid for him. I'm so afraid I'll never see him again."

"I'll be at your house in two days. I can't bear not being with you when you're hurting like this. I'd hop the next plane, but it's too late to cancel tonight and tomorrow's concerts."

"You don't have to cancel any shows on my account?"

"Detroit can wait. We'll reschedule. Then we'll take one day at a time."

She promised herself she wouldn't cry on the phone, but she did. He tried to soothe her with words, but they drowned in the sea of her sorrow. After a time she spoke, "Thanks and Cole?"

"Yes?"

"I love you."

"Me too. I'll see you soon, and if you hear anything, promise me, you'll call."

"I promise."

Shannon hung up the phone and hugged herself. Soon Cole would be here to hold her, to make her feel better and tell her everything would be okay. He would cancel concerts to be with her. Her lips curved into a smile even as tears blurred her vision. She thought no one would care enough about her to do something like that.

Since she was up and no longer tired, she showered and call Scott Danvers in hopes he had good news.

"Scott, it's Shannon, anything new?" she asked around the lump in her throat.

"Were your ears buzzing? I was just about to call you. I spoke with a bus driver for Greyhound and he remembers Cameron." Shannon heard him pause and drink something, probably coffee. "He said Cameron exited the bus with a girl, and they never came back on. The good news is he remembers the approximate vicinity of where they disembarked. I'm heading out the door now to Colorado then following the bus schedule for yesterday."

Shannon took a deep breath, trying hard not to get her hopes up. *But how could she not?* "That's great news. Call me as soon as you know anything. Okay?"

"You got it, boss."

Shannon collapsed with relief when the conversation ended. They were close. "Oh please God," she prayed out loud, "let my baby come home safe and unharmed."

When she entered her kitchen a few minutes later, she found John at the stove making scrambled eggs. This was the second night he'd slept here, and the second morning in a row he had made breakfast. He wore his two-day-old wrinkled clothes, but he was freshly showered because his dark hair glistened wet, and she could smell the body wash Cameron always used. It caused a piercing pain to her heart, and then she remembered her news.

She explained to John everything Danvers had said as she ate eggs, toast, and coffee. It was the first time she'd eaten hungrily in days, and it felt good to put something substantial in her stomach. Not long after they finished the conversation, Mitch entered the kitchen.

"What smells so good?"

"Eggs," John replied. "Sit and I'll dish ya out," he said, grabbing a plate from the cabinet.

Shannon filled her brother in on the news, and he was visibly relieved to have some hope.

"And oh, Cole's coming day after tomorrow." She paused and glanced at John, daring him to say anything negative, but he kept his mouth shut tight. "He's canceling two shows to be here."

John looked up from his plate of eggs. "That's nice of him," he said so nonchalantly, causing Shannon to almost slip off her chair in shock.

"You don't mind?"

"I said I was wrong to tell you how to live your life."

Reaching across the table, she took his hand in hers. John glanced down at their joined hands and then at her. Was she crazy or did he look longingly at her? How odd. She must be mistaken or more tired than she thought.

"Thanks," she murmured as she pulled her hand away to clean up from breakfast as John and Mitch talked and drank their second cups of coffee.

Once John finished his coffee, he decided it was high time he went home to his family and checked in with work to see if anyone there had any leads on Cameron. Also, there lay a thick envelope on his desk, an envelope containing everything he wanted to know about the Cole Jackson trial. Today seemed as good a day as any to bury himself in it. It would also take his mind off of his missing son.

A while back he'd pulled several favors and got the police and coroner's report and the court transcripts in the Jackson case. Now, he sat at his desk in his locked office and spent several hours reviewing everything with a fine-tooth comb.

He started with the autopsy, scanning to the actual findings. Mrs. Jackson had bruising on both wrists, showing a struggle, and one stab wound directly to the heart. There was no sign of rape or sexual assault. What surprised him the most was there was absolutely no physical evidence linking Jackson to his wife's death other than he was covered in her blood. Which in court could be argued in many ways by a good attorney, and Jackson had hired the best.

During Jackson's police investigation, he swore his innocence, never once wavering from his original story. A Grand Jury eventually indicted him. Never once was he offered a plea bargain.

The trial, in John's opinion, was a farce. The prosecution knew about the weaknesses in their case so they attacked Jackson's character and lifestyle any way they could. Jackson's attorney objected to everything he could, and the judge overruled, but the damage had been done. It biased the jury.

There was no murder weapon.

No witnesses.

Did he really do it?

Jackson never took the stand in his own defense. Sometimes that in itself was a sign of guilt, or he could have been protecting something or someone and didn't want to perjure himself.

Both the prosecution and defense's closing arguments contained dramatic and potent information, but obviously, the jury believed the prosecution. John thought that if there ever was a case in which the jury was prejudiced, this was it. That had to be it. There was no evidence against Jackson to warrant a conviction. He also couldn't believe he was never granted an appeal. It was as though they made an example out of him.

John truly believed in the judicial system. He had to. His job depended on it. But he knew guilty people often went free, and unfortunately, innocent people went to prison. In his opinion, even if Jackson killed his wife, the prosecution had no case.

Of course, he still hated the bastard's guts.

Cameron awoke with a smile on his face and feeling odd, different and changed. He wondered why? He'd spent yesterday having sex, and he couldn't even begin to count how many times. Amber was hot and sexy and oh-so inventive. He wondered where she learned all of it?

He'd been shy and tentative the first time and maybe the second, letting Amber take control, but after that he'd felt a surge of confidence and began leading. It was a day he'd never forget, and neither would he ever forget Amber.

She slept soundly beside him, lying on her stomach facing away from him, the covers riding low on her silky back. Her long hair fanned out on the pillow, and he felt his body waking up. Instead of doing anything about it, he threw on his clothes and walked to the busy diner. The parking lot once again overflowed with big rigs. All he wanted was chocolate milk and a bagel. He ordered two of each.

As he entered the room, she stirred on the bed. He placed the food on the night table and kissed the back of her neck. "Hey, you."

"Hmm, hey yourself. Where did you go?"

"The diner and I brought food."

Rolling over, she sat up in the bed looking sleepy with her hair tangled all around her and she pointed toward the floor. "Could you pass me my shirt?"

Cameron picked up her T-shirt, turned it right side out and handed it to her. He thought she seemed a little uncomfortable with him this morning. He hoped not.

He passed her the milk and bagel and sat next to her and ate his food in three bites. After not eating much for the past few days, he was starving.

Amber ate her bagel silently, watching Cameron. She felt a little funny this morning after yesterday and last night. Not necessarily because of the sex, it had been fun and hot, but her stomach did a little flip when she remembered she told him she loved him. He had said nothing, in fact, she didn't even know if he had heard her. God, she hoped he didn't hear.

She didn't want him thinking she was one of those clingy girls who once they had sex with a boy thought it was love. Then they would follow the boy around even when he told them he didn't like them anymore. He would be mean to them and they would beg him not to break up with them. They would do anything, did anything to keep him, and that anything turned out to be sex, when and where he wanted it.

Amber hugged her knees up to her chest as she fought the shivers raking her body. She had been a fool once like one of those clingy desperate girls, but never again. She'd embarrass herself once, but not twice.

"Hey," she said as she climbed off the bed. "I'm taking a shower."

Cole stopped by AJ's room before he left for his interview with Marlene Simpson. Nothing had changed. He still wouldn't let him in or come out. Once again, he told him he'd see him at the concert.

As Cole walked down the deserted hallway, he contemplated what was happening. Bloody hell, had the world suddenly gone nuts? Never would he ever have thought AJ, always Mr. Reliable, would go off the deep end about anything. Somehow he had to get him to talk, but right now he had to deal with the pain churning inside his stomach. He didn't have butterflies—he had an ancient family of Pterodactyls taking flight, causing constant pain with their expansive wingspan. *Weren't they extinct?*

He'd be damn glad when this interview stood behind him. He must have been out of his mind to have agreed to it. As much as he wanted to, he wouldn't go back on his word. Hell, it was probably high time the world met the real him, not some tabloid fabrication created to sell magazines regardless of the fact most of what it printed about him was false and created from imaginative writers' minds.

Marlene had wanted to send a car for him, but he'd refused, the studio was seven blocks away and he could use the exercise and fresh, crisp Chicago air. The wind blew relentlessly, whipping off Lake Michigan, as he made his way down Michigan Shore Drive, causing him to pull up his leather jacket collar, lower his baseball cap on his head and stuff his hands into his pockets. There was a strong nip to this October air. And damn, he mused, it felt good and invigorating. The thought of seeing Shannon had his spirits way up, and he suddenly felt charged and less nervous the closer he got to the television studio, which somehow seemed strange, considering what he'd felt like earlier. Considering what was happening with AJ and Cameron.

After giving his name to the young, pretty receptionist at the front desk, he stood looking out the window and watched all the people walking by. It resembled a kaleido-scope of people from all walks of life. It made him smile as he thought about how incredible this country was. The same people and same country that convicted him, and still he was glad to have been born here, to be part of this free country where opportunity knew no bounds.

"Cole, sorry to keep you waiting," a female voice said.

Cole didn't need to turn around to know Marlene came down personally to meet him. She had a distinct voice, and voices were a thing of his. He may forget a name but never a voice. He spun around to face her and replied, "You didn't keep me waiting. I just arrived."

She smiled at him and hooked her arm through his. "Good. Let's go to the recording studio. The cameras are ready to roll." She looked at him and her voice softened. "Are you still okay with this?"

She surprised him with her question. He figured she couldn't wait to shoot off her list of questions, and his respect for her rose another notch.

"Yeah, I'm okay. But don't forget I want to see the questions first."

Marlene laughed and patted his arm. "I knew *you* wouldn't forget. Read them and give me your input. Now I need to ask about Shannon Gallagher. Is the topic off limits?"

Cole chuckled and his eyes gleamed. "Yeah, it is."

Marlene laughed again. "I figured as much."

They were now in the studio. Cole saw no audience, just three camera operators and two chairs with a small table between them. A pitcher of water and two glasses rested on the table. Marlene gestured toward the sitting area. "Is this satisfactory?"

"It's fine."

"Then should we begin?"

"Yes." Cole waited for Marlene to show him which chair was his before he sat down. He removed his hat but kept his jacket on. A young woman came up to them. She fussed with Marlene's hair and makeup, then turned to him, holding some face powder.

"Do you mind?"

"No."

She powdered his face, smoothed back his hair, then she left them without another word. Cole liked people who respected other people's privacy. He turned his attention back to Marlene and held out his hand, palm up. "List."

"You don't forget a thing do you?" Marlene said, her voice laced with humor as she placed a notepad in his large hand.

"Not usually," Cole replied as he scanned the questions. Not one pertained to Lindsey's death just like they'd agreed. He handed the pad back. "It's fine."

"Good. Are you ready?"

His stomach took a dive. "As ready as I'll ever be."

Marlene signaled her producer, and the cameras began rolling. As the interview progressed, Cole relaxed more and more and as she said, it was an informal conversation, more like two friends talking versus interviewer and interviewee.

By the time the interview ended, Cole felt as though an encumbered burden had lifted off his chest, and he was breathing easier. He did not understand what the public would think of anything he said, but he thought he didn't care one way or another. And he wouldn't have long to wait, as Marlene planned to air the interview tomorrow morning in her usual time slot.

Cole walked back to his hotel and went directly to his room to prepare for the night's concert. The band's business manager, who'd been with the band from the beginning, sounded none too happy about postponing two concert dates in Detroit, but Cole knew he'd get over it. And hopefully so would their fans. He had a flight out tomorrow afternoon. An earlier flight would have been better, but there wasn't anything available. Now, with the later flight, he could spend time with AJ. His behavior at the concert last night was frightening, and he figured tonight to be no less.

He'd been right. That night's concert, AJ cloned his previous night's behavior and Cole became even more worried. He tossed and turned most of the night, flashing from Shannon, to Cameron, to AJ. It was a long depressing night.

AJ sat on the bed in his hotel room looking un-kept and exhausted. If one looked closely into his eyes, they would see eyes glazed and void of life. They would see no emotion whatsoever. He may look like a man void of any emotion, but his brain was active, thinking about money, fame, his terrific family, wonderful friends and one best friend—Cole.

And there lay the problem. Now that AJ finally opened his mind to the truth about Lindsey's death, he couldn't look Cole in the eye. He couldn't continue to work with him and he most definitely couldn't continue to let him take the blame for something he did. Cole had already paid dearly, and he deserved more out of life. He also deserved to know the truth about that night.

Earlier in the day, he'd purchased a small camera and tripod. He focused it on the bed and hit record.

"T'is AJ Macleod and ah have something tae say. I have done an injustice tae Cole Jackson, and ah have tae right the wrong." He closed his eyes briefly then cleared his throat. "Ah'm sorry Cole. Ah'm so sorry." He wiped his eyes. "Ah dinnae ken what happened or why it happened. Ah only ken ah did it. Ah killed Lindsey. Ah blocked it out for years, convincing myself someone else committed the murder because ah could never have done that tae her. But ah did do that tae her and not only did ah take her life, ah took yours away as well. You will never ken how sorry ah am.

"Ah dinnae expect ye to forgive me and ah'm not asking for it, but would ye please look after Elizabeth and my children. They should not be blamed for my sins. This has nothing tae do with them." He didn't bother wiping the tears away anymore. He let them flow freely. "All ah can say is ah'm sorry. Ah wish ye well, and ah hope ye find your happiness and all your heart's desire with Shannon. Love is precious, and it's a strong, precious love that binds ye two together. Don't waste a single day of it.

"Tae my beautiful wife, ah'm sorry for what all this will do tae ye and our children. Ah love all of ye with my entire heart, and that's why what ah'm about tae do is hurting me so. But it must be done."

AJ struggled to open the bottle of sleeping pills. When he did, he silently prayed and swallowed the entire contents. He was not taking any chances. He did not want to wake up, ever.

As he began feeling sleepy, he curled up on the bed in a fetal position. His last thought before his world ended was that he had forgotten to stop the camera from recording.

Chapter Seventeen

COLE SNAPPED AWAKE THE NEXT MORNING TO POUNDING ON the door and a woman's voice with a strong Brazilian accent calling out, "Mr. Jackson, Mr. Jackson, please open the door."

Not understanding what the fuss was about, he quickly pulled on his jeans and T-shirt from yesterday, combed his hands through his hair, and opened the door to a frantic-looking young maid. She grabbed his arm with surprising strength and pulled him forward. "Please come quick. Mr. Macleod. Something is wrong, he no wake up."

In that instant Cole realized the popular saying, "my heart stopped" was not just an expression. Pulling away from the maid he ran like hell down the hall to AJ's room. The door stood ajar and several hotel security guards graced the inside. Cole crossed the threshold, his hand on his pounding heart as he scanned the room, his eyes coming to rest on the figure on the bed. Oh God. He didn't have to get closer to know AJ was dead. Cole could smell death. The strong pungent smell of body fluids and waste hung in the air. He swallowed the bile trying to force its way up his throat while he stood there mesmerized by AJ's dead body. Death was not a pretty sight, nor was there any pride.

Cole suddenly felt old, tired and numb. AJ—his best friend—dead. It didn't seem possible. How? Why?

"Excuse me, everybody out," bellowed a plain clothes detective as he came into the room with two uniformed officers and a man carrying a medical examiner's bag.

Cole left the room on legs so unsteady they could have belonged to a ten-month-old baby wobbling along, taking his first steps. When he reached the hallway, he collapsed to the ground and sat stunned as silent tears streamed down his face. He waited and waited as people in law enforcement came and went. He stared at a dark spot on the wall for what seemed like an eternity. After a time the detective he had seen earlier approached him.

"Mr. Jackson?"

Cole climbed to his feet but leaned heavily against the wall for support. He didn't trust his legs just yet.

"Yes."

"Mr. Jackson, I'm Detective Silver. I'm sorry, but Mr. Macleod is dead," the detective said flatly.

"I know."

"Would you mind notifying his family? I think it would be better coming from someone close to them."

Jesus, Cole closed his eyes and hoped to God when he opened them he would be lying in bed, and this would all be a dream. There was *no way* AJ was dead. But when he slowly opened his eyes, nothing had changed. The harsh-looking detective still stood there waiting for an answer to his question, and AJ was still dead. Cole cleared his throat, coughed and finally answered the detective. "Yes. How... how did he die?"

"It's too soon to tell. Once an autopsy's done, we'll

know for certain. But it appears to be a suicide by sleeping pills."

His knees buckled, and he crumpled back to the ground. He could not breathe as claws gripped his lungs, and his heart pounded toward fatal speed. Burying his face in his hands, he fought the sobs bubbling up and fighting their way out.

"Was... was there a note?" He forced the words out, and after he said them, he thought, what a stupid question. But then again, most suicide victims left notes.

"No. However, he recorded a video."

Cole's head snapped up. "Excuse me?"

"Yeah, that's what I thought. I just watched it. And there's something you should know. It pertains directly to you."

Cole groped the wall with his hands as he stood up, locking his knees in hopes they wouldn't give way again. "How so," he asked, trying not to picture AJ swallowing pills and lying dead in bed in his own body waste not thirty feet from him. Guilt pounded him like a runaway freight train. He knew something was bothering AJ, and he had tried to talk to him, but shit, obviously not hard enough.

"I shouldn't tell you this, but before there's a media frenzy, which I'm certain there will be, I think you should know it was a confession and an apology."

Cole took a steady breath, not knowing if he wanted to hear this. "I don't understand."

The detective looked right at him, sympathy radiating from the same eyes that appeared hard earlier. "Macleod confessed to killing your wife."

Cole closed his eyes and leaned even harder against the wall. His whole body convulsed, and his heart pounded so loudly it caused severe pain inside his head. He knew if he moved even an inch his head would explode. What nightmare had he woken up in? This couldn't be right? Couldn't be real?

"AJ loved Lindsey. I don't understand," he choked out, feeling confused and sad and hurt. If it's true, his best friend killed his wife and let him take the blame. Let him go to jail. He didn't want it to be true, and he wouldn't believe it until he saw AJ's confession himself. And even then, he didn't know if he'd believe it. Not in AJ's nature.

"Can I see the video?"

"Yes. You'll have to come to the station house. I'm almost done here. I'll drive you."

"Th...Thanks," Cole mumbled.

Several minutes later, the detective came out of AJ's room with a small blue camera in a plastic bag. Cole followed him in a mind-numbing haze.

"Mr. Jackson, why don't we stop by your room so you can get your shoes?"

Cole glanced down at his bare feet. Christ, he would have walked out of the hotel barefoot and being as numb as he was, he never would have noticed.

The ride to the station house took less than ten minutes. It was the longest ten minutes of Cole's life. He stared, unseeing out the car window, everything blurring together as if a painter regretted his painting or possibly hated it and took his brush, swirling it across the canvas, washing all the colors and images together. Nothing was in focus. Cole couldn't concentrate, or was it his brain protecting him from the devastating reality around him?

When they arrived at the station, he stumbled out of the car and blindly followed Detective Silver into the station house. There, he found a small room with a laptop, a gray metal table and two metal chairs, unaware of the stares and hushed talk around him.

The Detective plugged in the camera, turned the

computer screen toward him and left the room to give him privacy. Cole watched as AJ's face appeared larger than life on the screen. His breathing became choppier and choppier as he fought not to sob, but it was no use. He buried his head in his hands, and as his whole body shook, he cried out in anguish. "Damn you, AJ. I would have forgiven you. You didn't have to take your life. I loved you, man." Then the rage boiled up and exploded. Cole began throwing and pounding everything in sight until Detective Silver came back in with several officers to restrain him. Cole could do nothing, think about nothing as numbness took over, and he buried his head once again in his hands.

"Shannon," Mitch yelled up the stairs, "come quickly. Cole's on the Marlene Simpson Show."

"What," she yelled as she descended the stairs in a hurry, her feet barely touching the steps as her fingers fumbled with the buttons of her blouse. "Did I hear you right?"

She slid onto the couch, eyes glued to the television. Sure enough, it was Cole. Her heart jumped at the sight of him. He was so gorgeous her breath escaped her lungs in one quick swoop. *How could she have forgotten the effect he had on her?* She clasped her shaky hands together and lost herself in the show, her attention never wavering until a commercial. Then she looked at Mitch, pride as well as tears in her eyes.

"I can't believe he gave an interview. He said nothing when I spoke with him." She sucked in air as the commercial ended and Cole's face took over the screen again. She had heard most of what he and Marlene discussed before from Cole, yet she was still moved greatly by what he'd gone through. And horrified about how cruelly some people treated him. And she couldn't believe he had broken his silence about Lindsey's death. Incredible as it seemed, he was the one to bring it up.

By the time the interview ended, she could barely breathe her emotions were running so high, never mind her feelings of love for him. She kept reminding herself that he would be here today. Tonight they could hold each other and make love and finally look to the future together.

Just as Mitch was about to hit the off button, a live broadcast from a local Boston station broke in. Shannon and Mitch sat stunned as they listened to the reporter tell the news of AJ Macleod's death by suicide. The woman reporter read from AJ's quote as the words appeared on the screen. They broadcast everything AJ said in his suicide video for the entire world to hear and read.

Shannon sat motionlessly, shocked by it. Mitch sat beside her and pulled her into his arms for comfort and silent support.

Oh my God! What was Cole going through? Where was he? The reporter said Cole knew about AJ's death and had watched the video. He also had been in AJ's hotel room and identified the body. Shannon clutched her heart as pain pierced through it. Cole must be brokenhearted to find out it was his best friend who had murdered his wife. Would life ever stop throwing curves in the path of his happiness? Yes, the world would finally know he was innocent, but still the cost to him was high.

Shannon knew he would still take the blame on himself for Lindsey's death, anyway. And he would definitely feel responsible for AJ's death. A thought suddenly occurred to her. Was he still on his way? She doubted it. He now had AJ's death to deal with, and Cole would make all the arrangements. He would not leave his best friend and bandmate in death regardless of the horrendous circumstances, regardless of the betrayal, the deceit and the open lies. Even with the years stolen from him, he would honor his friend in death.

She breathed deeply and sighed loudly as she wiped away her tears with her trembling fingers. She loved Cole so much, and she admired him for his loyalty and compassion and love. If the circumstances were reversed, could she be as caring as Cole?

"Mitch, please find me the phone. I need to call him." Her voice sounded hollow, distant and strange, as though coming from inside a deep, dark cave echoing off rock walls trying to find the opening to freedom, sunlight and life.

Shannon hugged herself and rocked back and forth. There was so much pain in her life right now and she was hurting badly, hurting for herself, for Cole and for AJ's family back in Scotland, but most of all she hurt for her missing son. She needed her son. She needed to see him, touch him and reassure herself that he still lived.

Mitch handed her the phone, and the concern and love pouring from his eyes helped steady her and allow her to make the call. She really didn't want to reach out to Cole on the phone. It was too impersonal, too sterile. She wanted to reach out in person so she could physically comfort him by wrapping her body around his and offering solace. But she'd call him and do what she could with the distance of miles between them—miles upon cold, lonely and needy miles.

She received his voicemail. Damn. "Cole, I just heard. I don't know what to say. I'm sorry. I love you. Call me."

Less than five minutes passed before the phone rang, and she jumped, still holding the receiver cradled in her hand. She read the caller ID, and her heart stopped. It was Cole.

"Hi." She held her breath, waiting for his voice.

"Hey," he said, sounding tired and numb.

"Are you okay?"

The sound of him exhaling came through the phone. "Not really, things are bad. As bad as they can get." As he spoke, his voice lowered. "I can't get the image of Lindsey's lifeless body out of my mind or the image of AJ lying dead in the hotel bed. It was awful." He cleared his throat. "I can't get the smell out of my nose. It's the second time I've witnessed death, smelled death. And it's two times too many."

He paused, and she heard him sob. "Oh, Shannon, I can't believe what's happening. It seems surreal. I keep expecting to wake up and I'll be twenty-three again, before Lindsey's death, before any of the other nightmarish stuff happened."

She didn't know what to say, and her heart ached for him. Her whole body burned in pain for him. "Oh, Cole," she whispered.

"I called Elizabeth, AJ's wife and broke the news. Without a doubt, it was the most difficult thing I've ever done. She's devastated. I don't know what she'll tell their children. Christ, they're so young, only five, eight and ten. How will this affect their lives?" he groaned out in despair. "The only good thing is they are isolated in the Highlands, but I'm sure the media will still find them and make a mockery of this."

"You watched the video?" It wasn't necessarily a question. She already knew the answer but felt compelled to ask.

"Yeah, it was awful. AJ looked and sounded terrible, not like him at all. It's no wonder he was confessing to murdering Lindsey and planning his own demise. Shit, he filmed his own death." He paused, and she heard him fighting for control, for air. "I watched him die. Right there in front of my eyes, and I knew the second it happened. There are no words to describe watching death happen. And I tried not to watch, hell I tried, I really tried, but I couldn't help it. And even though I know it to be true, I'm having a hard time dealing with it, accepting it, under-standing it. *No one* had their head screwed on straighter and tighter than AJ."

She heard what sounded like someone smack their forehead. "I'm not sure I'm capable of dealing with it now. Nor am I feeling much of anything but shock. I feel like my life is not my own. I'm watching it happen from the sidelines and have no control over anything."

Shannon's throat burned, and her lungs ached as she tried to breathe. Hearing him like this tortured her to no end. She wanted to wrap her arms around him and take his pain and anguish away. But even if she could take it away for a time, he would eventually have to face it and go on. She could be a much-needed salve for his hurt, but it would only be temporary.

"What happens now?" she asked.

"I'm sorry I can't come to you today. I know you're frantic with worry about Cameron and so am I, but I owe it to AJ and his family to accompany his body to Scotland and see him buried. It won't be for several days, until the autopsy report is complete and they release his body. Meanwhile, I'm staying here." His voice sounded hollow, defeated and foreign to her ears. "My lawyer's trying to speed up the legal paperwork involved in clearing my name so I can get a passport. I'm not sending AJ home alone. I could not attend Lindsey's service, and it's some-thing that will always plague me, but I'll be damned if I'll miss AJ's. We're all going. The whole band, that is." He paused and drew air. "I'd ask you to come, but I know you can't. Your responsibility is to your son." He cleared his throat. "Any news?" he asked.

She told him what she knew. "I'm trying not to get my hopes up too high, but I can't help it. I just want him home so I can hold him again, touch him again, and tell him I love him."

She sniffled and coughed. "In my heart I know it will be okay. But my imaginative mind is wreaking havoc on me, tormenting me, haunting me."

"He'll be fine. He's smart and resourceful. He'll come home soon," Cole said with more emotion in his voice than she'd heard during the whole depressing conversation.

Shannon hoped there was truth to his words. All she had left was hope and faith. "You were something else on the Marlene Simpson show. You handled yourself incredibly professionally and suave, and then I heard the news..."

"Great timing, huh?" he interrupted. "I'm glad I did it and Marlene is quite a lady. I have great respect for her. She's a woman of her word."

"Will you be coming right back after the burial?" Something inside her panicked as she waited for his answer. Waited to hear if her heart, her future and her happiness were at stake.

"I don't know what I'm doing. I can't think beyond burying AJ. Elizabeth might need me. Although I doubt it with her family nearby, not to mention I'm a stranger to her."

"I need you," she choked out, and her heart lodged up into her throat as she waited through the silence.

"God, I need you too," he groaned out. "I miss you. I can't wait to see you, hold you and know you're real. You're the one real thing woven into my unreal world. I'll call every day and promise me you'll be okay. I'm so worried about you and Cameron. I wish I could make it all better. But if there's one thing I've learned, it's that we're all just passengers in this thing called life. Our destinies are predetermined. And if God has any love or compassion in him at all, you and I are each other's destiny. We'll be together and soon."

Shannon couldn't contain her tears or her sobs any longer. When she could trust herself to speak again, she said, "When did you become so wise?"

He snorted. "I'm not wise, just trying to be a realist. And don't forget I'm good with words and expressing my feelings through them. It's about the only way I know how."

"That's not true," she said, lightening the mood. "I seem to recall spending two days with you. Two wonderful days spent together, and you expressed yourself in many other ways. Good ways." She paused and sighed as she remembered the feel of him against her body, inside her. "I miss you. It seems forever since I've seen you."

"Shit. I don't want to go. Promise me you'll never doubt my love for you?"

"I'll try not to. Never doubt mine for you," she cried into the phone then disconnected.

A long time passed before she felt composed enough to look at her brother, who had just re-entered the room. Her brother, always a gentleman, had left the room to give her privacy. If that Texas lady knew what was good for her, she had better reach out and hold tight to him. He was rare, as rare a man as her Cole.

Once she calmed down, she punched in the number for Kevin English. She hadn't spoken with him in a few days, and she needed to bring him up to speed on Cameron.

"Kevin English."

"K ... Kevin, hi, it's me."

"Shannon, how are you?"

Shannon took a deep breath and fought the tears stinging her eyes. She would not cry into the phone. She'd just cried into Cole's ear and enough. "I've been better, but I have some new developments on Cameron." She told Kevin all about them.

"Like I said before, if you need me, I'm here. Just say the word, and I'm on the next plane out," Kevin replied with his gentle, soothing voice.

"No. Stay where you are. There really isn't anything you can do here. I'll keep you posted."

"Okay, sweetie, anything you say. Love you and try not to agonize over this too much."

Shannon snorted into the phone. "Yeah, I'll try. Bye. Love you too."

For the second morning in a row, Cameron woke up naked in bed with an equally naked Amber. Only today they were checking out and hoping to hitch a ride to the nearest bus station and purchase tickets to continue on to California. He had to keep focusing on California because if he didn't, homesickness took over in suffocating waves. He missed his mom, and if he wanted to be honest, he also missed his dad.

He and his dad had said some awful, hurtful things to one another, and since Cameron had meant nothing he said perhaps the same thing pertained to what his dad said to him.

He also missed Matt, Heather and Taylor and Cheryl. But most of all he missed his mom. She was all alone without him, and he felt terrible having left her. What must she be feeling? Awful he imagined. And today his heart lay heavy, longing for everything familiar, even school. He missed school and his friends. He missed the ocean, the smell of saltwater and the feel of the sand between his toes. He wanted to hear the sounds of the waves crashing on the beach late at night from his bed.

But most of all, he felt guilty for what his running away was probably doing to everyone. Maybe he should go back and convince Amber to return. He imagined her dad was frantically missing her, especially since her mother had died recently.

When he got his license, they could see each other. He could drive to Newport. It only took a little over an hour to get there. Heck, that was nothing. Put some good tunes on the stereo, and off he'd go. A little Jason Aldean, some Eric Church, and a little rock-and-roll from BlackJack, and he'd be good to go for miles upon miles.

He knew what he had to do. He had to convince Amber because if he couldn't convince her to go with him, he'd be dammed if he'd let her travel alone. So if he wanted to go home, he'd have to be persuasive.

Cameron rolled onto his side, resting up on one elbow as he faced her, and his stomach took a tumble. He would miss waking up with her. And the sex, hell, he would miss that too.

Maybe he'd get himself a girlfriend when he got home. Perhaps Lacey Paranello would be his girlfriend. She was in some of his classes and she was hot. There was, however, one major problem. Lacey didn't know he existed, never mind the fact that she dated a senior and not just any senior, the captain of the hockey team, and everyone knew he was destined to go pro after playing for a division one college. Hell, he'd probably suit up in maroon and gold and play for the Boston College Eagles or maybe red and white for the Boston University Terriers, or even the Northeastern Huskies. One of the bean pot teams would probably recruit him, they would be crazy not to and when they did, what would Lacey see in him? Her boyfriend would head to play hockey for a division one school and what would he be doing? Still be in high school. Oh well, if Lacey wasn't interested there were other fine girls in school besides her. The problem was he'd wanted Lacey since seventh grade.

He focused back on Amber. Too bad she didn't go to his school. They would have each other. He reached out and combed his fingers through her soft hair, her thick, long and exotically dark hair. He tried to picture her as a natural blonde which she was, and he knew she would be even prettier as a blonde. She had taken all the rings out of her nose and eyebrows. That left several in each ear and her belly button. And Cameron had to admit the belly button being pierced and sporting a silver rod was sexy as hell. If he hadn't already been sporting a bona, he would have then.

She fluttered her eyes open and slowly smiled at him.

"Morning," he murmured.

She stretched and curled into him. "Morning yourself. What time do we have to check out?"

"Not for two hours," he replied.

She smiled a smile Cameron knew well. It was shy, sexy and sweet, but it meant she wanted sex and his body hardened even more just watching that smile cross her lips.

A little while later as they lay on the bed sweating and breathing heavily, Cameron went for it and told her his plan. She let him speak his mind without interrupting, but he knew she wasn't keen on going home.

"I'm not going back, you can," she said like it was no big deal. "I'll be fine, but I can't go home, not yet anyway."

"Why not," he countered.

Amber sat up and hugged her knees. "I don't know. I just don't want to. My dad probably doesn't even know I'm gone."

Cameron saw the tears pooling in her eyes, and he knew she missed home as much as he did, but she was one stubborn girl. "I'm sure your dad knows you're gone, and I bet he's worried sick. He's probably out looking for you right now."

She glanced at him, her lips quivering and tears in her sad, but hopeful eyes, and he knew he had her. He only hoped her dad really missed her so she didn't just run away again. "Please go back with me?" Cameron pleaded, his voice vibrating and his eyes beginning to tear.

"Okay."

He hugged her close. "Good. Let's get going. We need to hitch a ride to the nearest bus station."

Thirty minutes later they were out on the street with all their gear and Amber had her thumb out whenever a car or truck went by, which wasn't often. Finally, a trucker driving an eighteen-wheeler pulled over. "Where ya'll going?" asked the large, bald man with a southern drawl and a warm smile.

"The bus station," replied Amber.

"Hop in. I'll give you a lift."

He seemed friendly enough Cameron thought as the man drove and talked and he and Amber mostly listened. They pulled onto a highway crowded with truckers hauling everything from livestock to humongous logs. Welcome to the Midwest.

Even though the man had seemed nice, Cameron felt instant relief when they arrived at the bus station. Unfortunately, they had to wait until six that night for a bus. Cameron purchased their tickets. He figured it was because he was sick that they got off the bus in the first place, so he owed her.

They sat on the cleanest bench they could find and snacked on food from the vending machines and watched the one grimy television in the station. They were watching some game show when a news reporter interrupted and Cameron sat, frozen, his heart lodged in his throat.

He couldn't believe what he was hearing or seeing. There were three pictures on the screen, AJ, Cole and someone he presumed to be Cole's dead wife.

AJ was dead. He committed suicide. He killed Lindsey.

"Hey, isn't that members of BlackJack?" Amber asked, pointing to the television.

Cameron swallowed and cleared his suddenly dry and burning throat. "Yeah."

"How awful."

"Yeah." What else could he say? And now more than ever he was glad he was going back home. Six o'clock couldn't come fast enough.

They boarded the bus, sitting in the back. It was nearly empty. Cameron hadn't played his guitar in several days and he craved it. He wanted to play in tribute to AJ because if it weren't for him, he never would've played at the Garden with them, nor would his mom have met Cole.

He played as quietly so no one would complain. He played every BlackJack song he could remember. Amber's eyes fluttered closed beside him, but he didn't think she was sleeping. She was chilling out to his music, so he continued playing. He even played the new stuff he and Cole wrote together.

By the time darkness descended all around them, Cameron looked out the window and saw fog so thick he contemplated how the driver could see anything in the blanket surrounding them. He went back to playing. It helped pass the time. Playing always made him feel better. He played his heart and soul out on his guitar, and when his fingers were numb and his arms ached, he continued to play. Much later, he put his guitar back into its case, put his arm around Amber's shoulders, pulled her close, and drifted off to sleep. Sleep plagued with visions of AJ and Cole and his mom. His dreams replayed the day they all met, the day he played at the Garden, one of the best days of his life.

Something, a noise, a screeching metal against metal, struggled to pull him out of his dream. Yelling, screaming and someone shaking him pulled him out completely.

"Cameron, we're crashing," Amber screamed in complete terror.

The next thing he knew, he crashed into the seat in front of him, and then he tumbled toward the opposite side of the bus. He saw, or at least he thought he saw, Amber's head crash into the window. He tried crawling toward her, but the bus was sliding on its side. The noise was deafening; it sounded as though a freight train screamed through his head. Sparks flew everywhere, and when the bus finally stopped moving, pain exploded throughout his body. All around him people were crying, and he thought of Amber. He struggled to get up but something heavy had him pinned down. Black swirls blurred his eyes, and the world tilted. He closed his eyes shut, trying to fight the inevitable pull into darkness. His heart slowed and parts of his life flashed before his eyes. Was he dying? He didn't think so, but still he didn't feel right either. Exhaustion and weakness washed over him as he faded. He prayed to God because he didn't want to die, not now.

Chapter Eighteen

Startled awake by the sound of her phone ringing, Shannon's heart leaped up into her throat. One quick glance at the clock told her it was two in the morning.

"H..." she cleared her throat and tried again. "Hello."

"Mrs. McKenzie?"

Oh God. It was never a good sign when people called her Mrs. McKenzie. "Yes." Her head pounded in tune with her heart.

"I'm Doctor Splaine from St. Joseph's Hospital in Denver. There's been an accident. Your son Cameron is injured."

Shannon had a hard time replying because her entire body shuddered. She nearly dropped the phone. A huge part of her was afraid to ask how badly her son was hurt. So instead of answering the good doctor, she prayed to God to spare her son's life.

"He's pretty banged up. Broke several bones."

She felt a strange feeling in the pit of her stomach when she went to bed, almost as though she knew. "How...how bad is it?" She held her breath and waited.

"Unfortunately..."

Oh God, her hand flew to her throat. Here it comes.

"He suffered a severe blow to the head. He's unconscious. We had to operate on his leg because of a compound fracture, and he lost quite a bit of blood. However, that's not my concern right now. His head injury is. How soon can you get here?"

Shannon's life became a tunnel, and the phone and the person on the other end were billions of miles away. Miles she'd never be able to travel in time. This could not be happening, not to her Cameron. Somehow she reeled herself back to the situation at hand and answered with what she thought was someone else's voice entirely.

"First flight out."

"Good."

After the call ended, she stared at the wall, trying to come to terms with what the doctor told her. Cameron hurt. Hurt badly. His head injured. And then the reality of the situation slammed into her, and she cried for five solid minutes before she reeled herself in once again and dreaded what she had to do next. She had to call John. She'd dialed his number thousands of times before but couldn't remember it now. It took her three tries to get it right. Her brain had gone numb along with the rest of her body. When she heard John's clipped voice answer, she broke down again and blubbered. It was a wonder John understood anything she said. He would make the travel arrangements as she drove to his house.

Frantically she tossed clothes carelessly into an overnight bag, pulled on jeans and a sweater and grabbed her leather jacket on her way out the door. As she drove, squinting through her tears, she thought about the fact that Mitch had gone home. She wished he'd stayed because she wasn't confident in her driving skills at the moment.

It was a dark and drizzly night, and Shannon never did much care for driving at night in the rain. The glare from other car lights nearly blinded her. She leaned forward, white-knuckling the steering wheel, and drove as fast as she could. When she approached the exit, she said her silent thanks to God for getting her safely to John's and her hands loosened their grip on the steering wheel. Several miles later, she pulled up to his well-lit antique colonial.

Before she could knock, the door flew open, and she found herself wrapped in John's arms. He stroked her back as she quivered in shock and fear of the unknown. "I couldn't get us a flight until seven in the morning. Come in and get comfortable."

Shannon entered their family room and sat on the couch. The television glowed in the dark telling her John must've been watching it. He left her briefly and came back carrying a pillow and blanket. "You might as well sleep for a couple hours."

Shannon took the things he offered and tried to settle in. But she knew sleep would never be possible. "Will you stay with me?"

John sighed, ran his hands through his hair and her cheeks heated with embarrassment. Why would he stay with her when he had Cheryl's comforting arms waiting for him in their bed? She took a deep breath and let him off the hook. "Never mind, I think I might sleep after all."

He raised a brow. "You sure?"

She waved him off. "Go. Just don't forget to set the alarm."

Before he left, he shut off the television and Shannon found herself alone in the room. The glow from the night-light plugged into the wall gave her welcomed comfort. She lay on the couch and prayed. When she felt there was nothing left she could do or pray about, she turned the television back on, muted the volume, and rummaged around in her pocketbook for her cell phone. She desperately needed to hear Cole's voice. She didn't want to call her parents, her sisters or Mitch until she had a better understanding of Cameron's injuries. She scrolled through her address book, touched Cole's name and counted the rings until she heard his deep, sleepy voice answer on the third ring.

"Hello."

"Hi, sorry I woke you."

Bed covers rustled. "Shannon, honey, is everything okay?"

"No," she choked out. "I'm at John's house and we're on our way to Denver." She paused, hoping to stop her voice from vibrating. "Cameron was in an accident."

Cole groaned and cursed. "How bad is it?"

She explained what she knew, which wasn't much.

"I'll meet you at the hospital tomorrow."

"But...what about AJ?"

"I can't take his body back until it's released from the autopsy, probably three days. Besides, I'd go stir crazy here worrying about Cameron." He paused and added, "Worrying about you."

She cried. Jeez, she'd done nothing but cry lately, albeit she had plenty of reasons.

Shannon kept Cole on the phone for over an hour. They talked about everything and anything. Talking to him was easy. It seemed as if she could tell him anything, and he'd understand. Not to mention hearing his voice soothed her. He understood her so well. If she didn't already accept their connection, she'd freak out that someone knew her almost better than she knew herself. And hell, maybe he did. She finally let him go because her battery kept flashing low. So before her phone died, she hung up and lay there silently as her heart pounded so loudly against her ribs they hurt.

The hell with cardio workouts. All it took to get one's heart rate pumping was having a family crisis.

John came in to wake her not long after she hung up with Cole, and she was ready. The sun had yet to rise, but at least the rain had let up. As they walked to her car, John held out his hand. "I'll drive." Relieved, she gladly handed the keys over.

John drove in silence so she sat back and listened to her car stereo. When a BlackJack song played she witnessed John physically tense up. So even though Cole was innocent of Lindsey's death, John still didn't approve. Too damn bad for him. She was going for the brass ring. He had, so why not her?

They breezed into Logan Airport, as traffic was light this early in the morning. When they went through security, John removed his shoes. She almost laughed at his expression when she saw his big toe protruding through his sock.

"Did you forget you had to remove your shoes?"

"Nope. These were the only matching socks I could find."

"Having a hard time with the laundry?"

He rolled his eyes and muttered something under his breath, which Shannon was sure wasn't nice.

The flight left on time and was uneventful. They arrived in Denver almost on time to the minute. If only all of her flights went this smoothly. Which reminded her she had to contact her publicist and cancel her tour on the West Coast. Christ, with all the worries and thoughts going on in her head, how had that popped up?

They drove straight to the hospital from the airport and the closer she got the more nauseated she was. She'd not eaten anything, but that didn't mean her stomach didn't want to revolt and throw up something. She swallowed and fought the bile down as she clasped her hands on her lap to keep them steady. Her whole body ached from her trembling and tense muscles. When they pulled up to the hospital, she felt almost faint from stress and anxiety and shit—fear. Fear of the unknown. Without a word, she linked her arm through John's, hoping to help steady her legs and hoping his were steady enough for both of them.

They entered through the main lobby, went to the volunteer at the desk who gave them Cameron's room number. When Shannon walked down the long sterile hallway, it gave her the illusion of getting longer and narrower, making her wonder if she'd ever reach the end before the walls closed in on her, crushing her, suffocating her, causing her to never see her son again. With a huge sigh of relief, she finally did reach the end.

One nurse at the station outside Cameron's room stopped them before they could enter. "May I help you?"

John answered for them in his deep, commanding voice. "Yes. We're Cameron McKenzie's parents."

"Go on in. I'll page Doctor Splaine and let him know you've arrived."

"Thank you," John mumbled, practically sprinting toward his son's door.

When Shannon stepped inside the first thing she noticed was his left leg up in traction, his right arm in a cast and his head bandaged. She sucked in her breath as she took in the many cuts and bruises on his face. His ribs were bandaged as well. My God, he looked bad. But he'd survived. Yes, thank God. He'd survived. They'd heard a radio report about the crash on the way here. There had been over a dozen vehicles involved.

Heavy fog played a huge part in it. It started when a truck carrying logs jack-knifed causing a chain reaction. There were several fatalities. She tried not to let her mind drift into dangerous places. But it was impossible, and she couldn't help but think Cameron could become one of those casualties.

Shannon stood paralyzed on the floor as she thought about what-ifs. Jesus, she honestly didn't know how she would go on if the worst happened. And her heart bled for those families who had lost cherished loved ones in the crash.

She fought down her tears. She would be strong from now on and cry on the inside, not outside. Gently, she placed her hand on Cameron's unbroken arm and startled when his eyes fluttered open, one all the way, the bruised one only part way. He licked his parched lips. "Mom, Dad," he said, sounding weak and dazed.

The doctor had said he was unconscious. She expected to find him in a coma. Relief washed over her, and her knees nearly gave way so she rested against the side of his bed. She couldn't explain how it felt to see her beautiful son's hazel eyes staring at her. "Does it hurt badly?"

"I'm sorry," he strained to talk. "I was on my way back home. I got off and turned around. I missed you."

Shannon's heart fluttered, and she took his hand in hers, the one without the cast. The hand with the intravenous line feeding him much-needed fluids and medicine. Tears streamed down John's face as he rested his hand on Cameron's shoulder and said, "it's okay. It doesn't matter. What matters is you will be okay. You'll heal and be fine."

"Do me a favor," Cameron struggled to speak, and Shannon could well imagine the painkillers throwing him for a loop. "I keep asking for Amber and nobody will tell me anything." His eyes bored into hers, and she saw the fear and desperation in them. "Find Amber for me," he pleaded.

"I'll find her. Don't you worry," she breathed.

He closed his eyes and slept in a drug-induced state, leaving Shannon to wonder who Amber was?

"Mr. and Mrs. McKenzie, I'm Doctor Splaine. I spoke with you, Mrs. McKenzie, on the phone."

"It's Gallagher. Shannon Gallagher."

"I'm sorry, Ms. Gallagher." He turned toward John. "Are you Mr. McKenzie?"

"Yes." John shook the doctor's hand.

Doctor Splaine gestured toward the doorway. "Why don't we speak in the lounge, and I'll fill you in on everything."

Shannon and John followed the stone-faced, tall, slim, middle-aged doctor to a small waiting room at the end of the pristine white hall. There were several anxious-looking people waiting there. They took three seats in a row, and Doctor Splaine explained Cameron's injuries in great detail. Not only did he break his wrist, he broke his leg in two places, one resulted in a compound fracture and they had to insert rods. He broke several ribs and punctured his lung. He also had a serious concussion and many lacerations and bruises. Yet he was a lucky boy. Only nine of the fifteen people on the bus survived the crash.

Shannon reached for John's hand and squeezed it. A thousand questions raced through her mind, but they all seemed trivial considering the fact so many people perished and her son survived. There was one question, however.

"Cameron asked for a girl, Amber. Can you tell me anything about her?"

Doctor Splaine exhaled and his features turned grim.

Shannon didn't think she wanted to hear what he had to say.

"We came across her student identification card an hour ago and just notified her father. Unfortunately, it doesn't look good."

Shannon bit her lip to hold back an anguished cry for this Amber person she didn't know. She must, however, be the girl Cameron appeared to be traveling with.

The doctor continued, "Other than that, I can't divulge anything else without her father's consent."

"How old is she?" Silly question, but the only one Shannon could think to ask?

"Seventeen," he replied.

Oh God, the poor girl and the poor father. "Could you please let me know when Amber's father arrives?"

"Yes." He unfolded his long, lanky body and stood. "Is there anything else I can do for you?"

"Nothing now. Thanks for everything you've done," John replied as Shannon suddenly looked a million miles away, and the miles between here and there were laced with sadness and pain.

Shannon and John sat vigil beside Cameron's bed for the next several hours. He slept most of the time, but occasionally he'd wake up and try to smile. His nurse came and went. The lab came and drew blood. The respiratory therapist came in and checked his lungs. The orthopedic surgeon came to check his broken ribs and his handy work with his broken arm and his leg. It was, Shannon mused, as though Cameron's hospital room had a revolving door. But it was a good thing. They were taking very good care of him.

Shannon's body was completely drained of energy, and her brain barely functioned. She'd gone way beyond tired. The chair she sat in turned out to be comfortable and every few minutes she felt herself fading out and her head would drop forward and then she'd snap it back up. One of these times she would slither off the chair and hit the ground. At least maybe then she could get some much-needed rest.

A knock sounded on the door, causing Shannon's head to snap up again.

"Hey, can I come in?" said a gorgeous but exhausted-looking man, *her man*, and her heart fluttered.

"Sure."

He reached her in three long strides; she stood and then fell into his outstretched arms. He held her tight, stroking her hair and murmuring soothing words into her ear.

"I'm here. Everything will be okay." He pulled back and kissed her mouth, tasting her salty tears. He wanted nothing more than to inhale her, but this was neither the time nor the place. Reluctantly he peeled his lips from hers, looked at Cameron and sucked in air as pain pierced his chest. Cole dropped his arms, reached for Shannon's hand with one of his, and entwined them together. "How is he?"

Shannon explained everything she knew and what muscles Cole had that were not already tense, tightened up. Cameron looked awful, young, pale and fragile lying in the bed against the stark white sheets. He struggled to fight back his own tears, which was nothing new in the past twenty-four hours.

"He's strong, and he's a fighter. He'll be up and around in no time." Cole prayed his words rang true. They had to for Shannon's sake, for John's and for his own and especially for Cameron's.

Shannon squeezed his hand and leaned closer into him with her head resting against his. Her scent drifted to his nostrils, reminding him how much he'd missed her, missed everything about her. He dropped her hand and circled his arms around her waist, pulling her close. It was then he noticed John sitting tense and quiet in the corner watching them. Cole might be free from the stigma of being a murderer, but John still didn't approve of him being with Shannon. Well, hell, too bad. He'd have to get over it because nothing could keep him from being with her now. Nothing would stop him from loving her, marrying her and having a family with her. John be dammed.

"Hey, John," he drawled.

"Jackson?"

That went well, Cole mused.

Cameron coughed, and all eyes flew to him. His eyes fluttered open and when he saw Cole he smiled big time and his eyes sparkled.

***

Great, John thought. His son never looked at him like that. What was it about the guy that not only his ex-wife, but his son, went ape over? Just because he was some big-shot musician, didn't they know he put his jeans on one leg at a time like all working stiffs?

He mumbled something and left the room. Coffee, all he could think about was the fact he needed a caffeine boost and a bottle of his favorite pink drink. Suddenly his stomach had turned sour. He stopped his fingers just as they were about to comb through his thinning hair. If he didn't stop the habit, he'd be bald by next week.

"Excuse me," said a young nurse from behind the

nurses' station. But then again, everyone seemed young to John lately.

"Yes?"

She smiled hesitantly before she asked, "Is that Cole Jackson in your son's room?"

Wouldn't you know? A young, pretty nurse would never smile at him like that. He should have known. He almost said no. The word formed in his mouth, but for some reason he mumbled "yes" and continued walking toward the elevator doors. He hated feeling this way. God, he cringed. He was jealous of Jackson. Jealous of everything he stood for—his fame, his talent, his obvious way with people, but especially the way his son worshiped him.

It hurt him to see them together. It hurt to see Shannon and him together. He hated himself even more for those feelings. She had every right to date and even remarry if she wanted to. His whole body shuddered. What bothered him the most was he'd have to share Cameron with another man. There would be a stepfather in Cameron's life.

He wondered if Shannon had felt any of these feelings when he'd married Cheryl. Maybe, but somehow he doubted it. She was a caring, giving and loving person. Not someone to be plagued by petty jealousy.

Right this minute he made a promise to himself. A promise to stop being jealous of Jackson. Be happy for Shannon. Happy she finally found someone to love, and someone to love her back. No being jealous because his son and Jackson had the same musical talent. Could share things he never could with Cameron. And just stop being an overall prick.

Yeah right, sounded good, he just wondered if he could do it? He would start by buying three coffees. The old prick would have bought two and let Jackson be dammed.

It was a small peace offering, but it was a start. He paused at the doorway and watched the three of them talking and laughing and touching. Swallowing his jealousy, he walked in.

"Hey, I brought coffee." He winked at his son, and when he handed Jackson one, he said, "Truce."

Jackson seemed surprised by the peace offering as he took the Styrofoam cup and replied, "Truce."

"Hey Dad," Cameron said from his bed, which was raised to a more comfortable semi-sitting position. He pointed to the table beside his bed. "Look what Cole brought me. It's an autographed copy of an old Led Zeppelin album. Every member's signature is on the cover, and there's not a scratch on the vinyl. Isn't it cool?"

The exuberance in Cameron's voice killed John and made this jealousy thing hard to kick. But he'd made a promise to himself. He rolled his eyes and mumbled, "Way cool." Then to Jackson he shook his head. "You're killing me. How the hell can I compete with things like that?" He pointed to the album.

―――――――

Cole knew something had changed between the time John left the room and when he returned. He seemed visibly relaxed and less hateful toward him. Almost civil, he guessed one could say. His comment about competing, not made in anger, but in acceptance of him being a part of Cameron's life.

"It's no big deal. I've had it for years. I carry it with me everywhere. Kind of like a good luck charm."

John snorted. "That's what I mean. Shit. I don't have stuff like that sitting around my house."

"Dad," Cameron broke in. "It's no different from Mom

having autographed books by Lee Child, Sandra Brown, or Nora Roberts. She has bookcases full. Mom knows famous authors, Cole knows famous musicians, and you know..." He paused and smiled right at his dad. "Famous cops."

John threw his head back and laughed. It was Cole's first glimpse of what he thought and hoped was the real John McKenzie. Since the ice broke, they chatted about music, books and movies, and Cole realized that John and Cameron's tastes ran along the same lines as his, except for music. John was a country music fan all the way. *Ouch man, that hurt.*

Chapter Nineteen

WHEN CAMERON'S DINNER CAME, WELL, IF CHICKEN BROTH and Jell-O made up dinner, Shannon thought it was probably a good time to check into a hotel. She kissed her son and reassured herself he would be fine for several hours without them, and she shuffled Cole and John out the door. At the hospital's main entrance, John paused and Shannon could see he had something on his mind. His brows creased and his mouth set tight.

"There's a Sheraton down the street. Maybe we should stay there?" John stated as he stared across the street to the parking garage.

"Okay," Shannon agreed.

"Hey Jackson, Cameron's guitar was destroyed in the accident. I'd like to buy him another one." He raised his eyes and met Cole's. "Maybe you could...um...go shopping with me tomorrow?"

Shannon could not believe her ears. Was John making nice with Cole? Had someone hit him in the head? She smiled and kissed John's cheek. "Thank you," she whispered happily.

He narrowed his eyes and grinned. "For what?"

"You know." Even with Cameron in the hospital, Shannon suddenly felt like the luckiest person in the world.

Cole finally answered John's query. "I'll ask the concierge where there's a good music store." His eyes darted from John to Shannon and back to John. "I'd be glad to go with you."

"Great," John replied. "I'll see you two later. I'm gonna get me a room, a bite to eat, grab a quick nap and I'll see you two back here later."

Shannon and Cole stared at John's back as he walked toward the parking garage. "I think I might like this John," Cole said as he put his arm around her shoulders and they walked in the same direction as John.

"Yeah, I might like him again too."

"Do you think aliens have taken over his body?"

"Maybe." Shannon laughed. "Or maybe he finally realized what an asshole he's been, and he wants to play nice."

"Yeah." Cole laughed. "That's it. He finally realized the sandbox is big enough for all of us."

Anyone remotely close to them could hear their laughter echoing off the concrete walls of the parking garage.

Once in their hotel room, Cole shut and locked the door, leaned against it with his arms crossed in front. A grin plastered on his face, and his midnight eyes smoked with lust. Shannon's pulse soared and every erogenous zone in her body shot off the sensitivity chart. Her fingers worked the buttons on her leather jacket and it dropped to the floor. She peeled her sweater off and locked eyes with Cole, smiling again when she heard him groan.

Her fingers slid down to her jeans and after undoing them she tried to kick them off and then laughed as she remembered her boots were still on. *Smooth, Shannon, real smooth*. Cole strolled casually toward her and dropped to one knee. "Here, let me help you," he said with a quiver in his soft voice.

One boot hit the carpeted floor, then the other. Next he removed her jeans but didn't get up. He skimmed his warm fingers up the inside of her calves and continued up her now quivering thighs. Shannon bit her lip to hold back a groan as he slipped his fingers inside her lace panties, gently opening her folds and inserting first one finger, then two. His thumb found and teased her sensitive nub.

The pressure built and Shannon began floating, drifting until she realized Cole was carrying her to the bed. He laid her down, stripped off her panties and knelt between her open thighs. One glance at him and she saw the look of a man who would get some, and it stole her breath away.

Nothing else existed but Cole's hot mouth making love to her body and his tongue mating with her. She fisted his hair and pulled him in closer as her body trembled. Her head moved from side to side and she cried out, "Cole...oh God...Oh my God." She arched her back forcing her hips higher and higher as the orgasm hit her and kept coming and coming until she couldn't take it and begged for mercy by pushing his head away and trying to close her legs.

Cole slid up her body and held her as she trembled in a release that would not quit.

"I love when you come for me," he said in a raspy voice filled with desire. "You taste so good."

"Cole," she breathed out. "You need to take off your clothes. It's my turn."

Shannon laughed as he shed his clothing in record time and his gorgeous, naked body, standing at full attention, joined her on the bed, giving her full access to him. Before she tasted his body, she tasted his mouth and lost herself in his kisses.

Cole's tongue twisted and twirled with Shannon's. Kissing her resembled an intoxicating elixir, one he could never get enough of. She was addicting, and it was an addiction he never wanted to quit. A deep guttural moan rising up from deep inside was lost between his throat and Shannon's mouth. He heard her purr as she settled deeper into the kiss. He splayed his hands on her back, unhooking her bra and pulling her even closer to his scorching body. They'd gone way past separate entities and were entering the point where he couldn't tell where his body ended and hers began.

This was what love was—love and soul mates. She was the other half of his heart, and this time he would never let her go. He ended the kiss and nuzzled her neck as he fought to control his breathing. "I love you," he whispered breathlessly, lightly biting her soft, creamy neck. "I love you so much."

Shannon leaned up and looked at him. Her lips curved into a sensual smile, her blue eyes smoky with lust. "I love you."

Cole sucked in his breath and held it as she tortured him with her mouth and talented hands. When he thought he would lose it, he flipped her onto her back and entered her with one deep thrust of his hips. Then he froze as he tried to control his body. He didn't want to come yet, he wanted this to last, and he wanted to watch her when she unraveled.

Shannon lay still, her eyes closed as she waited for Cole, knowing he fought to control his body. She'd been bad, really bad. Then his hips moved and his warm palms cupped her breasts. His fingers rolled her nipples, and she thrust her hips up to his. He shifted and pulled her legs up and over his shoulders and thrust deeper still. The sensation boarded on painful, but not quite, as a burst of intense pleasure traveled through her body. Her insides contracted around him as she crested over and over. He tensed and moaned and collapsed on her as she felt the hot wetness from his seed enter her body.

"I don't think I can move," he groaned into her ear.

"Hmm, me neither," she purred. "I missed you."

"Me too, more than you'll ever know."

"Hmm, try me." She wiggled beneath him.

"I would if I could move."

She smacked his back lightly. "You have a dirty mind, Cole Jackson."

He laughed and nipped her ear with his teeth, causing her to gasp. "Don't all men?"

Shannon pushed him off and out of her. "I'm going to shower. You can join me if you'd like." She cast a siren's smile over her shoulder as she disappeared into the bathroom, knowing he'd be right on her heels.

***

One hour later, Shannon and Cole stood together at Cameron's bedside. They arrived just as Doctor Splaine entered the room, making his nightly rounds. They waited patiently through Cameron's exam and the doctor's questions. Then he turned to them, and Shannon saw a tiny flicker of recognition in his eyes when he looked at Cole. Then it was gone behind his doctor's facade.

"Doctor Splaine, I'd like you to meet Cole Jackson." She placed her hand on Cole's arm. "Cole, this is Doctor Splaine, he's taking care of Cameron."

Cole reached out and shook the doctor's hand. "Nice to meet you, and thanks for taking such good care of Cameron for us."

Shannon couldn't believe the stone-faced Doctor Splaine smiled. Well, it was almost like a smile. Maybe he was human.

"Cameron is a great kid and a lucky one at that. He should sleep now as we just gave him something to help him rest." He went to leave and then paused in the doorway. "Amber Sullivan's father arrived a short time ago. She's in room 327. He might like some company. From what I understand his wife passed away last year, and Amber's all he's got left."

Just as Doctor Splaine left, John came in, his face beet red and his breathing labored. "The media knows you're here Jackson. It's a zoo downstairs. One little asshole stuck a microphone in my face and asked how I felt about my ex-wife having a rendezvous at the Sheraton with Cole Jackson while my son's barely hanging onto his life." He held up his hand and put his thumb and index finger together with barely an inch of space between them. "I came this close to clocking the guy in the face. Instead, I told him you two went to the hotel to rest, and Cameron is recovering just fine. Somehow, I don't think he believed the resting at the hotel part."

Shannon felt the heat sting her cheeks. "No, I don't suppose he did."

"Anyway, I insisted on security at the main entrance and at all accesses to Cameron's floor. I'm not having our lives turned into a media circus." He looked at Cole sympathetically. "How can you stand it?"

"I can't. But if you like, I'd be willing to give a statement so maybe they'll leave us alone."

Shannon placed her hand on Cole's arm and shook her head. "No. I'll call Sharon White, my publicist, and have her do a press release. It may give us some time."

"Mom," Cameron moaned, looking sleepy. "You never told me about Amber. How is she? Can I see her?"

Oh dear. With Cole's arrival and Cameron not having asked again, she had purposely put off telling him. Shannon sat on the edge of his bed and decided the only way to tell him would be to come right out with the truth, no matter how much pain it caused her son. "She hit her head badly, honey, and she's in a coma."

"No." Cameron rolled his head from side to side and yelled out in anguish, "No."

Shannon watched as her son struggled with his emotions. She hurt for him. He was too young to know this type of pain and loss. She said a quick silent prayer, "please spare Amber's life, she's way too young to die."

"Will she wake up?"

Shannon blinked back her own tears and looked at Cole, then John who both appeared to struggle with their own emotions. "The doctor doesn't know sweetheart, but you could pray and maybe that'll help."

Cameron closed his eyes and silent tears slithered down his cheeks. His chest hurt, and he could barely breathe for the lump clogging his throat. Amber. He wanted Amber. If he hadn't insisted they turn back, they would have been on a different bus and she would be okay. He had only wanted to help. God, his head felt like a top, spinning fast and furious, barely staying on his shoulders. They must give him some potent drugs. He was tired and his body felt like an elephant stomped on it. There was a constant drum roll going on inside his head and the only time he got relief from the pounding pain was when he slept.

Right now, all he wanted to do was sleep and end his pain. And when he awoke he hoped this whole mess would be a dream, and he and Amber would be back at the motel making love. His last thoughts as blackness descended all around him was of Amber dying.

John watched as Jackson massaged Shannon's shoulders.

"You're tense and stressed out. Try to relax." Her head dropped forward slightly as his fingers gently massaged her neck, shoulders, and back.

"Hmm, that feels good," she said. "However good it feels, I think nothing can help how awful I feel inside."

Jackson looked at him. "Would you mind taking over here while I get Shannon some tea?"

"Stay. I'll get it," John said as he left the room. Visiting hours would end soon, and he knew only one parent could spend the night with Cameron. He supposed he and Jackson would head back to the hotel soon. Strange how, in twelve hours, John had a new-found respect and admiration for the man. And damn it, he didn't want to like the guy, but seeing firsthand how he acted with Shannon and Cameron and how much he loved them both, how could he not like him?

He supposed it was time to be happy for Shannon and to let her go into the arms of another man. Even though he had his own wife he loved, there would always be something special about Shannon. She would always possess a piece of his heart.

Before he left the hallway, he glanced into Amber Sullivan's room. He presumed the man sitting with his eyes closed in a chair next to her bed and holding her hand was her father. John swallowed the lump in his throat. That could be him and Cameron. It made John realize just how lucky they were.

Within the hour, Cole and John left Shannon to sleep on a reclining chair bed in Cameron's room.

"Do you want to leave your car here and drive with me to the hotel?" Cole asked John, not knowing how he'd react to the invite.

"Sure. Would you like to grab a drink at the bar? I'm in desperate need of a beer."

"Sure, but I'll have a club soda."

John suddenly looked embarrassed. "Sorry. I forgot. My brain's kind of mushy right now. Never mind, I think I'll just crash for the night."

Cole shrugged one shoulder. "Whatever."

"Care to meet me in the lobby at nine so we can shop for Cameron's guitar?"

"Sure."

They rode in silence to the hotel, valet parked and just as they were about to step into the hotel entrance, one lone reporter came out of the shadows ready to pounce. "Excuse me, Mr. Jackson, would you like to comment on AJ Macleod's suicide?"

"No, I wouldn't," he said with strong conviction and kept walking.

"Mr. McKenzie, is it true your son, the son you had with the writer, Shannon Gallagher, ran away and that's why he was on the bus that crashed?"

"I have nothing to say."

"Mr. McKenzie?"

Cole turned and stared at the reporter, stone-faced, rage barely under control and shoved the large burley man back, nearly knocking him down in the process and sorry he hadn't done just that. "Leave *him* alone," Cole said in a frozen, icy tone. "His son was seriously injured in an accident, and he'd like his privacy." The reporter tried to interrupt and Cole stared him down. "Shannon Gallagher's publicist will issue a statement tomorrow. Goodnight."

Cole turned, grabbed John's arm and dragged him inside the hotel doors. The reporter wouldn't dare enter, but they could hear him cursing Cole and vowing to sue for assault.

"Thanks," John mumbled, somewhat stunned.

"Don't mention it. I'll see you later."

Cole put the *do not disturb* sign on the door and took a long hot shower. He stood underneath the water as it pelted his naked body, the same body that shook uncontrollably as he cried over AJ's death once again. Being busy today with Shannon and Cameron kept his mind off his grief, but now being alone it consumed him. It swallowed him up, and he didn't know if he could find his way free.

If the running water hadn't turned cold, he would have stayed there all night. The heat from the shower soothed him, but now as he climbed into the empty bed, he felt the tension crawl up his body one muscle at a time until he could hardly move, and he prayed for sleep to take over. But Cole soon found out, there would be no peace in his sleep tonight.

He kept seeing the video of AJ over and over again. Seeing the life slowly drain from his body as he passed from this world to the next. His dreams took him to their first meeting and through all the years on the road, from

Lindsey's murder to his conviction. He dreamed about the years of loneliness and destitution behind iron bars to his release from prison to his love for Shannon, which brought him back to seeing AJ's death. Cole tossed and turned all night, never coming fully awake nor sleeping deeply. And when the sun rose and extended its fingers into his room, he was glad to get up and begin a new day.

Cole didn't want to be alone. He didn't want thoughts of AJ plaguing his mind. His grief was so strong and powerful it overwhelmed him. He needed to be busy. If he dwelled on AJ and the circumstances of his death and the lie that was AJ's life, nothing good would come of it.

Chapter Twenty

AT SEVEN IN THE MORNING, COLE NOTICED A FEW PEOPLE in the small café downstairs. He chose a seat facing the window which faced the street. He gazed endlessly, not really seeing as the blur of people and cars passed by the window. He barely tasted his coffee, although the waitress had refilled it twice. A short time later, he stared at his empty plate, not remembering eating his French toast. He existed in solid form but not really living inside.

"Jackson, mind if I join you?"

Looking up, he saw John standing before his table, his hair still damp from his shower, and Cole gestured toward the seat opposite him. "Be my guest."

John contemplated Jackson's aloofness this morning and decided the man had been through the axe grinder lately and maybe needed a friend to talk to. A friend, now that was something John never in a million years thought he would call Jackson.

"I want to tell you how sorry I am about AJ and everything that has happened."

Jackson inhaled deeply and cleared his throat. "Thanks."

"His wife and kids must devastated?"

Jackson snorted. "Yeah, I imagine they are."

"What will happen to the band now?" John asked, hoping to keep the conversation flowing.

Jackson signaled to the waitress for more coffee. "I don't know. I don't mean to be rude, but I can't talk about it now."

"I understand." John could to a point, but to completely understand he'd have to be in Jackson's shoes. No, thank you. His were crowded enough at the moment.

"I would like to tell you something that happened to Shannon while she was in Chicago," Jackson said seriously.

"Please do."

"Before I do, you must promise me you'll not fly off the handle. She didn't want anyone to know, but I can't stop worrying about it, about her."

John's heart pounded, not liking the sound of Jackson's voice. "I'll try not to."

"I visited her in Chicago. We spent the night dancing at the hotel lounge. I left her shortly after one in the morning." Jackson swiped his hand through his loose hair. "Someone broke into her room and he had a knife..."

"What?" John interrupted, not caring if people stared at him. "Why am I just hearing about this now?"

"There's more. He said he would kill her so I would go back to jail for murder. Fortunately, a hotel employee saw the masked man enter her room and security arrived, but the man escaped. As far as you not knowing, she didn't want you to. After that night she hired a bodyguard, but with all that's been happening with Cameron, she never got around to hiring a new one when she got home. I don't think the threat to her life is over. I don't believe AJ killed my wife. I think the killer's still out there and wants to send me back to jail by any means possible."

John's mouth hung open as his blood boiled inside his body. "I can't fucking believe this. She can't be alone for a minute until we hire bodyguards. If someone so much as looks at her, I'll be on them like handcuffs on a criminal."

"I don't know what I'd do without her. She saved me," Cole said, his body visibly trembling.

John didn't want to think about admiring the guy, but he was close. "I don't know what I'd do without her either."

Then he texted Shannon because he didn't trust himself not to yell at her. He told her to stay in Cameron's room that they would be there shortly, and that they needed to talk.

Bill Sullivan took a steady breath as he stared at Amber, his beloved daughter. He curled his fingers around her delicate, lifeless ones as stabs of guilt pierced his heart and he cried.

What the hell happened to his life? Two years ago, everything was grand. Amber was a sophomore in high school, an honor roll student and getting all the leads in the school plays. She resembled a happy, healthy and blonde teenager. Amy, his wife, had begun a new and exciting career in real estate. He almost smiled as he remembered how excited she was to join the workforce after being a stay-at-home Mom for many years. Oh, she loved being home with Amber, but Amber had grown up, and Amy needed something to make her feel wanted again.

She loved people, loved houses and loved Rhode Island. She made a terrific real estate agent until the news came, the news about breast cancer, and not just any breast cancer, but Advanced Stage IV Breast Cancer. She was tough through the double mastectomy and chemotherapy. Everything looked good for two months. Bill would never forget the day the doctor told them the cancer cells had spread to her lungs and her brain.

The chemo wasn't working to control the spreading—eight weeks later, she drew her last breath.

Bill wiped his tears with his free hand and stroked Amber's smooth cheeks. "Your mom loved you baby with all her heart. Her only regret had been leaving you at a time in your life when it was so important to have a mother," he groaned. "I tried to be there. I know I wasn't. I was so consumed with grief I neglected you. I broke a solemn vow I made to your mother on her deathbed. I promised to take care of you." He shook his head from side to side and sobbed. "I'm sorry. Please forgive me and come back to me. You're all I have."

When his dad and Cole arrived in his room that morning, Cameron's eyes bugged out of his head when he saw the guitar his dad carried. "Wow, Dad. Thanks. It's great."

His dad shrugged. "I figured I owed you. You have more color on your face today, and you seem more alert. How do you feel?

"My body's sore, but my head hurts less."

"Thank God," his dad said with a grin.

Cameron glanced over at Cole who stood close to his mom. "Hey Cole, would you play something? I'm so hung up with tubes and casts it will be awhile before I can play."

Cole stepped forward, took the guitar from the foot of his bed, and settled down into a chair. He played without hesitation, holding and strumming the guitar so naturally that it was like an extension of his body.

Cameron watched and listened to a song he never heard before. The words rang sad and haunting but beautiful at the same time. When Cole finished Cameron suddenly had an idea, and he thought it was a good one.

"Cole, Amber loves music, especially yours." He paused not sure what Cole would think about his idea. "Do you think if you played for her, it would help pull her out of her coma?"

Cole's heart clenched at the look of both sadness and hope shining from Cameron's eyes. At this moment, Cole would do anything for him, including play for a comatose girl, one who meant an awful lot to him. They would have to have a little heart-to-heart about Amber later. Cole wanted to know everything. And he wanted to make sure if things had progressed quickly, as in sex, Cameron had used protection.

Cole smiled. Christ, he was already assuming the role of a stepfather. His heart suddenly swelled with love and pride for Cameron and damn, it felt good.

He finally answered Cameron's question. "Anything to help."

Cameron beamed. "Thanks."

Shannon took Cole's hand in hers. "I'll take you to her and introduce you to Bill, her father. I had a nice long talk with him last night. My heart goes out to him. How tragic it is that his wife died last year and now his only daughter's hanging precariously to life."

They left Cameron's room and walked quietly down the hall. "You'll like him. Even though he's immersed in grief, I can tell he's a straight shooter," Shannon said, stopping outside Room 327. "Here we are."

Cole stood riveted just inside the doorway and took in the depressing scene staring back at him. The pale, frail-looking girl lying motionless in bed, tubes everywhere, the constant whoosh of the oxygen helping her breathe. She looked like she slept peacefully. Only Cole knew she slept anything but peacefully. She had crossed over to a land where she slept in an unnatural state, and Cole prayed her brain was healing and she would wake up soon. The alternative was to gut-wrenching to contemplate.

The tall, lean, slightly gray-haired man stood looking out the window, his back toward Cole, his head and shoulders hunched forward looking defeated. Although Cole couldn't see his face, he could well imagine the pain, worry and anguish it would show, not to mention the haunted look in his eyes.

Bill must have sensed someone's presence because he turned around and locked gazes with Cole. Cole had been right on the mark. He was devastated and looked even worse than he'd imagined.

Shannon spoke up, "Bill. I'd like you to meet Cole Jackson. Cole, this is Amber's father, Bill Sullivan."

Cole took Bill's outreached hand and said, "I'm sorry. I hope Amber recovers soon."

"Thanks," Bill mumbled back.

"Bill." Shannon gently laid a hand on his arm. "Cameron was wondering if Cole could play some music for Amber. He told me how much she loves music." She paused and swiped at her tears. "Maybe it can help."

Bill placed his large hand on top of Shannon's and squeezed. "Thanks."

Then he turned to Cole and said, "Thank you. I appreciate your willingness to help, especially when I know you're going through a rough time yourself."

"I'm glad to do anything I can." Cole quickly kissed Shannon's cheek. "Go be with your son. I'll be along shortly."

Shortly turned into several hours as Cole zoned out to his music, so intent on playing for Amber, he lost all track of time. Never noticing the hunger pains, or the ache of his arms, or the numbness of his fingertips, all he could do was play, and play he did. He played everything and anything he could think of.

He prayed to God his presence and his music were helping this girl. She was too young to die. She had her whole life ahead of her, a life that hopefully would include love, marriage, children and happiness. When, not if, she came out of this coma, she would have a long healthy and prosperous life.

When Cole heard Bill calling Amber's name, he stopped playing.

"She squeezed my hand." Bill looked at Cole, his eyes filled with hope, excitement and tears. "She squeezed my hand. My God, maybe she will come out of it after all."

Cole's spirits soared as he walked back down the hall to Cameron's room. He stepped inside, his eyes scanning the room. John slept in a chair in an awkward position destined to bring on a sore neck. Shannon lay in bed next to Cameron. They both slept, snoring lightly, like mother, like son, and his heart skipped a beat. Another man occupied a chair, staring at his cell phone. He glanced up as Cole's boots squeaked on the floor.

"Hi, you must be Cole Jackson. I'm Mitch, Shannon's brother."

He stood up and shook hands with Cole.

"Nice to meet you Mitch," Cole said as he glanced again at Cameron and Shannon on the bed. "I only wish it were under better circumstances."

"Yeah, I know what you mean, but hell, my nephew is a fighter."

Cole smiled. "Yeah, he is."

"My two sisters and my parents are down in the cafeteria would you like to grab a bite to eat?"

Cole's stomach flipped at the thought of eating with Shannon's parent and her sister Bridget. "I don't know."

"Come on, I heard you playing nonstop for the past three hours. You must be starving, if not thirsty and needing water. Besides, my parents don't bite. Rachel either, now Bridget..." Mitch threw his head back and laughed. "She's got mighty sharp fangs, but I promise I'll protect you from her blood-sucking ways."

Cole laughed and relaxed as he walked toward the elevator with Shannon's brother. He liked him. He seemed decent and friendly and nonjudgmental. Cole tried to remember what Shannon told him about Mitch. Oh yeah, he used to be a Navy pilot, now he flew a private jet for a large international company. Not a bad job, probably came with plenty of perks.

The hospital cafeteria looked crowded, but Cole spotted Shannon's family immediately. Even if he hadn't met Rachel and Bridget before he would have known Shannon's mother instantly, the resemblance was uncanny. Cole's legs turned a little rubbery the closer he got to the table as four sets of eyes stared at him. Was his imagination running wild? He didn't think so, they were staring and he could physically feel Shannon's dad sizing him up. Oh shit!

"Mom, Dad, this is Cole Jackson. Cole, these are my parents, Edward and Alberta Gallagher."

Edward Gallagher stood up to his full six-foot-something height. So that's where Shannon got her height from. They shook hands. Alberta Gallagher stood to an incredible height of maybe five feet and to Cole's surprise, she hugged him. "It's nice to finally meet you, Cole."

He didn't know what to do or say. Thankfully Mitch spoke up. "You remember Bridget and Rachel?"

Cole smiled at both sisters. "Yes, how could I forget?"

It was a stressful lunch for him, but he muddled through. Later, when they all piled into Cameron's room, claustrophobia set in. He excused himself and went outside the main lobby entrance. Relief washed through him immediately when he saw no reporters anywhere. Maybe Shannon's press release had done the trick, and they would get some much-needed peace.

"Hey." Familiar arms wrapped around his waist, and a warm soft body pressed up against his back.

"Hey yourself."

"I spoke with Bill and he told me about Amber squeezing his hand. He wanted to know if you would play again tomorrow."

Shit. He had to go back to Chicago tomorrow. "I can play first thing in the morning. My flight is in the late afternoon."

He felt Shannon's body tense up and he mumbled, "I'm sorry."

Shannon squeezed him tight. "Don't be sorry. You need to do this. I admire your strength and courage."

"Courage." Cole laughed. "It took every ounce of courage I possessed to meet your parents. I was scared out of my mind."

"They like you."

"Hmm, do they now?"

"Yeah, they said so."

"I like them too."

"I'm mad at you." She nipped his ear.

"Is that right?"

"You told John about the attack."

Cole's body trembled. "I had to. You aren't taking this seriously. Someone tried to kill you."

"I know." This time her body trembled, giving away her nonchalant attitude.

"I find it hard to believe, but it must've been AJ. Now that he's dead, I'm safe."

Cole reached for her arms and pulled her in front of him so he could see her face.

"Contrary to what AJ confessed to, he didn't kill Lindsey." He smacked his chest. "I know inside here he didn't do it. That means you're not safe. You may not notice them, but John and I hired an agency to watch you 24/7 until Lindsey's real murderer is caught. There are four security personnel on you at all times."

She turned her head looking all around them. "I don't see anyone?"

"Precisely," Cole said, trying to gauge her emotions. For the first time since the night it all happened, he witnessed fear on her face and in her lovely blue eyes. "If you can't see them, then neither can your attacker. But don't you fret, they're watching and keeping you safe."

She placed her soft hands on either side of his face and smiled while tears glistened in her eyes. "Thank you. I love you."

Now tears threatened his eyes. "I love you, too."

"Come back inside with me. Being cooped up in that room with my family is more than I can handle right now. Don't get me wrong. I love every one of them...it's just...it's crowded and..." Shannon laughed, but it was fake. "I don't know, the stress and worry from Cameron's accident and what we just discussed..." she fake laughed again, and he felt her hot breath on his neck. "When I'm tense or stressed or worried, I tend to seek solitude."

This time he cradled her face in his hands. He could see the strain and stress around her mouth and eyes. The dark circles under her eyes reminded him of a raccoon, not that he'd tell her that.

He kissed her gently. "Let me take you back to the hotel so you can get some rest?"

"Hmm, that sounds like a wonderful idea, but my family's here."

He kissed her again, only this time it was deeper. "They'll understand."

Shannon leaned into him and her body relaxed against his. "I'm going to stay. John asked me if he could spend the night with Cameron. I can sleep later."

This time she kissed him with the promise of doing much more than sleeping come nightfall.

When they returned to Cameron's room, Cole took Cameron's guitar again and played the afternoon away for Amber. Every time her dad called Amber's name, Cole's heart soared as he finally felt as though he were doing something worthwhile with his music. Nothing would please him more than making a difference in Amber's life, the difference between life and death.

She still didn't wake up that afternoon, but she squeezed her father's hand many times. Cole figured her brain still needed time to heal, and she would wake up when she was ready.

The night turned out to be a crazy one. Everyone but John went out to dinner to a French restaurant. Cole slowly became more comfortable around Shannon's family, and boy could they talk. He really didn't have to join in the conversation going around the table like a tornado because with all the Gallagher's talking at once, no one noticed his silence, no one that is, except Shannon, who kept silently apologizing with her eyes for the whirlwind which was her family.

What she didn't know was he thought it was great, and he had a touch of nostalgia as he remembered the last time he sat around the table and ate with his mom, stepdad and his two sisters. God, it seemed like a lifetime ago. He almost couldn't connect with the person he'd been then, and that scared the shit out of him. *Had he really changed that much in all these years?*

A side trip to Wales to see his two sisters would definitely be put on his agenda after, he shuddered, AJ's burial. Maybe he could finally put the past behind him and visit Lindsey's gravesite as well.

"Cole." Hearing Shannon's soft voice and feeling the warm touch of her hand on his knee brought him out of his private thoughts.

"Yes?"

"Are you ready to go?"

"Sorry I was…" He shrugged his shoulders and shook his head. "I was thinking about AJ and Lindsey."

———

Shannon would have to be blind not to see the sadness and pain in his eyes. God, would he ever find peace? Her stomach rolled. She hoped so because she loved him so much, and she wanted him to be happy and comfortable in his life again. He deserved it and it was high time he had it.

Hopefully, his trip and the burial of AJ would help lead him in the right direction. A pain knotted in her heart with worry for him. It would be hard burying AJ, and she wondered who he would lean on during his time of grief?

Thank God the other band members were going and

he wouldn't be alone. Although she knew Cole well, well enough to know he would be alone surrounded by hundreds of people.

"Hey," Cole now interrupted her thoughts. "I thought we were going," he said with a warm smile that melted her heart and made her forget her concerns and think about the night ahead. Think about the lovemaking that was sure to come during the long, cold, dark hours of the night.

She rose from her seat, bid her whole family goodnight and dragged Cole by the hand out into the night. Immediately cold air blasted them. They walked hand in hand in comfortable silence the short distance to the hotel. Shannon kept glancing at Cole, knowing he thought about the things she thought about. Where were her bodyguards? Did they see anyone suspicious following her? Tomorrow would be a much different day than this one. A day they would have to say goodbye once again. Only this time the goodbye would not have their future hanging over their heads. This time, thank you God, it would be under the knowledge of when they would see each other again. Not if.

Even though they never had the relationship conversation, Shannon knew in her heart and in her mind that they were now a team forever. A team to be reckoned with if anyone so much as batted an eyelash to keep them apart.

"Hmm, good morning," Shannon murmured as she snuggled closer into Cole's wonderful arms, the arms that had held her tight the entire night. There was nothing in the universe like making love and then being held the whole night long in the arms of the one you loved.

"Morning," he said as he kissed her neck.

Shannon regrettably pulled away. It was time to give John a break from spending the night with Cameron. She also wanted desperately to see her son. To see the progress, he made during the night in the healing department. She also wanted to stop by and see Bill, hoping he would have good news about Amber.

"Hey, where are you going? It's still early." Cole yawned and stretched. "At least I think it's still early."

"I want to get to the hospital." Shannon walked naked to the bathroom door, paused and said over her shoulder in a sexy voice to go along with her wanton look, "Care to wash my back?" She scooted inside the door laughing, knowing damn well he was already out of bed and halfway to the bathroom.

The morning flew by. Shannon rarely saw Cole as he hadn't left Amber's bedside once since they arrived. Shannon could only imagine how tired he must be, not to mention the soreness in his throat and arms. She stopped in now and again to bring him juice and crackers or coffee because he refused to take a break. He wanted to play as long as he could until his late afternoon flight.

Amber showed more and more signs of pulling out of the coma. Even Doctor Splaine was hopeful and that meant a lot.

Shannon watched and listened as Cameron argued and pleaded with Doctor Splaine to let him see Amber.

"Why can't I go see her?"

"Cameron," the doctor said, trying once again to reason with him. "I don't think it's in your best interest to be moved at this time. Your body has been badly damaged, not to mention your concussion. I'll revisit the idea in several days."

"But..." Cameron stammered, "I need to see her."

"Soon."

Shannon knew her son all too well, and she knew he was not happy about the doctor's answer, and she also knew Cameron would defy the orders and crawl down the hall to Amber if the doctor didn't give him the okay soon.

John had gone to the hotel to grab some sleep while Shannon's parents, Rachel, Bridget and Mitch crowded in Cameron's room with her. They all snuck out once in a while to listen to Cole play for Amber. My, Shannon mused, how times had changed. Everyone, including John, finally treated Cole with the respect he always deserved.

Before Shannon knew it, the time for Cole to leave had come, and she could visibly see him tense up. She couldn't blame him. The next few days would be tremendously challenging for him, the other band members, AJ's wife, and children. Shannon could only imagine the Macleod family's grief. Death was tragic enough—suicide had to be the worst. Never mind the circumstances leading up to it. They believed him to be a murderer.

Shannon did not envy Cole one bit for what the next several days would bring him. She only wished she could be there to offer her support, comfort and love.

She accompanied Cole to the parking garage, and as soon as they neared his rental car, he pulled her close and buried his head in her hair.

"I wish I didn't have to leave you. I'm worried about your safety," Cole said, sounding as though the weight of the world rested on his shoulders. "I wish I didn't have to leave Cameron or Amber. Cameron is looking better, isn't he?"

Shannon tried to make her voice sound light, but found it hopeless. Her heart was being eviscerated ever so slowly.

"He is. And Amber does as well. Thank you so much for what you did."

"Shannon." He cradled her face in his large, cool

hands. "I love you. I'd do anything for you." He brought his lips down to hers and kissed her deeply, lovingly and reverently. He finally pulled back, and she watched as a single tear slid down his cheek. "Stay safe. I'll call you."

Shannon didn't want to cry, she wanted to be strong, but damn if she didn't lose the battle and cry tears straight from her breaking heart. "I love you," she said before Cole left her alone, except for her bodyguards, she presumed, in the chilly parking garage. Her arms hugged herself as she watched him drive away and disappear completely from sight.

She'd been without Cole nearly her whole life. She could be without him a while longer. She hiccupped as she wiped her tears away and went back inside to be with her family. Thank God she could always count on her family. It was a good feeling and one she wouldn't, or at least would try not to complain about again, at least not anytime soon.

Chapter Twenty-One

Cole sat in first class, his hand gripped a glass of soda water like a vise as he thought ahead to Chicago where he was meeting his bandmates at the airport. Then they had an immediate flight out to Heathrow with a connection to Scotland. AJ's body would be on board the plane. Cole couldn't believe the laughter spewing out of his mouth as he thought what if the coffin got lost? If the airlines could lose luggage, they could lose a dead guy. As quickly as he laughed, he cried. Damn it, this sucked. He missed his best friend. He missed Shannon.

He knew he acted like, *oh poor me*, but he'd spent so many years wanting things. Things like Lindsey's love and his freedom from prison, why should his life continue to be any different now? The difference being, now he wanted Shannon, and he wanted AJ. One, lost to him forever, and one, God willing would belong to him. Correction, they would belong to each other, like equal halves of one whole.

Things went smoothly in Chicago even though he had a small moment of panic when he saw Kyle Ward enter the plane. What was he doing going to Scotland? He ignored him and found his seat just as a text arrived from Shannon.

"Thank you for coming to Colorado. I don't know if I could have managed without you." He cracked a smile as he read the next line. *"It meant so much to me having you here. Bill wanted me to thank you as well. Unfortunately, not much has changed with Amber. Dr. Splaine said Cameron can go home in a few days. Mitch's company has generously and graciously offered the use of their jet to fly us home. Cameron says he won't leave without Amber. We're working on that. I believe my boy's in love. Call me when you can. Not a second goes by that I don't think of you. All my love, Shannon."*

While he sat quietly, he concluded. Shannon needed him and he wanted to think his presence helped Cameron and he knew Amber responded at the times he played his music for her. So the big question was? Did he continue on this quest or go back to the people who needed him? AJ would understand if he turned right around and went home. Cole could hear his voice in his mind. "Life's too short, go for love. Nothing's more important than love. Without it, what would any of us be? Dull, empty, lonely humans wandering the earth in a lifeless haze, struggling to survive. Love, we all need love."

Cole knew Brad and Ted could handle everything. And when Cameron was better, they could travel to Scotland and pay their respects to Elizabeth and her children, AJ's children. He could introduce Shannon and Cameron to his sisters. And while they were in Wales, he would ask Shannon to marry him in this beautiful stone chapel near the house he grew up in. It was built in 1670 and was still used today for special occasions. And his marriage to Shannon fit the title of special occasion.

His heart pounded painfully, and he sweated profusely. Damn, what the hell was he doing in this tin box, flying over the black of the Atlantic, when he should take care of securing his future? Shannon meant more to him than anything. She should come first. She and her injured son should come first. If something happened to Amber? He would never forgive himself. He could make a difference in her life. AJ was dead, there was nothing he could do for him now, but Amber, my God, she was only seventeen and still alive.

His thoughts turned dark. What if the security people screwed up and Shannon was killed? He suddenly had difficulty breathing, and Cole fought hard to keep the anxiety attack at bay. That would not help the situation any.

In four more hours, the plane would land in London, and Cole would turn right back around. His gut told him he had to. He closed his eyes briefly and whispered, "AJ forgive me. But I know you of all people would understand someone in need."

"Cole," Brad said from his seat across the aisle. "I forgot I had this. The concierge in Chicago said this was dropped off by a messenger service this morning."

Cole took the sealed note from Brad, opened it and his world tilted once again. His stomach tumbled as though the plane did a barrel roll. Oh shit. His hands trembled as he read the typed note.

"I hope you said your goodbyes to Ms. Gallagher as you will never see her alive again. I may not be able to frame you for this murder, but I will have taken another person you love away from you. Possibly I'll take her son as an added bonus. This time, I hope you take a cue from AJ and join him in taking your own life. AJ was so easy to convince he killed Lindsey, I almost feel sorry for him."

Cole stole a look across the aisle and up several rows from him at Ward. Deep down in his gut he knew Ward killed Lindsey. If he just threatened Shannon and

Cameron, who had he hired to do the killing? Were they professionals? What a perfect alibi he'd planned. Although his gut could be wrong, and it was someone else entirely.

———

Cole ran through the Denver airport, his feet barely touching the ground, his breathing labored and his heart pounding. He had to get to Shannon. Ever since he read the note on the plane he'd been in panic mode. His stomach twisted up in knots as he felt desperate and on the verge of collapse. Everything that had happened lately came crashing down around him as he tried to crawl out of the dark abyss and into the light of day. Only he was lost in a labyrinth of endless tunnels and mazes.

He'd contemplated texting her about the note the second he landed in London but decided not to make her panic. She was safe. He had to believe that. Had to believe the security people and John were keeping her safe. *Just keep telling yourself that.*

He ran past the lobby desk at the hospital, past the nurses' station and straight into Cameron's room waving the note and mumbling like a lunatic. He handed the note to John and pulled Shannon into his arms and held her close and tight. He could feel his heart pounding inside his chest and knew Shannon could as well. But the longer he held her, the calmer he became. She centered him and led him out of the maze and into the light, into life. This one woman would never know how much she changed his life, more than changed it, saved it. Before he met her, he was a hollow human being struggling with life, and when he met her, she gave him life. Oxygen, love and everything else a person needed to survive. He now had to give the gift back to her.

"Cole. What...how..." Shannon asked, her voice breathless with surprise.

"I couldn't go. I'm needed here more." He pulled back and kissed her with all the love he felt for her. He didn't care if every member of the Gallagher family watched, and he was certain they were, and watching no doubt with their jaws hanging open. Let them watch because they would have to get used to this because he planned on kissing Shannon every chance he got for the rest of his life.

"We need more security," John said as he left the room with his cell phone in his hand.

Cole took Shannon's hand and led her out into the hall where he explained everything. His heart broke for her when he told her about the threat to Cameron's life. Her face lost all color and her body shook uncontrollably so he wrapped her in his arms and held her close, murmuring soothing words he would never remember later. "Will you be okay?"

"I…I think so. I can't believe this bastard would threaten my son. Who is this asshole?"

"Do you remember me telling you about Kyle Ward?"

"The senator?"

"The one and only. I think it's him. It all makes sense. He was having an affair with Lindsey at the same time she was with AJ. The only thing I don't understand is what did I ever do to him to make him hate me so? And how did he convince AJ he killed Lindsey?" He stepped back, looked at her and winced at the tears wetting her face. "He'll be caught, eventually. Meanwhile, we need to find out who he hired? John's taking care of all this right now, so I want you to sit with your son and not worry about anything." He brought his lips to hers for a quick kiss. "Do you think you can do that?"

"No."

"I figured as much," Cole said as he took her hand once again and led her back to her son. Then had a private word with Mitch. "Do me a favor and don't let Shannon or Cameron out of your sight unless John or I are with them."

Cole gave Mitch credit. He hadn't blinked an eye or questioned the why of it. He just said yes.

Knowing they were in good hands, he had one more thing he needed to do. He needed to play for Amber, and when he walked in the room and found her alone, he took a seat next to the bed and played. Halfway through the song he heard a soft female voice.

"You really were here. My father told me you were, but…"

Cole nearly dropped the guitar in shock. "You're …awake?"

She fluttered her eyes open. They were a brilliant shade of blue, much like Shannon's, and Cole's heart melted.

"Yes. Last night. I thought I had dreamed of all the music. I kept hearing it and trying to reach for it, but the darkness wouldn't let me through." There were silent tears dripping down her face onto the pillow. "Thank you. Without your music to guide me and make me strong enough to fight the force that kept sucking me into the dark, I don't know if I could have found my way out."

Cole wiped away his own tears and gently hugged Amber. "Welcome back." Then he ran down the hall and burst into Cameron's room. "She's awake and talking."

"Mom?" Cameron pleaded with wide eyes full of hope.

"Dr. Splaine said you can't leave your bed yet," Shannon said with a deep sigh.

"The hell with that," John interrupted. "Jackson, grab the IV bag. Shannon, carefully remove his leg from that contraption. We'll wheel his bed down the hall. My son wants to see his girl."

Cole stood off to the side and watched the tearful reunion between the two young people, with a lump in his throat. Before they took Cameron back to his room, they promised to get the two of them together once they were all back home and recovered.

Chapter Twenty-Two

"I CAN'T TAKE IT ANYMORE," SHANNON SAID AS SHE STARED at the snow falling fast and steady outside her home in Standish Bay. "When will it end?"

"I don't know," Cole answered as frustrated as she was.

Perhaps we need to meet with the head of the security company and plan a sting operation with me as bait."

"No way."

"If we don't do something, it may never end. I don't know about you, but I can't go on living like this. Tiptoeing around, looking over my shoulder and expecting Cameron to be killed every time he leaves the house," she sobbed. "I can't do it anymore."

Cole grabbed her and engulfed her in his strong arms, rubbing his hands up and down her back, trying to soothe her. "Shhh. I know it's wearing on you. You've been so strong. I don't know how you've done it."

"Please call John and security. Perhaps they can have someone pretend to be Cameron and me to draw the killer out?"

"Good idea. I'll see if they can get here this afternoon, weather permitting."

Shannon paced her great room early that evening as she listened to Cole, John and a Mr. Nash, who headed up her security detail, discuss plans for a sting operation.

"Ms. Gallagher," said Mr. Nash. "We will sneak you and your son out of the house and to a safe location and replace you with two of our best officers. With any luck, this will be over in a day or two. We'll make it look as though you've canceled your bodyguards, which will open the doors for the culprit to make his move. Questions?"

"No. Just end this. I want to get on with my life." She sat beside Cole and placed her hand on his thigh. "Our life."

"I'll do my best."

Cole checked and rechecked the gun John had given him to protect Shannon and Cameron with if need be. Just holding it in his hands had them shaking. Could he honestly pull the trigger and take another person's life? He hoped to God he never had to find out. John risked a lot, probably his career, by providing him with the weapon, but sometimes desperate times called for breaking the law. Not to mention he could go to jail for carrying a gun without a license. Small price to pay if he saved the people he loved with it. Technically, he was still an ex-con on parole and not able to get a gun permit, but once again semantics aside, it was worth the risk.

Shannon and Cameron played cards in the hotel room while he tried unsuccessfully to remain calm. They'd been here for two days already, and the walls were closing in on him. John, along with the lone bodyguard posted outside their door, kept them informed about what was happening at Shannon's house. Too bad there wasn't much to report.

At eleven-thirty, Shannon and Cameron slept soundly in the bedroom while he paced in the adjourning living room, barefooted and trying to be quiet when his stomach growled. Sure, why couldn't he have been hungry when dinner had come at seven? He flipped through the hotel's room service menu and was surprised he could order until midnight. Ordering a cheeseburger and fries, he flipped on the TV to the Late Show and muted the sound as he ticked off the minutes until he heard the door knock and the guard's words, "Your food is here, Mr. Jackson."

Cole opened the door and stepped aside while the security guard wheeled the dinner cart into the room. Just as Cole was about to grab the metal cover off the plate a loud crack reverberated in the room, lights flashed in his eyes and his head exploded as he crumpled to the ground, darkness swallowing him up.

"That was easy. Good job," Kyle Ward said as he entered the room and shook the guard's hands. "Thanks for your help."

"No problem. The extra money's come in handy, and I owe my boss nothing."

"Did you have your food delivered as well?" Ward asked as he handed the guard some sleeping pills.

"You bet."

"Eat most of it. Take two pills, open the other one and sprinkle it on the food that's left. That will ensure you're not accused."

Ward closed the door behind the guard, pulled Cole's body up against the wall and entered the bedroom, grinning at the two sleeping people. "It may have taken longer than I planned, but I'm gonna enjoy this," he muttered to himself.

Killing Lindsey had not been planned. She'd pulled a knife on him when he wouldn't take no for an answer. She had wanted to break it off with him and go back to her fucking asshole of a husband. He'd shown her, hadn't he? And when Cole had been convicted of the murder, he'd laughed his ass off. *My, how the mighty had fallen.*

Now he would get to enact his revenge against Cole once again. He walked across the room and placed the barrel of a gun against Shannon's temple, waking her up. "Shhh, don't say a word or I'll shoot your precious son."

The second something cold and hard rested on her temple, she opened her eyes to find a middle-aged man leaning over her with hatred in his dark, almost black eyes. She swallowed the lump in her throat and fought the panic threatening to take over her body and mind. Who was she kidding? She was in total panic mode. Her heart thumped wildly inside her chest, her body trembled violently as she stared, wide-eyed, at the man she knew had come to kill her and Cameron. Oh my God, where was Cole? Had he already been killed?

Tears slid down her cheeks onto the pillow as her mind screamed *do something*.

"No, no, no." The man pressed the gun deeper into her temple, causing her to wince. "Don't even think about it. And in case you're wondering, your lover is very much alive, for now."

"Why?" she whispered.

"Why?" he repeated. "Because I hate the mother-fucker. Now get up and do nothing stupid."

Fighting down the bile rising up her throat, Shannon

sat up slowly, afraid if she went too fast he might shoot Cameron.

"Move into the other room."

Her knees almost gave way when her eyes found Cole slumped against the wall with blood dripping down the side of his face. "Please God, let Cole and Cameron live," she prayed internally to herself.

"Sit down on the desk chair with your arms behind your back."

Shannon did what he asked. She knew if she didn't someone she loved would die. The man made quick work of using zip ties to secure her hands and feet and duct taped her mouth.

He swung the chair around, caressed his hand down her cheek and cupped her breast, causing her to cringe in revulsion.

"Too bad I don't have time to sample you. What I wouldn't give to take you and make Jackson watch. But alas, it's your lucky day, as I have a plane to catch."

He exited the room and Shannon watched in horror as he came back with her son. The barrel of the gun now against his temple. Cameron's eyes were full of fear as the man restrained him as he'd done her, only on the sofa.

"Now what to do?" the man said as he strolled over to stand in front of Cole. "Do I wait until he wakes and make him watch as I kill you both, or should I make you watch as I kill him? Decisions, decisions?" the man's deranged laughter reverberated throughout the room.

He kicked Cole's feet and slapped him across the face, sending his head and body reeling to the floor. "Wake up Jackson, time to pay the piper."

She heard Cole moaning, and then he pushed himself up, using the wall for support. "What the fuck are you doing here, Ward?"

"Come now Jackson, you're not that stupid?"

"What happened with AJ?" Cole asked as he wiped the blood out of his eye with his hand.

"Power of suggestion is well—a powerful thing." Ward shrugged. "Add some drugs and you convince a man he killed someone. Put suicide in a wounded soul's brain, and you get them to commit it."

"You bastard," Cole yelled.

What happened next happened so fast Shannon's eyes could hardly keep up. Cole moved at lightning speed. He swung his leg out tripping Ward, causing him to fall back. The gun discharged and Shannon screamed against the tape as blood pooled on Cole's shoulder. They fought on the ground each grappling for control of the gun. Where was the gun John gave Cole?" Shannon wondered as she and Cameron both struggled with their bonds. Her wrists burned as the zip tie cut into them. It was no use. She'd never get free.

The struggle continued. Ward got control of the gun but lost it when Cole punched him in the face and it skittered across the room. People were pounding on the door. But Ward had flipped the deadbolts, keeping everyone out.

Would it never end? She struggled to kick the rug and move the chair on wheels toward the two men. Her heart pounded because it was working. She had no idea what she'd do when she got close to them, but she intended to aid Cole. As she made headway, she watched as Ward raised up his arm, holding a deadly-looking switchblade. Once again, her scream was strangled in the tape, and she stared in horror as he tried to stab Cole in the neck. Cole deflected it with his arm, which now bled profusely.

She swallowed the bile crawling up her throat, she couldn't throw up, or she'd drown in her own vomit. "Please God, she prayed, please help Cole."

Determined to get closer, she scooted the chair and when she was in kicking distance of Ward, she gave it her all and swung her legs out, hoping to connect with his knees and take him down. Unfortunately, he saw her coming and his hand snaked out to grab her feet, but it gave Cole the chance he needed. He rolled across the floor, grabbed the gun, aimed at Ward's leg and pulled the trigger. The man's screams went on and on.

Cole stumbled to the door, flipped the lock, and fell back as an array of people entered, guns drawn.

Chapter Twenty-Three

Two weeks had gone by since their fight for their lives, and Shannon couldn't be happier. Snow was falling again, and she turned to Cole, who had his arm in a sling because of a gunshot wound. His other arm had had forty stitches removed yesterday.

Cameron's body had healed nicely since the accident and he now sported a walking boot, so getting around was much easier. This upcoming weekend they had plans to go to Newport and visit with Amber and her father. Cameron was beyond excited. His cast should come off his arm in several more weeks. But all in all, they had much to be thankful for and not a day went by that Shannon didn't remind herself about that.

"Come on you two guys, let's bundle up and head to the beach," Shannon said. "The snow's beautiful, and I'll bet big bucks I can whip your two sorry butts by making the best snowman this town has ever seen."

Cole and Cameron glanced at one another and nodded. Cameron grabbed his jacket, carefully pulled the sleeve over his cast, struggled into one boot and put a plastic bag over his walking boot to keep his foot dry. He grabbed a hat and gloves and left Shannon and Cole in the dust as he waded through the knee-deep snow. After Cole removed his sling, Shannon helped him into his jacket, then they headed down after Cameron and forgot about building snowmen as a snowball fight ensued. Cameron against her and Cole, and poor Cameron didn't stand a chance as he they continuously pelted him with one snowball after another. Shannon was proud of the way Cole made snowballs with two injured arms. Too bad Cameron didn't have as much luck, his cast hindered him big-time.

"I'll get you next time," Cameron yelled and laughed as he lay on his back, his arms blocking his face as snowball after snowball bombed him.

Then Shannon turned on Cole and threw half-formed snowballs at him, and it was music to Shannon's ears when she heard him laughing. Really laughing and looking happy for the first time in an awfully long time.

Then Shannon watched with love bursting inside her heart as Cole and Cameron pounded each other with half-formed snowballs. They were acting crazy and laughing loudly, making her realize how fortunate she was to have these two in her life.

Her son, born unplanned and not at a convenient time during her teenage years, was always wanted and loved. If she could go back, she would never do it differently. He was the best thing that ever happened to her.

The second best thing was Cole Jackson.

Her body tingled as she watched him. And, regardless of the freezing temperature, she felt warm and tingly all over. Warm from the love she had that overflowed for him and from being loved by him. Loved with the kind of true love that would stand the test of time and never die.

Epilogue

COLE JACKSON TOOK THE STAGE TO ACCEPT HIS GRAMMY Award for Best Solo Artist. He held the Grammy up in his hand and beamed. "You all know my life is an open book thanks to my talented wife, Shannon, who told it so honestly and emotionally with her words. Thank you, my darling for freeing me from my past.

"I dedicate this to my friend, AJ, who is no longer with us. I love you, man. To Brad and Ted, thanks for everything, and to my incredibly talented stepson, Cameron." Cole gestured toward Cameron in the audience. "This is as much yours as it is mine. Your magical fingers are in every single song on this album. And one day you will stand in this very spot, and I can't wait.

"To my beautiful wife, Shannon, I love you with every fiber of my being. Thank you for believing in me and giving me your unconditional love. I wouldn't be standing up here tonight if it wasn't for you."

THE END

About the Author

Christine Donovan is an international bestselling author who writes romance that touches the heart, soothes the soul, and feeds the mind. She self-published her first book in 2012 and has many contemporary and historical romances available, with more to come. She also writes for Dragonblade Publishing.

She is a PAN member of RWA and belongs to Novelist, Inc., Rhode Island, and New England Romance Writers.

Christine lives on the Southeast Coast of Massachusetts with her husband. She has four grown sons, two daughters-in-law, three granddaughters, one cat, and a black lab named Luna. In her free time, she enjoys spending time at the beach, reading, painting, or gardening. She loves taking on DIY projects. Please visit her at http://www.authorchristinedonovan.com

Please click here to sign up for her newsletter to receive advance notice of releases and contests

http://www.authorchristinedonovan.com/newsletter

Also By Christine Donovan

Morgan

<u>Single Title Contemporary</u>

Sunset Beach

MELCHIONNE FAMILY SERIES - NOVELLA

Venetian Holiday

Amalfi Coast Holiday